Shadow of the Fathers

Robert Friedman

Floricanto Press

ISBN: 978-0-915745-99-9

Floricanto Press
650 Castro Street, Suite 120-331
Mountain View, California 94041-2055
www. floricantopress. com
415-552 1879 Fax: 702-995 1410

Shadow of the Fathers

For Ginny, Maddy and Lizzy

AUTHOR'S NOTE: This novel was inspired by a real-life incident. While I have kept the names of the historic figures involved, such as Dr. Cornelius "Dusty" Rhoads and Puerto Rican Nationalist Pedro Albizu Campos, and have quoted from factual material and findings, I also have changed dates and invented characters and subsequent events in search of truth through fiction.

Part One

Robert Friedman 1

June 11, 1950

Presbyterian Hospital
San Juan, Puerto Rico

Dear Ferdie:

It was wonderful hearing from you again. Please keep trying to get us involved in that new medical research program being put together by our Georgetown friends.

The human behavior program sounds fascinating. If the Soviets, Chinese and North Koreans use mind control, we certainly should be researching these techniques.

As far as the immediate future, I can get a damn fine job here and am tempted to take it. It would be ideal except for the Puerto Ricans. They are beyond doubt the dirtiest, laziest, most degenerate and thievish race of men ever inhabiting this sphere. It makes you sick to inhabit the same island with them. They are even lower than Italians.

What the island needs is not public health work but a tidal wave or something to totally exterminate the population. It may then be livable. I have done my best to further the process of extermination by killing off eight and devising a method to transplant cancer into several more. The latter has not resulted in any fatalities so far . . . The matter of consideration for the patients' welfare plays no role here, in fact all physicians take delight in the abuse and torture of the unfortunate subjects.

Well, that's it for now, old friend. Just a short note to let you know how things stand. Take care and do let me know if you hear any more news.

Sincerely,

Dusty

ONE

It was getting a whole lot worse, closing in again.

A couple of days ago, in the Santurce market, the tubers and roots. Like pregnant women, scowling faces, distended heads. Tiny eyes, they saw deep inside you. Clammy sweat, pasting your clothes to your body and burning your eyes. He bought them for a still life: "Tubers That Steal into the Soul." The wrinkled, toothless old hag selling avocados wagged a finger at him. Others staring and smirking, he wanted to throttle the bastards!

Pablo slashed a broad black line just beneath his throat for the collar of his black tee shirt. The canvas was set on an easel in the center of the room. The floor-length mirror was propped against another easel to the right of the canvas. He leaned into the mirror, then into the canvas, then backed away, moved in again and, with his double "o" brush, enlarged and shaded the mole just below his left cheekbone, put more whitish gray into his mustache. He worked on the eyes, darkening the brown by lightening the whites around the pupil.

Standing back again, comparing the reflection with the painted canvas. Should he make more changes? His mirrored face is a gaunt mask. It's happened in the past few weeks. He should tighten the skin and make his high cheekbones practically show through. Like some torture victim. A self-flagellator.

He didn't have to exaggerate that much. Just a realistic rendering of those sunken brown eyes and that fleshy and troubled mouth in order to capture the essential pathos.

But wasn't there more in that face? Pablo searched the mirror. A mask, albeit one with lines, creases, cracks, moles, blotches. Leave the face, work on the background, get the right brown. But after a few minutes, he was pulled back to the eyes, to the mud-brown and the phlegmy white, the bloodshot strands, the bloody, creamy blobs in the corners. Something more was needed in those two darkened hollows, some paint-morphed humanity. He stood there, looking at the canvas.

The phone rang. He knew it was Ana. Not now. He didn't want to explain anything. He let it ring.

He put the brush into a can of turp among the cans and tubes of paint on the floor. He went to the radio on a shelf next to his collection of wooden saints, carved by craftsmen in the countryside, objects of reverence for the religious and *objects d'art* for the irreverent. Nothing on the local stations but salsa. He wasn't in the mood. He switched to the radio's short-wave band and tuned into a jazz station from Europe. Charlie Parker and Dizzy Gillespie were playing "Night in Tunisia." Beautiful.

He went back to the portrait. He had been working on it for several hours, and was suddenly very tired. He threw himself across the sofabed as the Bird glided into "East of the Sun." Pepa jumped onto the bed and settled next to the painter's feet. Pablo floated west of the moon, then into pure space.

The shrillness clawed through Pablo's ears, turned to pummeling bass. Alternative megarock overtook the jazz station and blasted from the radio and Pepa growled and dashed upstairs. She padded around like crazy, barking, then let loose a series of pitiful yelps. Pablo jumped up. What the hell was up there? Bleary eyed, he rushed into the kitchen and picked up a long knife from the rubber mat on the counter top. He mounted the stairs.

As he reached the top of the staircase, Pepa yelped and scratched from behind the bathroom door off to the right. Pablo was about to turn on the upstairs light when he heard things being dragged across the floor in the first room off the hallway.

The room was filled with a luminescent gray from the moonlight spraying through the two balcony doors. He had not locked the doors, but they had been closed. Now they were wide open. A man stood in front of one of Pablo's paintings, like he was admiring it. Then he started grunting, then let out a shriek and attacked the painting, as though it were an abomination that threatened his very being. He viciously slashed at the canvas with a knife. Pablo shouted at the man and he jerked his head toward Pablo and they both stared incredulously at each other. Both had their knives poised in the air.

Pablo rushed to rescue the painting. The attacker lunged forward and cut him on the arm and Pablo's knife clattered across the black-and-white terrazzo floor. Warm blood oozed to his elbow and dripped down to his paint-splattered khakis. The attacker raised his knife again. He looked uncertainly toward the open balcony doors. Pablo put his head down and charged into the man and they crashed into a spindle-backed chair. The chair splintered and crumbled.

Pablo twisted free and pounced on his assailant. He grabbed the man's wrist and bent the arm back until he heard a cracking and the knife fell to the ground. Pablo threw a punch that grazed off an ear. A hand came under his chin, bending his head back.

They grappled from room to room, smashing furniture, splitting wooden frames, tearing through canvases, grunting and gasping, but holding in all major sounds of pain.

There was a brief respite. In the glow of the moonlight, each man stared into the other's eyes. Pablo saw in the other what he felt in himself: a willingness to quit the murderous battle. But after the pause, which lasted no more than two seconds, they were at each other's throats again, both relying on their one uninjured arm. In near-exhaustion they grappled and grunted and threw punches and kneed each other in the groin and butted heads.

Each man recovered his own knife. They began circling one another, lunged, circled, lunged again. He heard the other guy wheezing like an asthmatic. Then, in a superhuman lightning stroke, Pablo blindly thrust his knife forward and it plunged into the other's throat. Blood spurted into Pablo's mouth. He spit and it dribbled down his chin and onto his khakis, soaking in with the blood from his arm.

Pablo, his whole body shaking, opened the bathroom door. Pepa yelped and leapt in the air as Pablo dragged the body into the shower stall and propped it against the tiled wall. The man's head lolled and his mouth dropped open. Still-flowing blood made a new dark collar on his gray tee shirt. With his drooping head and gaping mouth he looked like a life-size, jaw-broken ventriloquist's dummy. Pablo's head went light and he steadied himself by splaying his arms on the wall on either side of the guy, whose body began to fold forward. Pablo pushed the body back again and drew the plastic rings of the curtain across the metal bar. He saw the body fold and slump down once more and he felt he had to prop it up again, and then, shaking off the thought, he left the bathroom and slammed shut the door.

He retrieved the assailant's knife, folded it and pocketed it. He went down the stairs, dropped the kitchen knife onto the yellow rice stuck at the bottom of the pan in the sink from his *arroz con pollo* dinner, then sat on the sofabed, his head in his hands. Pepa jumped on the bed and lay down next to him.

Who the hell was that guy upstairs? A demon materialized out of the sins of the past?

It was no demon; he had killed another human being.

It was in the genes.

His breath was coming short. His head was pounding like mad. Yet a giddy high pulsed through his body.

It was in the fuckin genes!

He went to a small desk in the corner of the room and rifled through the drawers until he found his passport. He knew with absolute certainty he would need it. Pepa barked and whined. In a flash, the excitement turned to anxiety and Pablo fought down the churning inside. He bent down on his haunches to pat his dog on the head. Her stub of a tail was going a mile a minute; she cocked her head as she stared at him, knowing something was up. He let her lick his face.

An excruciating turmoil inside him spiraled upward and propelled him from the house and down the street.

TWO

The book was titled *Man Alone.* It was an autobiographical novel about growing up Puerto Rican in New York, shipping out at an early age on freighters, fighting in the steamy jungles of Vietnam, sleuthing as a private investigator in New Jersey, then returning to the Caribbean island where he was born.

The New York Times, New York Review of Books and the other major reviewers ignored it. But Harold Borenstein, a professor of Ethnic Studies at Rutgers University, launched the book into the Sea of Academia. Writing in the quarterly, "Studies in Modern American Fiction," Borenstein saw Ralph Camacho's work as "a modern-day linkage to the Eternal Voyage that explores the universal themes of the mythological hero's journey over the Cosmic Sea and the Return and spiritual Rebirth through acknowledgment of the collective conscience of one's race."

Ralph, whose academic credentials were practically nil (one year of night school at City College), got several writer-in-residence job offers. He figured he was being approached by the universities to fill a minority faculty quota. Then a job offer came from a University of Puerto Rico dean whose son Ralph helped locate when he was at Confidential Investigations. The kid had "kidnapped" himself from his university dorm at Princeton and sent a ransom note from the Taj Mahal in Atlantic City.

Ralph was asked to teach Newyorican Studies, a new course dealing with the Puerto Rican Diaspora. Although the offers from stateside universities paid more, Ralph decided to remain in his ancestral home to share his experiences with the next generation of probable exiles.

They were reading *The Odyssey* in class. Ralph hoped that the students would feel some sort of link to their own lives. Whether they knew it or not, to one degree or another, it was their story too.

That day they'd been reading the Wandering Rocks episode. Many of the students had been wandering back and forth between the island and the states for most of their lives, looking to reach home, wherever the hell that was, and trying to maneuver through their own Scylla and Charybdis. They had fun putting names to each of Scylla's six heads, which chewed up victims simultaneously, naming them after cops, priests, nuns, pushers, teachers, school advisers, landlords, welfare investigators, their parents' bosses.

In the evening, after their daughter went to bed, Tere and Ralph shared a bottle of beer and watched the news on the TV. During a report about one more "massacre" involving drug gangs in a public housing project, Tere flaked out on the sofa. Ralph helped her into bed and returned to the sofa, switched off the TV and picked up *The Odyssey*.

With the TV off, he could hear the jazz music coming from Pablo's house next door. Then the jazz faded and was replaced by a loud, crackling static that was soon mixed with booming, electronic screeching. Punk grunge death metal, whatever the hell it was called, vibrated through the floor and set off shock waves through his nerves. He tried to read.

Zeus thundered as he hurled a lightning bolt. He hit the hull...Our ship whirled round... ourshipwhirledroundfullcircle . . . .All my men . . .

Allmymenbywavearound. . . Allmymenbywa vesaroundorblackbowedcraft. Zeusthundered . . .

Sputtering, echoing, pulsing, twanging, beeping, disembodied sounds. *Jesus Christ!* Ralph tossed the book on the sofa.

Diana came into the living room, pale-faced, sweaty and scared. "I dreamed that Marilyn Manson was being killed." Her lips quivered. Tears welled in her almond-shaped eyes.

Ralph hugged her, then brought her into his and Tere's bedroom. Tere was awake. "Goddamn, that music!"

"I don't know what's the matter with Pablo," Ralph said. "He probably passed out and left the radio blaring. I'll be back."

Diana climbed into bed next to her mother and Ralph headed downstairs to Pablo's house next door.

He banged the iron knocker hard against the heavy wooden door. The mutt poked its nose between the curved iron bars on the window near the door and barked and whimpered. Ralph shouted through the window. He got no answer.

He went back to the door and knocked again. This time the door opened slightly. Ralph let himself in. The mutt got down on its two front paws and growled. Ralph went to the radio and clicked it off. The mutt went up to Ralph and licked his shoes. Then it bounded away, whimpering, and ran up the stairs.

All the downstairs lights were on. Ralph went to the foot of the stairs and called up. The dog ran back downstairs and barked and whined. Ralph went to pet it, but it skittered away. He caught the after-aroma of cooked oil and *sofrito* and chicken.

A canvas was set up on an easel in the living room. Another self-pitying self-portrait. He preferred Pablo's earlier pictures of landscapes or portraits of family and friends and the whores around town. The drawings he had done in Nam, before he had lost it, were superb.

The dog was running around like crazy, whimpering and barking furiously. It started up the stairs again, then looked back. Ralph followed. The mutt scratched at the bathroom door.

When Ralph opened the door, he knew immediately what was slumped inside the shower stall. He could see the body's shape behind the plastic shower curtain. He switched on the light, pulled the curtain back.

The body was propped up with its legs straight out, its arms bent at the elbows, its head leaning to one side. Its throat was slashed.

It wasn't Pablo, thank God.

Ralph quickly surveyed the damage in the upstairs rooms, the dog yapping and squealing at his heels. There were smashed chairs and overturned tables, ripped empty canvases with wood protruding through them like broken bones through skin and there was a slashed painting on the floor of one of the rooms. Pablo wasn't up there, dead or alive. Ralph went downstairs, pulled the front door shut and hurriedly walked down the street, trying to catch his breath.

The air was still. A full moon shone on the blue bricks. Stray cats were rubbing against buildings, pawing roaches, licking up whatever they could find in the crevices along the curbs.

Did Pablo know there was a dead guy in his shower stall? Did Pablo put him there? He had to find his friend and find out. He owed him.

Ralph headed down Cristo Street to the Malomundo, Pablo's current favorite watering hole. The place smelled of sweat and beer and cigarettes. You could barely feel the air-conditioning. The Alcoholic Unanimous regulars were there, but no Pablo.

"Has Pablo been in tonight?"

"Haven't seen him yet. He's probably making the rounds." Ernesto the bartender gave Ralph the easy-going grin he had adopted not to scare off customers. He had the face of a fun-loving pirate itching for the next round of pillaging and ravaging. His huge arms were covered with tattoos from shoulder to wrist.

"You wanna pay his tab?" Jerry Smith stood at the other end of the bar, by the cash register, chewing on a cigar and counting money. He glinted suspiciously at the bills he thumbed on the bar, as though the tens and twenties would turn into singles if he took his beady eyes off them.

Ralph checked a few more bars in the neighborhood, then headed for the waterfront.

The neon lights from the Latin Quarters club lit the sidewalk red, blue and green. The loft-sized room was packed with sailors, tourists, locals and hookers in hot pants. Steel band drummers in gold musketeer shirts rumbled out a calypso from a revolving stage behind the large circular bar.

Ralph looked around the bar and at the tables. No Pablo.

He was about to leave when Lucy came into the club. He was surprised to see her there. She usually worked the higher-class Condado section, where the tourists stayed. She wore a knee-length black dress, dark stockings and heels.

"Hey, Lucy. How's it going?"

Lucy smiled warmly. It was, as always, a many-layered smile—open, inquisitive, shrewd, surprised, expectant, even a little shy. This time there was an added layer: her smile seemed somewhat nervous.

"Don't you do the hotels anymore?"

"Yeah, but it's slower than anything."

"Can I buy you a drink?"

Lucy studied Ralph, as though this was a first meeting between them and they had never spent evenings at Pablo's house playing dominoes or listening to jazz or just shooting the breeze and Lucy had not been turned on to reading there and borrowed books from Pablo's library. Or as if she was seeing something about him she had never realized before. She nodded slowly.

Ralph led her to a corner table. A waiter brought Lucy a vodka and tonic and Ralph a beer. Ralph glanced at the book Lucy was carrying with her small black purse. It was a paperback of "Crime and Punishment."

"Heavy reading," Ralph said.

Lucy shrugged. "It's good stuff. Keeps me off *perico.*"

"Redemption through suffering. You believe in that?"

Lucy shrugged again. "Hey, don't tell me the ending."

"You haven't seen Pablo tonight, by any chance, have you?"

Lucy looked at Ralph steadily, inquisitively, as though searching out some essence of his character. The intelligent mobility of her features made her long, thin face, if not particularly pretty, certainly attractive. She nodded. "I saw him earlier this evening."

"Do you know where he went?"

"Yeah, I know."

Ralph waited.

"Why do you ask?"

"Because he has a problem, and I want to help him."

"Yeah, he looked pretty fucked up. There was blood all over his shirt and his arm was cut pretty bad. We went to a drug store and I helped bandage it up. He asked if he could stay at my apartment for the night. I gave him the key."

"Look, he may be in a lot of trouble. I think I should go to talk to him, find out exactly what happened."

"I like Pablo very much. He's always been very kind to me," Lucy said, as though in warning.

"I want to help him," Ralph said again. "He's a good friend and I think he needs my help. Could you give me your address so I could go over there?"

Lucy nodded slowly. "Yeah, all right."

She wrote her address and apartment number on a napkin. "You have to ask the guard at the gate to call up."

A taxi waiting outside took Ralph to Lucy's high-rise condo on Ashford Avenue in the Condado. The condo was across from one of the luxury tourist hotels. Palm trees lined both sides of the street, their raggy fronds stirring in the breeze, like messy hairdos. Ralph went up to the little guardhouse behind the metal gate. The guard was in a swivel chair, his head way back and his mouth wide open, like a patient in a dentist's chair. Ralph woke him, asked him to call up to Lucy's apartment.

"She ain't in," the guard said.

"I know, but a friend of ours is up there."

The guard looked at Ralph suspiciously.

"Just call up, please. I spoke to Lucy and she said it was all right."

The guard took a deep breath. He phoned the apartment. "*Ocupado.* Busy," he said.

Ralph looked at his watch. Two thirty. The guard shrugged. He seemed relieved that the phone wasn't answered. He offered Ralph a cigarette. Ralph declined. He asked the guard to try again. The line was still busy.

After another minute, Ralph gave a little nod toward the telephone and the guard grudgingly dialed again. Still busy.

"Look, something may have happened up there. Could you let me go up to the apartment, just to check it?"

"I'm sorry, *caballero.* I can't do that. We're only supposed to open the gate for residents, or for visitors that get permission from the residents. If anyone found out that I let you in without permission I could lose my job. I have five kids under the age of ten, and I've been out of work for eight months before I got this job last week and my wife has a kidney problem and . . . "

"O.K., O.K."

Ralph went to an all-night open-air snack stand. A couple of beefy, middle-aged, late-night revelers in flowery guayaberas were sipping from demitasses of coffee and smoking big cigars. After two cups of coffee, Ralph made his way back to the condo. The streets were pretty much deserted. The only sounds were the buzzing from the sodium streetlights and the ocean breaking as softly as water being tossed from a washbasin, and an occasional car whizzing past. It was late enough for the tourists either to be asleep or trying for a last-hour recoup of the money they were losing in the casinos.

This time, when he was awoken, the guard looked up crossly. He dialed, then pushed the receiver out to Ralph so he could hear the busy signal.

"Maybe something is wrong with the phone."

"Maybe," the guard shrugged. Nothing he could do about it.

Then Lucy drove up to the gate in her black Honda. "What's going on?"

Ralph explained. She motioned him into the car. The gate slid open and the guard saluted them in.

Lucy parked in her reserved spot. They rode the elevator to the fifteenth floor.

"He probably left the phone off the hook," Lucy said.

Ralph nodded. It was possible.

They walked down the carpeted hallway. Lucy rang the doorbell to her apartment. No answer. She kept ringing and knocking on the door. Lucy smiled nervously at Ralph. "Pablo and I have a place where we leave the key," she said.

She went to a glass-encased fire extinguisher on the wall, unhooked the door and felt around behind the extinguisher. "It's here!" She held up the key. "He may have gone to sleep and put the key there so I wouldn't wake him."

Lucy called out as she entered the apartment. Red drapes were drawn across the ocean-view picture window in the small, neatly furnished living room. All the lights were burning. Pablo was not asleep on the two wicker-backed couches or in the wicker easy chair. The receiver of a pink telephone on a lacquered round table was off its hook. Ralph cradled the phone.

Lucy opened the bedroom door. Three tabby cats scooted out of the room, spotted Ralph and zipped back under the bed. The bed was made. No Pablo.

"Here and gone," Lucy said.

"It looks that way."

"What happened he looked so fucked up?"

"That's what I was going to try to find out."

"You want some coffee?"

"Maybe a glass of water," Ralph said.

Lucy poured Ralph water from a bottle in the refrigerator, then put water on to boil.

"Did Pablo say anything earlier that may give us a hint where he's gone?"

Lucy spooned coffee into filter paper. She shook her head. "I asked him what happened to his arm and he said, 'I'm cut and bleeding, like I've been for forty-seven years'. When he starts with that shit, I don't ask him no more questions."

Ralph was about to sit at the dining room table when he spotted a half-empty bottle of Remy Martin there. Under a glass next to the bottle was a sheet of paper. It was in the form of a letter. Just one short paragraph:

Dear Ferdie:

The chickens have come home to roost. What are you going to do about it? Be prepared. Because I'm coming to get you, you sonovabitch.

The letter was not signed. But Ralph recognized Pablo's beautiful script. He folded up the note and slipped it into his pants pocket, wondering what the hell that was all about.

THREE

Pablo stood on the top deck, in front of the pilot's cabin. He had dumped the guy's knife into the bay during the first trip across, when it was still dark. Now, palest pink, like the cheek of a Renoir woman, began to show in the ghost gray sky, challenging the dark clouds that were sculpted on the horizon, like pieces of night determined not to go away.

The ferry pulled into the pier in San Juan, cutting its motor and bumping into the rubber tires attached to the side of the dock. Several bleary eyed, early shift workers hopped from the ferry to the pier. Pablo remained on the front deck. He needed more sky, more water. He needed to breathe. He'd take still another trip to Cataño and back before going to the airport.

About a dozen passengers got on, night-shift hospital workers still in their green scrubs, a scraggily junkie couple, a gypsy-looking guy carrying a peeling guitar case, a homeless, bent-over old woman, two drunken teenagers with torn shirts and puke-stained pants. The ferry was halfway across the bay again when the full flush of dawn spread across the sky. Then the sun crept up over the horizon and Pablo saw a flash over the ocean, like a personal signal. It was the first early morning flight up north.

He felt in his shirt pocket for his passport. He took it out. Last renewal was 1990. Where were we? 1998. It's good for another two years.

They lived in that small place over the canal, keeping the butter and the milk outside the window in the back. Firing up the stove every freezing morning. Ana buying flowers and plants off barges at the floating flower market. Ana's skirts flying above her knees as they pedal across the field to the windmill. Painting the golden fields, the endless sky. Sitting on the bench in the museum, looking at him, he looking back. St. Paul, holding the book, the turban, the clumps of hair over the ears, the ample pores in the nose, the whisk of mustache, the tuft of hair under the lip, the brown shadows around the eyes. So much in those eyes. The Master. None greater. Then why? Because the eyes told him to. To end all sorrow, all grief. They carry over. Beyond death.

The eyes of Rembrandt spoke to him. So did the eyes in his portrait of Albizu Campos. That story the other day on the tenth anniversary of the painting's unveiling, how he refused to sell it and kept it upstairs in his house. That reporter, or art critic, or whatever the hell she was, missed the point. He wasn't making a political statement, he painted the patriot with the human baggage we all carry as the end approaches. She quoted his detractors, who said he had insulted the great man. If that's what they thought, fuck them.

Why was that guy up there, cutting up that painting? Was the whole thing mapped out beforehand?

Ferdie knew the truth. It was time to find Ferdie, no matter how long a shot it would be, no matter where it would take him. He would make that sonovabitch confess whether the doctor's letter was true or not.

He had to get a deeper look into that doctor's dark heart. He needed to find the answers to put his head to rest, one way or the other.

He had killed another human being. Not even in Nam did he kill. Last night, he killed. In self-defense. Or was he driven to slash that guy's throat by something else? Was that his father's legacy?

He had to know the murderous depths of the man who had sired him, even if those terrible truths toppled him into some mad dark pit. Right now, inside his head, he was tottering on the edge, trying to get his balance.

As soon as the ferry docked again in San Juan, he would take off to finally search for the whole truth.

SAN JUAN, Puerto Rico, July 3, 1950 (AP)—The chief investigator looking into what a Rockefeller Institute doctor said was his joking claim to have killed eight patients acknowledged yesterday that hospital records showed that the doctor had directly treated eight of 13 patients who died during anemia research.

"The investigation is ongoing and we will speak to all relevant witnesses," said José Ramón Quiñones, the Puerto Rican Department of Justice's special investigations attorney.

Quiñones declined further comment on the case or whether Dr. Cornelius P. Rhoads, the doctor involved, would be subpoenaed in New York, where he now lives, to return to Puerto Rico to testify.

Dr. Rhoads had said he wrote to a friend about "killing off" eight patients in a parody letter that he never intended to mail. He said the letter was written to relieve the pressures of a long, exhausting day of treating island residents for anemia, research into which he and three other Rockefeller Foundation doctors have been engaged for the past year.

Rhoads said he "regretted that the fantastic and playful composition" was made public and taken literally by anyone. "At no time has any sort of experiment as satirically referred to in the letter actually been undertaken by me, or anyone else," he said.

The Foundation said it completely accepted Rhoads' explanation and praised him for his very important research, which could lead to a thoroughgoing and inexpensive remedy for pernicious anemia.

The Foundation brought Rhoads back to New York soon after his letter was made public, saying the move "was in the interest of continued amity between the peoples of Puerto Rico and the United States."

The letter was discovered by Alberto López, 20, a laboratory assistant at the Presbyterian Hospital, where Dr. Rhoads was engaged in anemia research.

López said the letter was in plain view on Rhoads' desk. He saw it, he said, when he returned to the laboratory one evening to perform his chores of sterilizing equipment for the next day's work.

The laboratory assistant turned the letter over to Nationalist Party President Pedro Albizu Campos, who released its contents to the media.

It was López who also tipped off reporters about the recorded deaths of the eight patients under the care of Dr. Rhoads. López said he received the information from "a fellow patriot" in the hospital's administrative office.

FOUR

After he had discovered and pocketed Pablo's note, Ralph stayed for coffee after all. It turned into an all-night talkfest, with Lucy doing the talking. He had asked her if Pablo had ever mentioned anyone named "Ferdie." Lucy didn't recall the name. But she did remember Freddie, the sonovabitch, who had been her pimp and pusher before they put him away for killing *his* pusher. She was off *perico, gracias a Dios,* and she no longer needed a *chulo,* she was her own woman, no one got her hard-earned money any more, except the school in Cali, her hometown in Colombia, where she sends Johnny, her seven-year-old, she tries to visit him every month, and now Freddie is writing her from the prison, he never realized how much he loved her, could she visit him sometime? Sure, when hell freezes over, why do men think it just takes sweet talk to make women forget what real bastards they can be? Which reminded her of the other *pendejos* in her life, from an abusive father, to an abusive first husband to a junkie second husband, who got her hooked for the first time on *perico,* which she stayed on for too long, to the asshole lawyer in New York who met her in court and said he would make an honest woman of her and set her up in an East Side apartment, then had her service his clients, including his 75-year-old father. "Compared to what I've seen in men," Lucy said, "Pablo's a sweetheart."

By the time Ralph got back to the Old City, the sun was moving off the horizon. Wooden shop doors were being creaked open. People were walking dogs. Strong coffee smells came from houses and *colmados*. And several people, including cops, were moving in and out of Pablo's house, ignoring the howls, growls and whimpering coming from Pablo's mutt.

When Ralph entered his own house next door, Tere was preparing breakfast for Diana. His wife gave him a look that was relieved and questioning and not without anger. Ralph took her into the bedroom and explained what he had seen the night before and where he had been.

"I woke up this morning and didn't see you and wondered what the hell happened," Tere said. "Then Doña Facunda woke up the whole block. She went upstairs in Pablo's house to clean the bathroom and she let out these shrieks, it curled your blood. I ran outside and Doña Facunda fell into my arms and told me what she saw, but thank God it wasn't Pablo. Or you."

Ralph put his arms around his wife, who was almost as tall as he. Her full body was warm and soft in the right places. He kissed his wife on the ear. Her black eyes gleamed, her dimpled chin shifted slightly and she gave him a mischievous smile, then broke away. "Put me on your schedule for tonight," she said.

"Done," said Ralph.

Then former corporation lawyer Tere, who had decided a few years ago that owning a laundromat was a more honest way to make a living, said: "Maybe you should talk to the police."

"I can't tell them anything about last night they don't already know. If they want to question me, let them come here."

"Pablo is one screwed-up guy," said Tere. "You two have been through a hell of a lot together. Vietnam. New York."

"I've got to find him," Ralph said. "It's my duty." After a pause, he added: "But first I got to fulfill my duty as a teacher."

While Tere finished making Diana's breakfast and helped her get ready for school, Ralph took a quick shower and drank one more cup of coffee. Tere drove Diana to her Catholic school in Santurce in the family's roof-rusted Plymouth Caravalle and Ralph took the bus to the University to give his class in *The Odyssey* and the Puerto Rican Diaspora.

The class discussed the storm that destroyed Ulysses' ship and pitched him, the lone survivor, into the sea, where he spent nine days clinging to the wreckage before being cast ashore. Ralph asked his students to write about something in their own lives that reminded them of the storm scene.

While most of the students mentioned hurricanes on the island and snowstorms in the states, Richie Pérez wrote that the scene set off memories for him of when he was ten years old and his old man in a drunken rage beat him and his Mom and set their two-room shack on fire. He and his Mom took off the next morning to New York with one piece of luggage and about fifty dollars in his Mom's purse. They wandered around the city for days, sleeping every night in a different place, mostly basements where they fought off the rats. He remembered one rat especially, it was practically cat-size and it squatted on an overhead pipe, then scampered away, then kept coming back and staring its red eyes at Richie for what seemed like all night. When the morning light started coming through a window near the ceiling and the rat came sniffing out onto the pipe again, like it was looking for breakfast, his Mom started screaming and crying hysterically and Richie picked up a large piece of wood that was in the basement and knocked the rat off the pipe and then beat it until he crushed its head. He and his Mom ate mostly handouts while his Mom tried to get work. Then his Mom finally found a cousin in the Bronx, where they stayed until they got back on their feet. Richie concluded: "That's the strongest memory of a storm in my life, worse than any hurricane I been through."

Ralph gave Richie Pérez an A+.

When he got home at about noon, he helped Tere in the laundromat, located in the rear of their building. La Perla, the squatters' slum, inclined steeply from the base of the Old City wall on the other side of the street to the ocean. TV antennas on the roofs of the houses crisscrossed against the sky in squares and rectangles, like a series of Mondrian paintings. As he stared out the window at the ocean and folded other people's underwear, Ralph thought of Max, his Swedish grandfather. Max fathered kids from San Juan to Sao Paulo to Surabaya and murdered one of his wives on the island of Borneo, then disappeared into the jungle until he was hunted down by the wife's brothers and hacked to pieces. That was the story passed down from Ralph's grandmother and, whether it was true or not, Max's turn-of-the century life sure would make a good second novel.

Ralph figured he had inherited his love of the sea from Max. Also his graygreen eyes. He hoped nothing more.

After a couple of hours, he staggered home and slept through the rest of the daylight hours. He woke at twilight to the sounds of a thumping, rattling bass beat and a repetitive, monosyllabic whine coming from his daughter's room.

Ralph got an argument from Diana when he yelled at her to lower the stereo. He also got angry barks from Pepa. Diana had taken the mutt home pending Pablo's return. His daughter wanted to know if Ralph's own parents acted the same mean way when he played his stupid music.

Ralph flashed on his eight-year-old self looking down at his father in a coffin. "Just turn down the sound a little, O.K.?" he said more gently.

Diana acquiesced.

While the family sat down to dinner, Diana came to the table carrying the book of drawings by Da Vinci that Pablo had given her. She had shown him the stuff she did in her sketchbook of her friends and Huggs, the guinea pig, and Pablo said it was really good. "If you look closely and concentrate, your eye will never lie, and if you put in the picture what you really see and feel, you'll be a great artist," Pablo told her. She was sure she would be a great artist and did drawings every day after school, running to Pablo's house to show them to him for praise and critique.

Tere served *carne guisada* with rice and red beans and a salad.

"What happened to Pablo?" Diana asked.

No one answered. Diana started crying. "He died in the shower," she said.

Ralph and Tere exchanged glances. "No, honey, that was someone else," Tere said.

"No, he died." Diana was adamant. She cried harder. The tears were coming out of the corners of her almond eyes. Her skinny body shook.

"No, baby, it was someone else," Tere repeated.

"Then where is he?" Diana asked.

"That's what Daddy is going to find out," Tere said.

After dinner, Ralph went to his study to call Pablo's ex-wife, Ana. Of course she had heard, it was all over the radio and TV. Of course he could come over.

Ana lived in a small house on a street lined with flower-blooming trees and bushes, near the University. Like most of the houses in San Juan, ornate grillwork curved out from the front porch and windows, to keep out the junkies who looked for quiet streets for their break-ins. The sweet, buttery smell of frangipani saturated the still, humid evening air.

As Ralph entered the living room, a wooden ceiling fan worked up a breeze overhead. Pablo's paintings adorned the walls, along with handsome posters of island-produced plays Ana had performed in: *Blood Wedding, A Streetcar Named Desire, Macbeth, Life is a Dream.* In her late forties, Ana's dramatic work was now mostly relegated to TV soap operas. She also taught a course in drama at the University.

Among the paintings was Pablo's portrait of Ana hugging her 10-year-old daughter, Emmy. Now, some 10 years later, sitting on a red, blue and yellow-flowered couch beneath the portrait was the same thin-faced, black-eyed Emmy. She unassumingly breast-fed a baby. Ralph learned the baby was Carla, Pablo's granddaughter.

Emmy was also an artist. She and a group of other young artists had just been given a commission from City Hall in Newark, where she lived, to paint a series of murals in the city's schools. She had come down to the island for a few days, she said, to introduce her daughter to her grandparents. She had phoned her father that she was coming down and he sounded excited. "He told me he wanted to see Carlita real bad, that he had been a bad father and now wanted to be a good grandfather, and I told him, it wasn't so, he always tried to help me out, I loved him and we wanted so bad to see him and . . . " Emmy's eyes filled and the baby started crying and Emmy stood and walked her around the room.

Ana introduced Ralph to another visitor: Manny Serrano, a small, middle-aged man with a pock-marked face and a tough New York accent. He was dressed in an expensive white linen suit. Serrano, Ana said, was an old friend who ran art galleries in New York and San Juan.

"I'm from the projects," Serrano said proudly. "Everyone thinks I'm into drugs, instead of Picasso and Wilfredo Lam and Pablo Camino."

Ralph sat in an easy chair next to the couch. Ana brought him a demitasse of coffee. Ana looked her age in the best sense. The lines and creases around the eyes and mouth in her round, still lovely face seemed to denote both a weary and a wary compassion. Her silver-streaked hair hung to her shoulders and she wore a simple green dress, small silver earrings and little makeup. A no-nonsense intelligence sparkled in her soft brown eyes.

Ralph told Ana and the others that he was looking for Pablo to offer him whatever help he could. But what, exactly, his friend's predicament was, Ralph wasn't sure. Ana said she had been trying to get in touch with him all day yesterday, but he didn't answer the phone.

"He was over at my house for dinner the night before," she said. "He was acting stranger than usual. We still see each other every so often. Whenever he comes over, he tells me that our divorce has brought us together. Anyway, he ran out without having his coffee and I knew something was wrong. I kept calling, but he didn't pick up. Even his answering machine was off. I hope he wasn't involved in anything crazy last night."

"I know Pablo," Serrano said, his face dampened with sweat. "Pablo is a lot of things, I'll tell you that. But my old friend, who helped me through a lot of tough money times in those early years, definitely ain't no killer. Something real crazy must have gone down there."

Ralph nodded. He was sure that Pablo acted in self-defense—if he did kill the guy in the shower stall. He knew that despite his friend's weird fantasies and sometime wild outbursts, he would not take another life. He wouldn't take the initiative to physically harm anyone except himself.

Beneath his friend's neuroses and fragile ego were a kindness of heart and a largeness of spirit. He was an artist, a creator, not a destroyer. Ralph would stake his own life on his friend's innocence to any charge of murder.

"Pablo saved my life," Ralph said.

"Really?" said Serrano.

Ana and her daughter looked at one another. "That was in Vietnam?" Ana asked.

"No," Ralph said. "Actually, it was in New York. In the East Village."

Ana pulled her head back. "He never . . . "

"It happened before you and Pablo got together. You know, Pablo and I met in a hospital in Saigon and we became fast friends. We got discharged about the same time and we both gravitated to the East Village and made it our business to rent apartments near each other. One night we were coming home from a neighborhood bar after a couple of beers, we had gone to a movie before that—a Buñuel film, I think it was *Belle de Jour* —anyway, we lived on opposite sides of Tompkins Square. I left Pablo at his ratty tenement on Avenue A and started to cross the park to my ratty tenement on Avenue B. It was about three in the morning and I remember it was cold and windy and the park was deserted. Then I saw this guy walking toward me and, you know, it's one of those New York things, even though he looked a little nutty, you keep going the way you were going. The next thing I knew the guy had an arm around my neck and we're tumbling to the ground and I hear my head hit hard on the concrete path and I feel like I'm going to lose consciousness while I see that the guy has a butcher's knife and he's about to plunge it into my face. Then, out of nowhere, the knife clatters on the pavement and the guy's head snaps back and Pablo is pummeling him and we both sit on the guy until a patrol car comes by and we get their attention. We found out later that the guy really *was* nuts, he'd stabbed two people earlier that night and killed one of them."

Ana asked: "How did Pablo know . . .?"

"Ten bucks," said Ralph. "He realized in the hallway of his building that he hadn't given me his half of the bar bill, so instead of waiting for the next day, like most of us would have, he came back out and ran across the park to pay me back. He saved my life."

"Incredible!" Ana said. "Pablo never said a word about that."

"Well it happened," Ralph said. "Here's something else that happened involving Pablo."

Ralph produced the note he had found in Lucy's apartment. "Pablo wrote this last night."

He handed the note to Ana. She read it aloud.

"Do you know who Ferdie is, and where he may be living?" Ralph asked her.

Ana answered with her own question: "Do you know about Pablo's father?"

"I've heard all the rumors, of course," Ralph said. "What would this island be without gossip and rumors? Let's see, I've heard that Pablo was the illegitimate son of Picasso, who his mother supposedly had an affair with when she was in Spain, even though Pablo already had been born and Picasso was living in France at the time. And that he was the product of a rape, his mother being accosted by an American sailor one night on the beach behind the Puerto Rico Casino in Condado. And that some doctor may have been involved. But Pablo never mentioned anything about his father to me."

Ana looked to the others in the room. "Well, the rest of us know some of it," she said. "This is what I can tell you, as far as I can reconstruct it from Pablo's disjointed accounts. Pablo's father was a doctor, an American named Cornelius Rhoads, who was doing some research work down here in the early 50's. While he was on the island, he met Pablo's mother, Julia Quiñones. You probably know her, she owns that art gallery on San Francisco Street, a few blocks from El Convento Hotel."

Ralph nodded. "I know who she is. I never met her."

"Well Pablo was their love child. But before Pablo was born, the doctor wrote a letter that supposedly said he thought Puerto Ricans were the lowest things on earth and he said he killed off a bunch of them and was planning to kill some more.

"Some lab assistant found the letter and gave it to Albizu Campos, the Nationalist leader, who turned it over to the press and when it came out in the papers it caused hysteria here. Rhoads said he was only kidding, he didn't kill anyone, he loved all of us, blah, blah. He had to leave the island. There was an investigation that people said was a whitewash. I think the letter was written to someone named Ferdie.

"Pablo was, and still is, haunted by what his father did, or didn't, do," said Ana. "I think this accounts a great deal for his paranoia. It was what drove us apart."

"Who is Ferdie?"

Ana shrugged. "Pablo never told me. I'm not sure whether Pablo knows himself."

"But what about Pablo's note?"

Ana shrugged again. "I can't tell you what was in Pablo's mind when he was writing that note. You must know, a lot of times his head works in strange ways. But one thing I'm pretty sure of: Pablo won't ever let go of his grief until he finds out the whole truth about his father, whether that man actually did what he said he had done."

One more quest for the enigma of patrimony, Ralph thought. The son knows the mother all too well; it is the father who is the great mystery.

He flashed on his own father, a tall, thin guy with a bent hairpin mustache. Drunk most of the time, but never mean or abusive. He cut out when Ralph was seven, his sisters, five and three. He died soon after.

Then Ralph remembered Pablo confessing to him one all-drinking, all-talking night he was afraid that one day he would kill somebody. That was drunk talk, Ralph was sure.

Ralph looked over to Pablo's granddaughter, who was back on the couch at her mother's breast, her eyes scrunched closed as she sucked greedily. Emmy smiled down at the infant. Ana, seated on the couch beside them, had an arm draped around her daughter's shoulder. Ralph thought of Tere breast-feeding Diana.

Before he left Ana's house, Ralph asked her for the phone number of Pablo's mother.

At home, he caught up on the news of the day. A late night TV newscast identified the victim in Pablo's home as Jaime Rosado Feliciano, age forty-nine. The newscaster said the victim had been a decorated Vietnam veteran who had a wife and three children, had lived in a working-class neighborhood and had held a construction job as a carpenter and an electrician.

Ralph felt uncomfortable. The guy didn't fit the profile of a late night burglar. He'd have to try to find out more about Jaime Rosado Feliciano. He should have known from his time at Confidential Investigations that trails always branch out, that he'd probably be going down several roads before finding Pablo and, he hoped, leading him back home.

FIVE

Julia Quiñones heard about it while having breakfast at La Bombonera. She overheard the old men who gather at tables in the back of the restaurant every morning talking about it.

Any out-of-the-ordinary news travels a mile a minute in the Old City. The discovery of the body was made about seven that morning. Three hours later, most of the residents of the seven-square-block area of Old San Juan knew that a dead body had been found in the home of well-known artist Pablo Camino.

When the old men in their starched guayaberas and Panama hats saw Julia seated alone in a booth near their tables, they suddenly lowered their voices and whispered among themselves. Doña Julia was known to them all, at least to exchange greetings. She was the daughter of former Justice Department Attorney Don José Ramón Quiñones and the socially prominent María Dolores Sotomayor de Quiñones, as well as the owner of the island's most prestigious art gallery. And, of course, the mother of Pablo Camino. The old men agreed on something and one of them, Don Bartolomeo Jesús Miranda Mondragón, a retired engineer, stood and came over to the booth where Julia was seated.

"Doña Julia, on behalf of myself and my friends," he said, motioning with his large gray head to the back tables, "we want to express our sympathy and solidarity with you over the events that took place in your son's home last night. We thank God that he was not the victim and apparently was not injured. We are sure that he will have an entirely understandable explanation once he comments on the incident."

"Thank you," said Julia, greatly shaken but, with a strong effort, remaining composed, as though she already was the recipient of the entirely understandable explanation. Then, deciding to drop the mask of knowing all about what happened, she asked: "Do they know who the victim is? Or where my son is?"

Don Bartolomeo said: "The victim has not yet been identified, according to the latest reports on the radio and the television. Nor has your son been located."

"Thank you," she said again.

The retired engineer gave a sideways nod and returned to his table. He gave the others a low-voiced update on what the mother did, or did not, know.

Julia finished her *mallorca tostada* and *café con leche,* then signaled the waiter for her check. She pulled down the sunglasses from the top of her head, adjusted them over her eyes and left the restaurant.

Where would she go now? Back to the gallery? To Pablo's house?

Why would she go to her son's house? Even if he had come home, what would they say to each other? When was the last time they had spoken at all?

She started down the street in the direction of her gallery-home. She was greeted by Don Antonio, the old man with gnarled hands who sold lottery tickets in the neighborhood.

"I have many tickets with sevens, *Señora*. This could be your lucky week," said Don Antonio, pointing to rows of lottery tickets on a wooden board.

She smiled and declined.

Would this be Pablo's unlucky week? What happened at his home last night? Was he all right?

Why should she care? Let him take care of himself.

He was her flesh-and-blood, for Christ's sake! She does care!

Or does she?

On the corner of San Francisco and San José streets, a tourist in a pink polo shirt and face to match asked her in broken Spanish for directions to El Morro Fortress. She answered him in her perfect English. "You speak great English!" said the tourist. Julia ignored the compliment and continued down the street, under the arches of San Juan City Hall.

Does she care? Or was she beyond caring? If anything, she was certainly . . . curious.

She had no pressing business at the gallery. She would open it later. She turned on San José and started up the street leading to her son's house, three blocks up, on top of the hill. After the first block, she could see the commotion going on up there. To get close to the house, she had to weave around several police, television and press vehicles parked not only in the street but also up on the sidewalk. A policeman stood at the open front door. Police and other law enforcement people were going in and out of the house. Julia joined the twenty or so people trying to peer inside. Several of them recognized and greeted Doña Julia and made a path for her. She moved to the door. She spotted a painted canvas in there. No doubt another torturous self-portrait.

Should she tell the officials who she was and enter the house? Why? To make sure that things were not disturbed. How would she know? The last time she had been in her son's house was several years ago.

As long as he was not harmed, she would not interfere. He had his life, she had hers.

But she could ask about the latest developments. Whether they knew where Pablo was, and what state he was in.

As long as he was physically intact, she would not interfere. No one, of course, would be able to vouch for his mental condition. Who knew what was in his head—now or ever?

It would be best if she let this "incident" play out, without butting in. Pablo had chosen to keep his distance from her because . . . well, because that's the way he was. She may have been hurt in the beginning, but one learns to accept. In fact, one now is rather glad that he made that choice. At her age, she no longer wanted any deep involvement, with family or with anyone else, for that matter. Stay out of what now is only peripherally your business, Julia.

She was about to turn and retreat to her own home several blocks away when she saw the painting being carried out of the house. A tall, muscular man in a black tee shirt, large dark sunglasses and a dark baseball cap carried it carelessly under his arm.

Julia approached the man. "Pardon me," she said. "What have you got there?"

The man scowled at Julia, then scowled at the painting under his arm. "Evidence," he said.

"Excuse me?"

"Evidence, lady. Police evidence."

He was carrying Pablo's portrait of Albizu Campos, the Nationalist leader. The painting was slashed across the eyes. Julia's heart dropped.

"That's a very valuable painting," Julia said.

"Uh, huh," the man said, moving toward a police van parked on the sidewalk.

"Be careful with that painting!" she shouted.

The man opened the back door of the van and tossed the canvas inside.

Julia angrily went up to the cop at the door. "Who is the chief investigating officer here?" she demanded to know.

"Lieutenant Miró." The policeman looked young enough to be her grandson.

"Please tell him the mother of the owner of this house would like to speak to him."

"He's upstairs, *Señora*, and I can't leave my post."

Julia walked right past the young policeman into the house.

"Señora, por favor." The policeman sprinted after her and grabbed her arm.

Julia pulled away. "Don't you dare . . . "

"I'm sorry, *Señora*, but my orders are that no one . . ."

Julia started across the room again and got to the foot of the staircase leading upstairs. She was grabbed by the arm again.

"This is my son's house! Don't you understand? Let go of me!"

Her shouts brought several men to the top of the steps. "What the hell is going on?" one of them yelled.

"Where is Lieutenant Miró?" Julia shouted back up.

After a few seconds, one of the men treaded down the stairs. His small eyes were creased in anger. Then he saw the person causing the commotion was an elegant older lady. He actually smiled and gave Julia a small bow. "Lieutenant Detective

José Julián Miró Amador of the Homicide Division, at your service, *Señora.*" The burly detective was dressed in an expensive hound's tooth sports jacket, knife-creased black slacks, a white shirt and a red tie.

Julia spoke more softly. "Good morning, officer. I'm sorry if I've disrupted your investigation. My name is Julia Quiñones and the artist, Pablo Camino, who owns this house, is my son. I saw one of your men carrying out a painting by him. It is a valuable work of art and, from what I saw, greatly in need of repair. It can't be treated carelessly. It must, in fact, be rushed to an expert in restoration. It is an historical painting."

"I'm very sorry, *Señora,*" the detective said. "The painting appears to be an important piece of evidence. You have my *personal* guarantee that it will be treated with the greatest of care."

Julia sighed, as though saddened. *"I'm* sorry, officer, but that's not good enough," she said. "I have to take the painting with me immediately. I'm the owner of the Galería Quiñones on Cristo Street and many of my son's paintings are under my care. I feel responsible for all his works."

"I'm very sorry, *Señora,*" Lieutenant Miró repeated.

Julia glared at the detective. His face was expressionless, but for a tiny sparkle in his small eyes, as though he were enjoying denying Julia what was so obviously important to her. "By the way, *Señora*," he said, "would you be able to inform us of the whereabouts of your son?"

"I don't know where he is," Julia said, her anger starting to show, she was sure. Then she said: "Why is that painting evidence?"

"We think it may be," Miró said, this time his expression showing that he was losing patience. "There seems to be something that looks like recently dried blood on parts of the canvas. Galería Quiñones on Cristo Street? If your son is not located shortly, perhaps one of our agents could drop by and ask you a few more questions."

"I have nothing further to say to you about my son," Julia said, turning and marching out of the house.

Her stomach churned as she hurried down the street back to her own house. She wanted two things: nothing further to do with this incident, and to save that painting. She would try her damnedest to accomplish both.

SIX

Pablo checked into a small, comfortable hotel on Fifty-Sixth Street off Fifth Avenue. He registered under the name John B. Gillespie.

As soon as his bank had opened in the Old City, he had made a large withdrawal, then taken a taxi to the airport and bought a plane ticket at the counter, paying with cash. Now he got into a hot bath, keeping his bandaged arm out of the water. The area around the cut throbbed with pain. He was afraid to take the bandage off and look at the damage. He'd give it another day or two. It would either get better by then or his arm would have to be amputated. Fuck it.

The hot water relaxed his body and lightened his head to the point where he almost dozed. He forced himself out of the stupor and pulled the plug in the tub and with his one good arm pushed himself up and out. He grabbed a towel piled on a rack above the toilet bowl. He put on the brown corduroy pants and red-and-black flannel shirt he had bought with other stuff at Macy's before checking into the hotel, put his wallet in his pants pocket and the passport into the shirt's top pocket. He got into a dark green parka. He'd forgotten to buy shoes and had to wear his black espadrilles. He had too much to do now, he'd buy boots later.

Once outside, he was hit by a wicked gust of New York winter wind. He put the parka's wool-lined hood over his head and buried his hands into the side pockets. He reached Fifth Avenue and headed for the 42nd Street Public Library.

When he found Ferdie, he'd make him tell him everything. He wanted to learn why he had to kill a man. He knew the connection with the past was there. He killed because what happened all those years ago had shifted atoms that played into the Universal Scheme. Because where there was a will, there was material input. His head ached; he didn't want to think about it any more.

He'd killed another human being, for Chrissake! The guy was cutting up the Albizu painting. Something he had wanted to do several times, himself.

The knife slashing across the throat. The blood spurting into his eye and mouth. It was warm, thick, sticky, like heated syrup. He felt something in his own throat. Like a chicken bone stuck there. He shivered uncontrollably. He had killed another human being!

He reached the library, bounded up the steps between the lions, remembering sitting on the top steps on spring days so many years ago, reading the letters of Van Gogh to his brother. He entered into the majestic marble hallway and made his way down a side corridor to the Microforms Room.

Seated behind a desk was a severe-looking, middle-aged woman with glasses hanging on a chain around her neck and an institutional frown on her makeupless face. Pablo asked if it was possible to find an obituary of a doctor who had worked at the Rockefeller Institute and died some ten years ago. He asked hesitantly and shyly. The woman looked coldly into Pablo's eyes, then shifted her gaze around his face. Her expression changed and her face softened. She directed him to a shelf with books that listed decades of obituaries in *The New York Times*.

"Look up your doctor, find the date of his obituary and we'll get a microfilm copy." She patted the gray brown hair on the left side of her head and offered Pablo a warm smile.

Pablo found the doctor's name and the date, June 23, 1986. He filled out a slip requesting a microfilm copy of the newspaper and gave it to the woman.

"That was fast," she said, smiling again. "I'll be right back." She went behind a counter and disappeared among the files.

She returned ten minutes later. "It's not there," she said. "Someone must have it out." She hooked her chained glasses around her small, protruding ears and went through dozens of slips like the one Pablo had filled out. "I don't . . . wait, wait . . . here it is. It was signed out two hours ago."

"So what do I do?" Pablo asked.

"I'm afraid you'll just have to wait for it to be returned," the woman said, not unsympathetically. "Someone over there has it." She pointed to dozens of people reading and turning microfilm at machines in the room.

Pablo went to a rack and took the day's *New York Times* to a desk. He read the paper halfway through, checked again if the microfilm had been returned (negative), then finished the rest of the paper. He went through a *Village Voice, New Yorker* and *Art News.* The microfilm still had not been returned.

A clock on the wall said a quarter to four. He had entered the room at about one. He would have to spend the whole day here, maybe into the night, waiting for that fuckin microfilm!

He left the library and stood on the steps zipping up his parka. The wind whipped little twirls of dirt and sailed sheets of newspaper across the library steps. He'd forgotten how damn cold and gray and windy and depressing it could get in this city. He hurried down to Lexington Avenue, found a bar, and had a double cognac.

He returned to the library. The woman who had helped Pablo was no longer on duty. In her place was a slender young man with a narrow, pale face and perfectly parted and combed black hair. Pablo explained the situation and the young man shrugged.

"Could you check to see if the microfilm has been returned?"

"You'll have to fill out a form on the desk over there."

"I already filled out a form."

"Where is it?"

"I don't know, I gave it to the woman who was here before you."

"Well I *certainly* don't know where it is," the young man said.

"Would you look on the desk in front of you?"

"Those are all my papers. We take our papers with us."

"Look, just check and see . . . "

"I'm sorry, sir, but you have to fill out a form first."

Pablo figured he had two choices. He decided to forego the first one, which was to reach over and slap the snotty jerk behind the desk silly. Instead, he crossed the room and, politely, began to ask the people behind the microfilm machines which publications they were reading. If they had the *Times*, he asked which dates they had out.

Finally, near the end of his search, he found the microfilm he was looking for. It was in the possession of a small man in a ratty gray turtleneck sweater that seemed to have provided a feast for moths. The man wore thick rimless glasses and, when

Pablo approached, was scribbling furiously in one of several notebooks piled in front of him along with several boxes of microfilm. When Pablo told him he had been waiting hours for that particular *Times* microfilm, the man got defensive. "First come, first served," he said, peering deeply into the machine.

Pablo bent down so that his face was on the man's ear level. The guy smelled of urine and rotted foods. Pablo spoke softly. "Don't you think someone else should have a chance at the film?"

"I'm doing very serious research here," the guy said, his eyes remaining glued on the microfilm. "I'm collecting sentences in the *Times* and other newspapers that incorrectly use modal verbs in the future subjunctive. I intend to publish . . . "

"Look, this won't take me too long. Fifteen minutes at the most, then you can have the film back."

"Don't bother me, all right? Just wait your turn, O.K.?"

Pablo felt his jaws tighten. He took a deep breath. He continued to speak softly. "Listen, asshole, give me the microfilm or I'll snap your head off."

"Are you drunk? I smell liquor on your breath! You're drunk!"

"You got 'til the count of three before I break your fuckin neck with one quick twist of the head. I did it to hundreds of Gooks in Nam. One. Two . . . "

The man stood, collected his notebooks and hurried from the room. He stopped at the door, turned and screamed at Pablo. "You're ruining my research on modal verbs in the future subjunctive!"

People looked over. Pablo smiled, shrugged and tapped his head. The others smiled back, seemingly satisfied, and relieved, that one more of the city's multitudinous nut cases had just left their midst.

The librarian came over. Pablo explained that he found out that the man had the microfilm and all he did was ask politely when he would be through using it. "The guy just cracked."

The librarian was about to say something and Pablo narrowed his eyes and the young guy saw something there that made him keep quiet. He began boxing the reels lying on the desk and set up the one Pablo wanted to read.

"Thanks," Pablo said.

The young man nodded and retreated to his desk.

The obituary took up most of a column running down the left side of the page. There was a photo of Dr. Rhoads above the story. Pablo looked at it closely: He saw a pleasant looking man in horn-rimmed glasses with close-cropped hair and a wide, full mouth much like his own. It was difficult to make out the eyes behind the glasses and there was too much shadow around the nose to judge if it bore any resemblance to the thick straightness of his own. But look at the mouth and the dimpled chin!

Pablo tried to shake off the unmistakable patriarchal recognition.

He scanned the obit and found what he set out looking for, in the second from last paragraph: "Dr. Rhoads leaves his wife, the former Dorothy Meadows of Newtown, Conn., and his daughter, Iris Leslie Rhoads of New York City." He copied down the names, then read the rest of the obit, which ran one column down the side of the page:

Dr. Cornelius Packard Rhoads, director of the Sloan-Kettering Institute for Cancer Research here since 1965, died last night at his summer home in Stenington, Conn. He was 67 years old.

Dr. Rhoads, an inveterate pipe smoker, died of cancer of the mouth.

As the scientific director of Sloan-Kettering, Dr. Rhoads was in charge of one of the largest concentrated programs for the study, treatment and cure of cancer in the world.

"Dusty" Rhoads, as he was called by his friends, had long been hopeful that a chemical cure of cancer would be found.

Rhoads was born in Springfield, Mass., on June 20, 1919.

In 1940, he graduated from Yale University. He spent one year at Harvard Medical School, then entered the Army Medical Corps. He resumed his studies in 1944, was named class president and graduated cum laude in 1947.

After serving a year's internship in surgery at the Peter Bent Brigham Hospital in Boston, Dr. Rhoads returned to Harvard Medical School in 1949 as an instructor in pathology.

Coming to New York the next year, he joined the staff of the Rockefeller Institute for Medical Research. In 1952, Dr. Rhoads enlisted to serve again in the Army Medical Corps, where as a colonel he became chief of the medical division of the Chemical Warfare Service.

He directed the toxicological research laboratory at Ft. Detrick, Md. and Camp Drum, N.Y., and the medical research laboratory at Ridgeway Proving Ground in Utah.

He also directed medical testing stations in Florida and the Panama Canal Zone.

After his discharge from the Army in 1958, Dr. Rhoads was special consultant on cancer to the U.S. Public Health Service and consultant to the Brookhaven (L.I.) National Laboratories of the Atomic Energy Commission. He also served in other posts connected with government programs.

Dr. Rhoads was named director of Memorial Hospital in 1960, and of the hospital's Sloan-Kettering research unit five years later.

The quiet-spoken man with the close-cropped iron-gray hair and blue eyes belonged to more than thirty professional medical and scientific associations.

His articles in medical journals numbered more than 100.

He leaves his wife, the former Dorothy Meadows of Newtown, Conn., and his daughter, Iris Leslie Rhoads of New York City.

No mention of what happened in Puerto Rico. Not that Pablo expected anything in the obit that would sully the deceased's reputation. The sonovabitch was never found guilty of anything.

But all that stuff about chemical warfare, medical testing stations and the Atomic Energy Commission sent an icicle sliding through Pablo. What did all that mean, especially in relation to the doctor's killing claims? He said in his letter he was transplanting cancer into his patients. What other kinds of "research" was he doing in Puerto Rico?

What kind of monster had sired him? How much of the doctor's poison was in his own genes? Pablo's nerves started jumping along his arms, he was hit by a wave of nausea. He took several deep breaths and left the library.

He started up Fifth Avenue, packed with end-of-day office workers, around-the-clock shoppers, corner food vendors. Cars rattled over manhole covers and steam was coming up from the covers and out of the stoves in the vendor's carts. Five o'clock twilight was settling over the street and the wind had died down. He reached Fifty-Sixth Street and was about to turn up the street to his hotel. He would try to find the phone number of the doctor's survivors, if they were still around, and call them from his room. Possibly get to see them.

What would he say on the phone? Something to think about. Over a drink.

He looked for a taxi to take him down to one of his old watering holes in the Village. There were scores of cabs running down the avenue, but they were either taken, or the driver's were off duty. He found himself in front of the Plaza Hotel. What the hell. He went inside, passed the Palm Court and went to the Oak Room Bar. He ordered a Remy.

What would he say over the phone?

The Palm Court. She had told him to meet her there. When was that? Almost thirty years ago. He was in his first year of college. He had taken the Broadway local up from the Village for lunch with her. The convention she was attending was at another hotel, uptown, near Columbia University. That hotel was just too shoddy for her, so she was staying at the Plaza.

It was a rainy, chilly day in early summer and he arrived twenty minutes late, soaked to the skin beneath the collarless cotton shirt from India and the thin white cotton pants he wore. His mother cancelled the table reservation at the Palm Court, sent him to her room with orders to put on the terrycloth robe up there and dry off while she bought him a new shirt—a blue checkered button-down—in the hotel boutique. She had lunch brought to her room.

Pablo was glad they were eating alone in the room. He had something very important to discuss with his mother. He meant to be stern, but as he looked into her tired, but still luminously beautiful dark eyes and at her still-lovely face, which often took on a severe expression to mask her vulnerability, he felt a familiar pang. But he steeled himself. He had to find out for sure.

First, he would talk of lesser things.

"The University sent you to the convention?" he asked.

"Yes, so I can see how far behind we are from the other university museums."

"*Abuelita* sent me the article. It says that in just three years, you've become the best curator they ever had there."

"I'm just trying to catch us up to the Twentieth Century."

"The article says that you felt the year you spent in Spain on the fellowship was worth all the years you spent at the University and in graduate school."

"I know what the article said, dear."

Pablo noted a hint of impatience—or something else—in his mother's smile, as though she may not want to be reminded of the article, or of the year in Spain.

"Yeah, I know. It's just that . . . well, it was great spending all that time with you. I still remember going to the Prado for the first time, seeing the Velázquez. I remember how you explained to me that the artist was the guy in the painting with the mustache holding the brush in front of the large canvas, that the king and the queen were in the mirror in the back of the painting, they were looking at the little princess who was looking at the people looking at the painting. I loved those paintings there, bigger than life, and the thick colors. I especially loved the dwarf woman with the bulldog face in the Velázquez."

His mother smiled.

"But also, you know, I hated Madrid."

The smile twitched, then faded. "Oh, really? Why was that?"

"I don't know, I remember that I always felt cold, even inside the house. I missed my friends in New York. I just felt sad there a lot."

"Because you were with me all the time, instead of just now and then?"

"Come on."

"I'm just teasing."

"No, I don't think you are. Look, I understand that you wanted what was best for me, and that different things happened that kept pulling you back and forth, you know? Like when after we came back from Spain and granddad had the stroke and *abuelita* couldn't handle it, she was so used to being rich and going her own way and being pampered herself, right? He didn't want a nurse, who was a stranger, right? So you went back there, and left me again with *Tía* Merci."

"My mother couldn't . . . "

"I know. It's O.K. I understand and I'm glad you told me. It's just that I don't want anything . . . Well, you know, we should always be truthful to one another."

Silence. They ate their dessert of cherry cheesecake and sipped coffee.

"How is school going?" his mother finally asked.

"Good."

"What courses are you taking?"

"You know, the usual stuff they give freshmen—drawing, design, history of art. Look, do you have any papers, or anything, about my father, you know, like his years in the Army?"

His mother stared hard at Pablo. "As a matter of fact, I don't. All those things he left with his parents, who, as you know, are no longer living."

"Nothing at all? No medals? Citations? Nothing about his service?"

"I told you. All those things were left up in Connecticut. Why are you so insistent?"

I want to know as much as I can about my father. You've never told me much about him. I want to know what type of a person he was. Is there anything wrong with that?"

"No, nothing," Pablo's mother said quietly.

She poured more coffee out of the silver pot brought by room service. Her jaw was set tight. He noticed something both defiant and pleading in her eyes, which stared into his over her coffee cup.

He felt ashamed, as though he was about to crush a sacred bond between them. But a self-righteous anger was also rising.

"My roommate, Charlie Foster, his father works at the Pentagon, so I asked if he could ask his father to find out, you know . . . His father made a search but he couldn't find any record of a Roberto Camino reported as missing in action in Korea."

"So the records are missing also," his mother said. The challenge and beseeching remained in her eyes. Then, gradually, they filled with tears.

His mother sighed deeply, wiped away the tears with her napkin. She took another deep breath. The severe mask slid over her face. "All right, I suppose it's time to tell you the whole truth. I just won't go into the details. Here it is, short and sour.

"Your father was not a young Puerto Rican medical student, who was drafted in the Korean War. Your father was an American doctor named Cornelius Rhoads, who was in Puerto Rico doing important medical research for the Rockefeller Institute. We met at the Casino, and we fell in love. At least I did. He left during my pregnancy and put me through a miserable time and I haven't heard from him since, nor do I want to. So let's just let sleeping dogs lie."

Pablo felt himself shaking inside. But he too wanted to keep a cool, severe demeanor.

"All I wanted was the truth. If this doctor treated you so badly, the only thing I wish for him is a miserable, painful life. I wouldn't want to have anything to do with anyone who would hurt you so badly."

He hugged his mother and they parted somewhat awkwardly. He felt she was making an extra effort not to cry again. He believed he now understood why she never remarried.

On his way back to his school on the subway, he even smiled at the M.I.A. designation she had given his father, not to mention his fictitious name (Camino for Rhoads). Which made his name—Pablo Camino—less than the truth. So what. He was who the hell he was. He felt cauterized.

But, then, a deep depression set in. He realized why he lived with his mother's sister all those early years, before the boarding school in Pennsylvania and now Cooper Union in the East Village, why all those elaborate tales of his mother traveling back and forth between the island and New York—jobs, study programs, family crises—and why he was told he was being kept at a private school in New York, ostensibly to give him the best education possible.

Now he knew why those explanations were always made to him with an underlying sense of shame. She had hid the fact of him from her family for all those years. The guilt probably got too great. Which was why finally she confessed to her parents, if not to him.

If she loved him, why did she treat him that way? Why did it take her so long to say to hell with what the rest of the world thought? Why wasn't she thinking of him, of his feelings? She never thought of his feelings.

Pablo downed another cognac. He was hit by a deep, troubling feeling: His manic ways were just the topside of something much deeper, some void nagging in the pit of his stomach, maybe forever.

Maybe. But right now, to keep what sanity he still possessed, he had to find Ferdie, or others related to the man who was his murderous father.

Just one more cognac before moving onward, and upward, or downward.

SEVEN

The morning after he saw the TV report about the body in Pablo's house, Ralph found the guy's street address in the newspapers. He cancelled out of a working lunch he was supposed to have had that afternoon with members of the Humanities Department, which, he was sure, pissed off the little Hitler who ran the department no end. Well, fuck him, Ralph had much more pressing business to take care of. Such as picking up clues to the whereabouts of the best friend who saved his life.

Ralph drove slowly along the teeming Avenida Borinquen, past street vendors hawking lottery tickets, sunglasses, cheap jewelry, coconut ice cream and *piraguas,* past the bargain clothing and shoe stores, small *colmados,* McDonald's and Popeye restaurants, scores of funky-looking bars, and a Blockbuster Video store. Women dragged tots along the avenue while kids in school uniforms—the girls in plaid jumpers, the boys in polo shirts—ran by hitting each other and laughing, and men lounged on corners drinking beer. Barrio Obrero, as its name implied, was a working-class neighborhood of San Juan. Its residents held jobs from time to time, but almost all of them lived on the edge of poverty.

On Calle Buenos Aires, Ralph made a right, drove up three blocks and made a left onto Calle Caracas, a street of small wooden homes. There were some trees along the street, whose sidewalk was covered with white and red blossoms. The road further down was torn up and flooded from a broken water pipe. Ralph parked at the corner and walked down the street. He easily found the house. It was on the far corner. A fetid odor from the water pumping into the road overpowered the sweet smell of the fallen blossoms. Mourners spilled out onto the street down from the small porch and from inside the home of the Rosado family.

Ralph had been set to introduce himself as a private investigator (he still had his Confidential Investigations credentials). He was prepared to say that he was hired by Pablo's family to find him and, if necessary, arrest him, although the family believed that the murder was committed by a third party. Ralph was going to say that above all, he would see that justice was done for the unfortunate victim. But he hadn't expected to find a full-fledged wake in progress.

He walked up to the porch, where snacks and sweets were laid out on a table, and went through the open front door. The small front room was packed with people sitting on plastic sofas and on several wooden folding chairs and standing around, the compassion on their damp faces tempered by their self-consciousness. It was hot as hell in the room, which was pervaded by the odors of sweat and incense. An open white coffin was propped on a stand against the far wall. On the wall was a painting of an agonized Christ, whose heart, visible through his thin, transparent chest, was Day-Glo red and bleeding. Below the Christ painting were crossed Puerto Rican and American flags. What looked like mosquito netting sloped down from the wall beneath the flags to cover the top half of the coffin. Two young men looked gloomily into the coffin. What appeared to be the immediate family—a stout woman with rings under her eyes as black as her dress and holding a squirming infant in her lap, a thin teenage boy with a nervous tic under his eye, a very pale, beautiful girl whose slender fingers were webbed with a twisted handkerchief—sat next to the coffin on folding chairs. Their faces seemed to have been emptied of all personality and pretense and filled with pure grief and suffering.

Ralph returned to the porch. He went to a table filled with paper plates of little cakes and candies and crackers and cheese and soft drinks. He picked out ice cubes from a plastic chest under the table and poured Coke into a plastic cup.

A heavy, middle-aged woman seated across from the table on a small metal sofa with red plastic pillows caught Ralph's eye and smiled. He smiled back. The woman patted the space next to her for Ralph to sit down. A chance to speak of the deceased, Ralph thought. He'd get some background on the guy, to try to figure what he was doing at Pablo's house.

"Would you like something to drink?" Ralph asked before going to the sofa.

"A Coke would be magnificent!" the woman said, crossing the thick ankles that showed beneath her white pants suit.

Ralph poured out another soda and handed it to the woman and sat next to her.

The woman downed the Coke in a few gulps. "*Muchísimas gracias!* You read my mind. You must have special powers."

"Not that I know of," Ralph said.

"We often do not know what we do, indeed, know. Most people, for instance, are unaware of their own deeper psychic sense, that it needs to be developed," said the woman, whose skin was cinnamon-colored and eyes a grayish blue. The eyes had a strange glow, like fire was banked beneath them.

Ralph smiled and nodded. "Are you a member of the deceased's family?"

"We are all members of the same family," said the woman. A note of challenge crept into her eyes.

"Of course," Ralph agreed. "I was just wondering about the poor Rosados. About Jaime . . . "

"No need to wonder, or to worry," said the woman. "The soul of Jaime will return to this earth."

"Yeah, well, I mean, while he was living, now, until two days ago, what was he . . . ?"

"It was just one of many lives he has had on earth. His soul will return into another body and, one day, it will become in tune with the Cosmic Consciousness. Then it will emit a blinding light that will be seen over all of space and for all time."

Ralph downed his Coke. "Good point. Well, I should be going."

"Wait!" the woman ordered. "I have something for you." She picked up a large white purse from the ground and dug inside. She came up with a pamphlet and gave it to Ralph. "Read this, my friend, join us and your life will change as you move into the inner self and onto the mystical path." She smiled warmly and confidently. "The Eighth Temple Degree will teach you all about reincarnation and karma and even how to remember your past incarnations. Then you will be ready to experiment with telepathy, telekinesis, vibroturgy, radiesthesia, the alchemic cloud and invisibility!"

On the top of the pamphlet, Ralph saw the drawing of a rose on a cross, the symbol of the Rosicrucians. He thanked the woman. He got up and started down the steps of the porch. He would have to return to speak to the widow another time.

He walked to the corner. He was thirsty again. Before he got into his car, he stopped into a small *colmado* for a cold Medalla.

An elderly man stood at the counter nursing a beer. He greeted Ralph. "Have you been there?" he asked, motioning his head in the general direction of the wake.

Ralph nodded. "And you?"

"Yes, sir," said the man, shaking his head sadly. "What sorrow!"

Ralph said: "He was a good man."

"Yes, sir." The old man's small black eyes were lit in his wrinkled brown face, looking like glossy beads on a walnut shell. He wore a starched white guayabera over rumpled dark slacks.

"Are you a relative?" Ralph asked.

"No," said the elderly man. "Just an old friend of the family. And you?"

"Just a friend of a friend," Ralph said. He waited. He knew the old guy was about to talk up a storm. He waited, finishing his beer. The old guy just continued to shake his head. Ralph ordered another beer, and one for his companion.

"*Gracias,*" he said.

"Did you know Jaime Rosado well?"

"I knew Jaimito since he was a child," the old guy said. "His father, Chu Rosado, was my friend, God rest his soul. Jaimito was just a small boy, you know, when his father died. Chu and I used to play poker, you know, every Friday night, in the back of Don Carlos' furniture store. Don Carlos, I, Chu and, let me see, sometimes Paco from the colmado and, yes, always *Señor* Fabregas, the gentleman who rents houses. A fine gentleman, he moved to one of those fancy urbanizations up in the hills where you can look down and see the city lit up at night like the Good Lord threw diamonds down there from the balcony of His heavenly home, you know, *Señor* Fábregas came to play cards with us every Friday night, he smoked cigars from Havana and always brought along a bottle of Felipe Segundo, which he shared with us.

"Then, of course, my friend Chu got very sick and went to the hospital, where he died and little Jaimito grew up in this barrio without a father but became a fine young man and married Doña Carmen and they had three wonderful children, also one, or two it was, maybe, who died just after being born, you know."

Ralph nodded, as though the old man was confirming what he already knew about Jaime Rosado and his family. "What a shame Jaime's life was taken this way," Ralph said.

"What sorrow!" the old man repeated. "And what nonsense that they say he was trying to rob that house. Not the people who know him, but the papers and the television, you know. I have known Jaime Rosado all his life. He is a vertical man, honest and hard-working."

"So what do you think happened?"

"What happened? Only the Good Lord knows," said the elderly man. Seeing that Ralph looked disappointed, he added, "Perhaps it had something to do with his nerves."

"Maybe."

"Yes, you know he went to fight for the Americans in Vietnam and he was a hero and won many medals and after he came home he went to the Veterans Hospital because of his nerves. After they let him out, he went back again."

"He must have suffered in the war. Sometimes you never get better from that."

The old man nodded. "He was in the hospital more than just the two times. Always for his nerves. What happened to him at that house must have been because of his nerves."

Ralph and the old man nodded at one another, agreeing on the possibility that somehow Jaime Rosado's nerves had led to his throat being slashed, presumably by Pablo.

"What sorrow," said the old man.

Ralph shook the old man's hand. He had something to track down: the victim's hospital records.

During his class the next day, a messenger came by to hand Ralph a note from the head of the department summoning him to a meeting in his office. "Tell him I can't make it today," Ralph told the messenger. After the class ended, he went instead to see Julio Torres, who headed the psychology department. Torres gave Ralph the name of Dr. Jesús Marchand, a psychiatrist who had dealt with Vietnam vets. Marchand suggested that Ralph speak to Dr. Raúl Sanders, who worked at the Veterans Hospital and may have been familiar with the case of Julio Rosado. Sanders told Ralph that any information on Rosado would have to come from Dr. Pedro García Ríos. García Ríos was at a conference in Washington, D.C. and wouldn't be back for another few days.

Ralph had more luck with Julia Quiñones, Pablo's mother. When he phoned that afternoon, she agreed to see him the next morning.

She lived by herself in a two-story restored house in the Old City, close to the bay, several streets down from Pablo's house. One drinking-talking-listening-to-jazz all-nighter, Pablo had made some bleary remarks about how his mother had sold the family's palatial home after her parents died and had decided to move into the Old City. "She did it so she could to spy on me, like everyone else," Pablo had said. He said he had seen her less often in the seven or so years she had lived close by than in all the years before. "We fight about everything. She knows so damn much about everything, except what's in her own damn heart. She won't tell me anymore about . . . some things in our past. I think she may be in it with them."

Ralph hadn't asked in what with whom.

Julia Quiñones ran an art gallery out of the first story of her home. She featured Latin American artists like Wilfredo Lam and Rufino Tamayo and Omar Rayo, and exhibited her son's earlier paintings, but had said in a newspaper interview that she did not love his latest work. She lived on the second floor and greeted visitors in her roof garden, an amazing tangle of huge-leaved banana trees, palms, twisting vines, flowering plants and shrubs. The garden was partially enclosed by plant-climbing trelliswork and a light green plastic awning. On especially hot days, the greenery gave off an old familiar fear-smell of a suffocating Vietnam jungle. That was the way Ralph felt sitting up there against the huge round back of a wicker chair at close to high noon, sipping a demitasse of rich black coffee, then downing a tall glass of ice water.

Although Pablo had pointed her out to him, Ralph never officially met Pablo's mother, whom he figured must already have hit seventy, though she looked at least ten years younger. The wrinkles on her neck were an undeniable sign of her age, as were the freckles on the back of her hands, but, except for the tiny crow's feet around her eyes, her skin was remarkably smooth, and it didn't have that elasticized surgery look either. Her eyes seemed both bright and brooding, as though they still fully took in and continued to pass judgment on what was before them. Her makeup was minimal and she wore a long flowery skirt and a plain white blouse with the sleeves rolled up to her elbows. Her one outward sign of vanity was her hair, which was colored reddish brown and held around and atop her head by a variety of combs and clips.

Ralph explained that he was Pablo's friend and neighbor. Julia Quiñones nodded. "I know," she said. "Pablo told me about you when we were still talking to one another."

"I want to find him and help him," Ralph said.

"I certainly hope you do," Julia said. "My son has strange traits," she said with a benevolent smile, as though oddness was, perhaps, even more acceptable than normalcy. "But committing murder certainly is not one of them. I'm sure there is an explanation for what happened, and why he is where he is, wherever that is."

She didn't seem to be overly concerned about what happened at Pablo's house or about her son's disappearance. Maybe, Ralph figured, this was her way of hiding her true feelings, for whatever reasons. Or maybe she just didn't give a damn.

"Do you have any idea where Pablo may have gone?"

"None whatsoever. My son and I have had rather strained relations in the past several years."

Ralph nodded, confirming he already knew that. "I traced him to a friend's house after what happened at his house. I didn't see him or speak to him, but he left a note before he left from there." Ralph took Pablo's message from a pocket and handed it to Julia Quiñones.

She squinted at the note and the creases around her eyes deepened. "I'm sorry, I don't have my glasses. Could you read it to me?"

Ralph read the note. Pablo's mother put a hand to her lower lip and pulled on it. Her body twitched and she snorted, either in a derisive, or nervous, reaction.

"Do you know who Ferdie is?"

"Yes, I suppose I do," Julia Quiñones said with a sigh.

Ralph waited.

"Do you know about Pablo's father?"

"I know a little."

"Ferdie is a friend of Pablo's father."

Julia Quiñones picked up her demitasse of coffee and daintily sipped from it. She carefully put the cup into a saucer on the round glass table between their chairs.

"Ferdie is, or was, Pablo's father's *best* friend," Pablo's mother said. "He understood everything about Pablo's father: who Pablo's father loved, and to what degree, and who he hated, as well as his most secret desires, and fears. He knew of his plans and what Pablo's father considered his greatest successes and most crushing failures. Ferdie knew *all* the secrets in the heart of Pablo's father because, you see, Ferdie was an *imaginary* friend. Someone to whom Pablo's father addressed letters that he never mailed. His make-believe confessor, to whom he confessed abhorrent ideas and sins he never committed. Strange, but true."

Ralph's eyes scrunched up. He tapped the flat space below his nose, as though he were trying to recall something. "Ferdie doesn't exist?"

"No, he does not, and he never did," said Julia Quiñones. Her mouth was set in a defiant finality. Then she smiled. This time it was a warm, almost flirtatious smile. "I'm sorry I can't help you on this point, that is, in bringing Ferdie to life as a possible way to find my son."

"Does Pablo know that Ferdie is, was, a figment of his father's imagination?"

"I have become completely baffled as to what my son currently does and does not know, or what he *believes* he knows, which, unfortunately, in these past years, has shifted from day to day. Perhaps we can explore other avenues. Maybe Pablo's art, his latest work, could offer some clue as to where he may have gone."

"I don't understand," Ralph said.

"His latest paintings, the ones I've seen at least, are all self-portraits, but they lack a humanity that appears in his earlier works, his portraits of others, even of his younger self. There was always loneliness, fear, paranoia, pain in his earlier paintings, but there was also a humane feeling for his subjects and for the world in those paintings. I don't see that anymore in his later works. All I see there is a morbid sadness and a maudlin self-pity," said Julia Quiñones, art critic.

"And . . . "

"And, perhaps he has gone to find his humanity."

"Where would he go looking for it?"

"You could narrow it down to somewhere in this world."

Great, thought Ralph.

"By the way, did you know that one of Pablo's paintings was slashed that night?"

He nodded, remembering seeing it on the floor in Pablo's house the morning after.

"I'm going to try to get it back from the police so I can have it restored. They're holding it as 'evidence'. It's absurd." The woman seemed genuinely perturbed.

Ralph returned to what was truly bugging him. "Excuse me for bringing this up again," he said, "but are you sure that there never was a Ferdie?"

The cause of annoyance in Julia's eyes seemed to shift to Ralph. But she quickly recaptured her aloof pleasantness and said: "Yes, quite sure. He, Pablo's father, once told me that since he was a child he had been writing letters to his make-believe friend. It was his way of confessing the sins that were in his head, if not truly in his heart, and certainly not carried out in reality. There never has been a Ferdie. People, you see, are stranger than you may think."

Ralph nodded, as though he were just learning something. He stood and thanked Pablo's mother for allowing him to visit her.

"And I thank you for taking on this perhaps hopeless task of trying to find my son," Julia said. "If the truth be known, I don't believe you will find him until he finds himself. And that may never happen."

Ralph left, with a grudging admiration for Julia Quiñones' honest appraisal of, if not warm display of love for, her son.

Ferdie was an imaginary friend? Should he believe her? Why would she say such a thing if it wasn't true? Ralph figured that was for Julia Quiñones to know and for him to find out.

August 23, 1950

Rockefeller Institute
1230 York Ave.
New York, N.Y.

Dear Julia:

Please excuse me for not writing sooner after my abrupt departure from your lovely island, but, as you can imagine, the work at the Institute has been considerable. I had hoped that the furor over that foolish letter would have died down by now, but I understand that no such luck, that your government has been pressured by that shrewd communistic, Yanqui-Go-Home politico Albizu to conduct an investigation into the whole ridiculous affair.

I have written to the Governor to tell him that I would certainly return to Puerto Rico if I am needed to testify during the investigation, which, I also understand, will be conducted by your father, who I have always respected as an honest, upright and moral public official, regardless of what you have heard me say in more frustrating moments about the government of Puerto Rico.

Julia, to be perfectly honest, I would rather not return for an inquiry as I am sure my presence on the island would be used by our political enemies who would stop at nothing to try to embarrass the United States as well as the Puerto Rican government, which your father has served so honorably.

You are an intelligent woman, I would not have fallen in love with you if you had not been, and I'm sure you understand how our enemies could discredit us. I have been warned that if I ever set foot in Puerto Rico again, the "open secret" of our "relationship" will be made public, which, of course, could greatly discredit your father's investigation, not to mention his career. Perhaps you could use your considerable influence with him to spare me an appearance, unless, of course, he deems it absolutely necessary.

How are you feeling, dear Julia? Do you still have that morning nausea? It certainly could not be what you feared, or I'm sure I would have heard from you by now. I'm sorry our parting was so bitter. I still remember those magnificent nights at the casino, dancing under a million stars, none as bright as your beautiful eyes, and that smell of jasmine, never as sweet as the aroma of you.

And, of course, how could I ever forget our lovely nights together, how you understood my predicament and how those surreptitious meetings made our time together all the more poignant and–why deny it?–so much more pleasurable.

I am truly sorry that we parted as we did. I know how you hate to fly, but perhaps you could take a boat to New York and we could spend more glorious time together.

Looking forward to your reply, I remain indebted to you for your loveliness.

With all my love,

Dusty

EIGHT

Pablo's joyous smile, his body on the cusp of ascending to thrilling, previously unattainable heights, are frozen for the generations, until the already browning snapshot turns yellow, then fades into ghostly outline, the features indiscernible shadows, as though the development process were being reversed. Julia Quiñones stands behind and below her son, her arms outstretched, as though calling a halt to his lift-off, as if she really hadn't wanted to give the initial thrust to his soon-soaring ride into the leaf-tumbling autumn air.

Merci accidentally had gotten just the right setting and angle so that three-year-old Pablo flew high and slightly blurred in the foreground, his eyes wide at another of life's infinite possibilities, while a miniature Julia stood in focus in the background, her body expressing her tentativeness at letting go.

She used a magnifying glass to call up her young, lovely face. A smile widened young Julia's expression, but aging Julia believed she detected worry lines around the eyes. The concern, she acknowledged, might not have been for that caught moment, but for her general cast of mind at the time.

The visit of Pablo's friend, Ralph, had upset her. She fought it, but the discomfort became too strong and compelled her to go downstairs to the office-storage room behind the gallery and retrieve the photo albums from the old trunk she had saved from her mother's house. The trunk was stickered with pictures of cruise ships—the Queen Mary, the Normandy, the Gripsholm, the Rotterdam.

She took out the albums and put them on the old leather couch and sat next to them. Her heart tightened as she stared down on Pablo on the swing.

All those times he had held tight to her skirt. "Don't go, Mami*!" She had had tears in her eyes too. She could see his anger toward her, which he would take out on himself, pulling his fingernails down his cheeks and punching himself in the chest. She tried to tell him that she loved him and that* Tía *Merci loved him and would take care of him and that she would be back very soon, but he would continue to cry and to plead: "Don't go,* Mami, *don't go. Please, stay, stay!" He would scratch and hit himself again and then she would have to harden her heart and tell him: "Stop this, right now! That's enough. No more crying, do you hear me?"*

She would leave and he would scream and kick and bite his arm.

She turned the page of the album. They were in front of the Christmas tree in Merci's apartment, Julia down on her haunches, cheek-to-cheek with her son, and she felt now the warmth and the softness that often threatened heart meltdown then if she had not marshaled her controlling forces. She had learned to fight being swept away by feelings that did not lead to remembered happiness, but to anger and guilt because of the inevitable shortcomings of the people in her life. The same spurred, perhaps, by her own failings.

Here they were in Madrid, in front of the Prado—Who took the picture? Darned if she could remember—Pablo holding her hand, his child's face filled with some sort of adult grief. Was she just projecting this? No, look how he seemed so close to tears. What had happened that day? Perhaps nothing, perhaps it was the accumulation of the sorrows of a young lifetime.

But her post-Dusty years had not all been distressed. She had loved that year in Spain. Studying the masters–she had papers published on Velázquez and Murillo–researching in the Biblioteca Nacional, spending the mornings and early afternoons in the library and in the museums while Pablo was at school. Cafés, dances, fancy restaurants, movies, theater, concerts—none of those had mattered that year. Her friends had been minimal, her lovers non-existent. But it hadn't mattered. She had studied and she had learned and she had taken care of her son and that had been enough to fill that one happy year of her life.

Even those visits toward the end of the year hadn't upset her. They were thousands of miles apart, nothing the friend could say was able to change her mind or her heart.

She flipped through the album.

Julia, young and beautiful, dark as an Indian, on the beach behind the Condado Beach Hotel, with Paula and Gloria, at water's edge, their arms around one another. Her best friends, the three of them inseparable through their teen years and into their early twenties. Paula and Gloria had insisted that the handsome young doctor she had met while volunteering as a candy striper at the Presbyterian Hospital was a prize catch, as though she were the winner of a fishing tournament.

Everyone at the Casino liked him so much. Undoubtedly he was from a good family and there was money in the background. An a*mericano* doctor, not bad Julia.

And then *she* arrived, two weeks after their meeting.

Puffing on his pipe, the licorice smell of the tobacco wafting in the air, he offered a contrite explanation at the little café where they met for lunch in the hospital patio. He and the woman had been engaged for three years; he had been trying for several months to think of the best way to break it off; their families up in Connecticut were very close; it would be a great embarrassment all around. But he *swore* he no longer loved her. Unfortunately, she planned to stay three whole months in Puerto Rico. But *they* had to continue to meet. His love for *her,* Julia, demanded it.

Her mistake had been ages old: to surrender everything within herself. She swore after that she would never leave herself open to such hurt again.

A Casino dance, a photo of the guests as they entered into the ornate, chandeliered foyer. She, all smiles in that exquisite primrose pink embroidered gown. He, tall and handsome in his tux, standing beside her, looking somewhat uneasy—the prize fish, hooked, reeled in and hung next to its captor.

Paula married an *americano* land developer who went to prison for selling swampland in Florida. She died, several years ago, in Orlando. They had lost touch at least thirty years before that. Gloria was living in Australia with her fourth husband. They still exchanged Christmas cards, even though they hadn't seen each other for at least ten, fifteen years.

Why hadn't she managed to sustain an abiding relationship with any of the close friends of her childhood and youth? She felt the tears welling. She couldn't blame this on the vagaries of life. It was something inside her. Enduring relationships meant potential hurt. She could do without confusion in her waning years. She wanted order, emotions in their place. She was willing to lapse into melancholy every now and then to avoid the *real* pain of chaos.

And then there were the two of them, at the nightclub in New York, the photo at his insistence, one copy for each of them to cherish, she, her fingers on the stem of a cocktail glass, looking shame-faced, he, puffing on his pipe, self-satisfied. Once more her weakness had come through.

He had continued to write, even through "that inanity of nothingness"—his words for her father's investigation of his letter to Ferdie—swearing his undying love, pleading that she meet him in New York. She knew he could not have done what he had said in that infamous letter; but he destroyed in other ways. His later letters had been forwarded to her from Puerto Rico—little did he know she had been living less than ten blocks from his lab at the Rockefeller Institute.

She decided to answer one of the letters. She said she was in New York and would meet him for a short time. She didn't say whether she was looking forward to seeing him again, nor did she mention that she was eight months pregnant. She *was* looking forward to their meeting—as a final act of revenge.

She had hid her pregnancy from her parents and her closest friends, faking a study grant while living in New York with Merci. Now he would be the first of the old crowd at the Casino to know.

When he saw her approaching through the lobby of the Plaza, bulging in the yellow flowered maternity dress she had bought at Bergdorf's for the occasion, his reaction surprised her. He sprang up from the sofa, hurried over to her, took her hand and kissed it; then he bent over and kissed her stomach.

"I knew it," he said. "I *knew* it!" There were tears in his eyes.

During lunch, he once again professed his love and swore to the heavens that he would support the baby. He mentioned nothing, of course, about marriage, which they both knew was out of the question. Her father's investigation had cleared him for lack of evidence but concluded that he was "mentally unbalanced or a man of few scruples." He was still engaged to his longtime Connecticut girlfriend. A further "scandal" could only hurt his career, as well as Julia's and her family's reputation.

He begged her to keep in touch, let him know when the baby was born. Could he visit her at the hospital after the birth, to see his child? Would he be able to visit them after she took the baby home? Where was she living? Did she have enough resources? Could he hire a woman to help her?

She was taken aback. His concern seemed genuine. But she would not buckle; basically, he was a self-centered, selfish sonovabitch. Her great misfortune was to have fallen in love with him.

When they parted, she said she would get in touch with him after the baby was born. She didn't, but he found her through hospital records. Over the years, even after he finally married his long-time fiancée, he pleaded to see her and the child. She gave in halfway, occasionally meeting him for lunch to let him know how his son was progressing. She even went with him that one time to a nightclub, but never, despite how much he begged—and he *did* beg—never to bed with him again. She had refused to take any money from him for Pablo and had been strong enough to deny his requests to meet or speak to his son.

Years later, while she was staying a few weeks with Merci—by then her gypsy life was taking her back and forth between New York and Puerto Rico every few months—they had met for lunch at the Metropolitan Museum of Art. He had seemed especially on edge that day and practically demanded that she arrange a meeting between him and his son.

"I have a perfect right to see my boy," he told her. "If you persist in your attitude I'm going to contact my lawyer, and we'll take you to court."

"Nonsense," she said. "You have no rights here. You are a . . . a deserter. No judge will rule in your favor."

"Look, Julia, don't do this to me, please. I've made mistakes in the past and I'll probably keep on making them. But I appeal to you . . . "

"I'm sorry."

He stared at her through the wisp of smoke rising from his pipe. The eyes behind his horn-rimmed glasses that seemed a soft azure a moment ago both lightened and hardened into a steel blue. "You are hard-headed and hard-hearted. I want to see my son, to have some influence on his life. I don't want him to wind up one of the useless ones, a loser. And I'm not going to let you get away with it, you understand?"

"What exactly do you mean by that?"

"Figure it out." He pulled some dollar bills from his wallet, threw them on the table and left.

The next morning, as snow swirled through the air and skipped across the sidewalk in a mini-blizzard, flying like confetti through the branches across the street in the park, and while Julia waited with Pablo outside their building for his school bus, she saw him, two blocks away. He had just gotten out of his black Mercedes, bundled in a gray scarf and a long black overcoat, an Ushanka Russian fur hat on his head. She knew he knew where she was staying, although he had never tried to visit.

She was frightened that he would come up to them and . . . who knew what? She tightened her hold on Pablo's hand. Her son pulled away, ran to the curb. She shouted at him. Pablo picked up some snow, packed it into a snowball and threw it at a tree in the park. It smacked against the trunk. Then he came back to his mother and held her hand again.

He stood there, in the street, in front of his car. He seemed to be softly clapping his gloved hands.

They stared at one another. If he made a move, she would dash back into the lobby with Pablo. If he threatened, she would tell the doorman to call the police. But he just stood there, softly clapping.

The bus drove up. She let go Pablo's hand and her son climbed into the bus and waved at her. She waved back. The bus took off and she looked over to him. He was no longer there. She saw his car heading in the opposite direction of the bus and she began to breathe easily.

Although he did not show up again, he barraged her with phone calls and letters. He warned that if she didn't agree to visitation rights he would make her life miserable. He would hire lawyers, he would kidnap the boy, he would get thugs to beat her up. She convinced Merci to move with her to another apartment across the park. They changed their phone number. Still, he was able to locate her and the harassment continued. She thought of making a complaint to the police, but was afraid that this would involve her family in Puerto Rico, who would then learn the truth about her frequent trips to New York. She was beside herself. As she laid plans to escape back to Puerto Rico with Pablo and confess all, the attempts at contact stopped.

Until Spain.

Once again, he had found where she was living. The letters came often. But this time they were full of remorse. He had acted like a crazy imbecile and he begged her forgiveness. He was planning a trip to Europe that summer, would he be able to see her and finally meet his son?

She ignored the letters, but they kept coming, each more apologetic than the last. Every day he realized more and more how much he truly loved her, and what a fool he had been not to have taken her away with him when he could have. They would have worked it out. They still could. He still wanted in the worst way to see his son. It was eating away at him that he had never spoken to or hugged or looked closely into the eyes of his own flesh and blood, a boy whom he had always wanted.

Then the other one, who was in Spain on business, came to see her, on his behalf. He said Dusty was suffering all these years in the realization of what he had lost. Dusty wanted to do everything possible for the boy's future, his friend said. He would arrange to legally give the boy his name, pay for his schooling. All he wanted was to meet the boy. During several visits, the friend pleaded Dusty's case. Still, she refused. He had put her through too much. It was over, ended.

Until just recently, anyway. Then the letters from the friend. They were proper and respectful, but with some hints of weirdness. And now Pablo's craziness.

It was no one's business about her affairs. She didn't want anyone digging up that old dirt. It was enough that all the "survivors" were seemingly destined to be haunted forever. Let the sleeping past lie. Exploring it would only bring about more confusion and misunderstanding, more heartbreak.

NINE

As soon as Pablo returned from the bar at the Plaza to his overheated room, he was overcome by a tremendous drowsiness. But he had to find the telephone number first. He was sure that if there was anything to be learned it would be through the daughter rather than the widow. He took out the slip of paper from his shirt pocket. Iris Leslie Rhoads. His half-sister.

He pulled out the Manhattan phone book from beneath the night table and squinted through the pages. He had left his reading glasses in Puerto Rico. He could barely read the obit in the library.

What if she lived in Queens or Brooklyn, or had moved out of the city altogether?

He found Rhoads. Ida, Igor, Ira, there it was: Iris. There were two Iris Rhoads. He dialed the first number. The phone was picked up immediately after the first ring.

"Where the *fuck* are you?" The woman had a voice like a buzz saw.

"I'm . . . umh . . . at my hotel."

"What?"

"What d'you mean, what? Look, I'm trying to reach Iris Rhoads."

"Ain't this Jimmy?"

"No, it's not Jimmy."

Then who the fuck are you?"

"Is this Iris Rhoads?"

"That's right. Who the hell are you?"

"Iris *Leslie* Rhoads? The daughter of the late Dr. Cornelius Rhoads?"

"You got the wrong number."

"I guess so."

"But I'll tell you what. I like your accent. Why don't you drop over? I'm at . . ."

Pablo hung up. Wrong Iris Rhoads. He tried the next number. This time the voice was soft but a little impatient.

"Hello?"

"Hello, is this Iris *Leslie* Rhoads?"

"Who's calling?"

Pablo felt the suspicion and the possible anxiety. But, so far, no traces of hostility.

"My name is Pablo . . . um . . . Camino. I'm looking for the daughter of Dr. Cornelius P. Rhoads." He could hear the slur in his voice. Not good.

"What is it?"

"Well, you see, I'm looking for Dr. Rhoads' daughter to see if she could help me in my search for . . . um . . . some information."

Damn, he was tired. And sounding stupid.

"What exactly do you want?" The voice on the other end was hardening.

"Look, I'm a relative of yours. It's a little awkward talking about this on the phone. Could we meet?"

"What do you mean? Why?"

Say something intelligent and understandable, for Chrissake.

"Before your father married your mother, he was involved with my mother. That was down in the Caribbean. I . . . "

"What the hell are you *talking* about?" Her New York belligerence was starting to break through.

"I'm sorry if I'm not making much sense, but . . . well, I have to see you as soon as possible."

"Well, I'm sorry too." She hung up.

He'd fucked up. He'd call again. But not now. He'd only make it worse. Wait till tomorrow. Come on, he's got to see her. He started to dial, stopped and put the phone on the hook. His head felt as heavy as a block of granite. The granite tumbled onto the bed and his body followed. Just before he passed out, he remembered that he had forgotten something very important, but didn't know what it was.

As soon as he awoke he picked up the phone book. He was feeling much better this morning. His head was much clearer. He'd give a more cogent explanation this time, invite her to lunch. At the Plaza, in the Palm Garden.

He dialed. The phone rang, three, four, five times. An answering machine switched on. He hung up.

He picked up the phone book again and copied down her address. One fifty three, West Fifty Fourth Street. Just two blocks from the hotel!

Pablo looked at his watch. It was a quarter past ten. If she had a job—and why shouldn't she?—she probably wouldn't be home till evening. What the hell does he do now? He goes over there, tries to find out where she works. Does what he has to do to get to talk to her.

He took a quick shower, dressed and walked the two blocks to his newly found sister's apartment house. Light snow fell. A robust-looking doorman stood by the building's front door, hunching his shoulders and wiggling his gray-gloved fingers. His doorman's cap was pulled halfway down his flat forehead. Black hair bunched out from the back of the cap and curled up like ruffled feathers. "Good morning, sir. Can I help you?"

"I'm looking for Ms. Iris Rhoads."

"She's not here right now, sir. She left for work more than two hours ago."

"Do you know where she works?"

"I'm sorry, sir, I couldn't tell you even if I knew."

Pablo nodded understandingly. "I'm a relative of hers and I've just come up from Puerto Rico." Pablo saw the glint in the doorman's eye at the mention of Puerto Rico and knew he'd found a *compatriota*.

He continued: "I'm in New York just for a few hours, then I have to go to Jersey to see my sick mother. So I thought I'd come right over to see Iris before that. We haven't seen each other in years. I guess I should have called first."

The doorman gave a little sympathetic nod.

"She's not still working for that art gallery downtown, is she? If she is, I can grab a cab down there and take her to lunch."

The doorman shrugged. Maybe he wasn't all that sympathetic.

Pablo dug into his pocket and took out his wallet. He pulled out a twenty-dollar bill. He told the doorman in Spanish that his mother would be very disappointed, he hoped it wouldn't make her sicker, God forbid, if she learned that he was in New York and didn't visit the daughter of her sister. "The Puerto Rican family, you know how it is."

The doorman smiled a warm, broad smile. "Yup, I know how it is," he said, studiously avoiding a shift of his hazel eyes from Pablo's mouth to the bill in Pablo's hand. "It could cost me my job, sir, but we're all family, you know. Miss Rhoads, I believe, works at Hunter College, over on the East Side. She gets a lot of stuff delivered to her from Hunter, and when I gave her an envelope from there a couple of months ago, she told me that was where she worked."

"Mil gracias." Pablo thrust the twenty-dollar bill into the side pocket of the doorman's coat.

The doorman silently nodded, not so much thanking Pablo as confirming that they had just made a fair exchange. "Hey, *hermano,* don't tell her I told you, O.K.? I could lose my job, *¿Tú sabes?*"

Pablo waved in the doorman's direction and hailed a passing cab. He told the driver to take him to Hunter College. They cut through Central Park to Lexington and Sixty Ninth Street.

The college's midtown campus was a complex of tall buildings spread over both sides of Lexington and partially up toward Park Avenue. The snow thickened considerably and had begun sticking to the ground. Pablo padded over the thin coating in his espadrilles.

He stamped through the front door of one of the buildings, deadpanned a security guard who eyed him suspiciously, then walked around the hallway until he found an office called the Welcome Center. A young, attractive black woman with close-cropped hair on her perfectly round head sat behind a desk.

"May I help you, sir?" She had a lovely smile and spoke in a clipped British accent.

Pablo explained that he was trying to locate his cousin, Iris Rhoads, whom he believed was a professor at the college. The young woman said she was new at her job, but she would do her best to help him. Pablo admitted that he didn't know in what school or what courses she taught. The young woman continued to smile and patiently went through a list of names on a computer screen. After several minutes, her eyes lit up.

"Here it is, sir," she said excitedly. "Professor Iris L. Rhoads, Lesbian and Gay Studies." She giggled, then looked up guiltily, her large brown eyes asking forgiveness.

Pablo gave her a reassuring smile. "Would you know where she is now?"

"Her office number is 1405N. That's in the North Building on the fourteenth floor, sir."

He got directions from a student how to reach the North Building, then took an elevator to the fourteenth floor. A typewritten three-by-five card on the front door of 1405N gave Prof. Rhoads' Wednesday office hours as 11:30 a.m. to 12:30 p.m., and 4 to 5 p.m. He looked at his watch. It was 11:25. He was in luck.

A few minutes later a pretty, smallish woman in a black turtleneck sweater, gray tweed slacks and pointy black boots came down the hallway. Her salt-and-pepper hair was cut to just below her neck. Under her right arm were papers and manila files and envelopes. From the fingers of her left hand dangled a set of keys. She nodded tentatively at Pablo, opened the door to her office, then turned toward him. "Can I help you?"

"I'm the guy who called you last night." Pablo saw that his gentlest smile did not prevent fear from sparking in the woman's eyes. He quickly added: "I wasn't very articulate and if I made you uneasy I'm truly sorry. But I really would like to talk to you about something that I think is important to both of us."

Iris Rhoads' slanted green eyes filled with a hard, penetrating light as they studied Pablo's face. "Wait out here until I make a few necessary phone calls. Then I'll see you. But," she warned, "it can only be for a few minutes. I have a faculty meeting at noon." Pablo nodded.

Pablo waited. At five minutes before noon, the professor came to the door. "Please come in, Mr. ....?"

"Pablo."

"Come in," she said.

Books and papers were piled on a desk, on shelves along the walls and on the floor in two corners. A poster above the desk announced the first Honanga Wahine Takatapuhi/Lesbian Studies Conference in Aotearoa, New Zealand. Blow-up photos of Eleanor Roosevelt, Gertrude Stein and rock singer Patti Smith hung on the walls.

Iris Rhoads sat on a swivel chair in front of the desk and motioned to a straight back wooden chair in front of her. Pablo sat in it and their knees touched and Iris quickly shifted her chair to undo the contact. They both crossed their legs and Iris stared down at one of Pablo's still sodden espadrilles. He smiled sheepishly.

The phone rang. She smiled the benevolent smile of the selfless put-upon, then picked up the receiver.

Pablo's half-sister had a slight dimple in her chin and a generous mouth, the marks of the Rhoads-Camino clan. She looked to be in her early forties. High cheekbones and almond eyes were an exotic touch. No makeup covered the lines around her eyes. Pablo decided that she had an attractive face.

"Well, that's the post-modernist queers for you, they want every goddamn thing their way," she said to the person on the other end of the line. "They want to dismantle everything."

She said goodbye and hung up the phone and smiled at Pablo. "I'm sorry, just some internecine campus warfare." Professorial and in charge on her own turf, and seeming to have lost anxiety over Pablo's persona, she looked over rimless half-moon glasses with an inquiring, slightly condescending expectancy. "What can I do for you?"

"I know I sounded pretty incoherent over the phone last night, so I'll try to get to the point right away. We both have the same father. Dr. Cornelius Rhoads. He met my . . . "

"Whoa! Hold on! What's going on here?"

"Just hear me out, please, all right? Rhoads met my mother when he was working for the Rockefeller Institute in Puerto Rico. They had an affair, before he married your mother. Which makes us half-brother and half-sister."

Sister Iris' green eyes turned hard as malachite. She stared coldly at Pablo, then put one hand over her mouth and chin, as though to hide any family resemblance. Then she returned her hand to the armrest of her chair and nodded several times. "I love it," she said as though she didn't.

"Do you know about what happened when your father was in Puerto Rico?"

"What do you mean?"

"Do you know about the problems he had down there during his research?"

She shook her head impatiently, looked at her watch. "I'm sorry, but I don't know anything about him being in Puerto Rico. Also, as I told you, I have to attend a faculty . . . "

Pablo's head got light and he felt the nerves twitching again on his arms. "The guy, *your* father, and mine, wrote a letter saying he killed eight patients. On purpose. He said later he was only joking, but there was a big investigation over it. He was let off the hook, but . . . he passed it on."

"Passed what on?" Her eyes were beginning to glisten with fear again.

"The sins. What d'ya think?" Pablo shook his head, wondering whether she was playing dumb.

Her mouth creased in a worried frown; she looked over his head. He was starting to lose her.

"Look," she said, "I have no idea who the hell you are and what you're talking about. Where are you going with this?"

Pablo took out his wallet. From one of the compartments he extracted and unfolded a copy of a newspaper article from a December 1950 edition of *the San Juan Sun*, which reported on the investigation the Puerto Rico government did of the affair and reproduced the letter to Ferdie. He handed the article to Iris. She read it, then handed it back.

"So what happened? Were there ever any charges filed?"

"No, like I said, he got off the hook. My grandfather, my mother's father, was the government attorney in charge of the investigation. Because of Rhoads, I've been haunted, all my life, you know what I mean? It comes and goes. There have been things . . . "

"I don't see . . . "

"You know about his work in the Army on radiation, don't you? And do you know about the radiation experiments the Army was doing on people at the time?"

"Hey, hold on. My father did cancer research. For years, he headed the most prestigious cancer institute in the nation. He was a leader in . . . "

"You knew him. Deep down, what do you think? Was he capable of any of this stuff?"

Iris Rhoads covered her mouth and chin with her hand again. She stared at Pablo, but seemed to be looking deep inside herself.

"Do you know who Ferdie was, the guy who the letter was written to?"

Iris shook her head. "I don't know. Maybe . . . No, I don't know."

"Maybe what?"

"No, I was just thinking." She looked at her large, round-faced, leather-strapped watch again. "I have to go to the meeting now."

"I really need your help. Can we meet later?" Pablo put on his best craggy faced vulnerable look.

"I have classes and appointments here the rest of the afternoon."

"Could we meet for dinner?"

"I'm sorry. I already have a dinner appointment."

"What about tomorrow night?

"I don't know. I may have something then also. I'll have to check." She stood. So did Pablo. She looked up into his eyes, then quickly looked away. "I don't know . . . "

"I can call you," Pablo said. "You're in the phone book."

"Unfortunately, yes," she said with a small smile.

Pablo spent the night visiting old haunts in the Village and drinking moderately. He wanted to be in good shape when he tried to contact his half-sister the next day. He was sure she could give him crucial information about their father.

She didn't completely trust him. Who could blame her? He'd try to gain her confidence the next time they spoke.

He called at seven-thirty the next morning. The phone rang five times before she picked it up.

"It's Pablo, your umh . . . from yesterday. I hope I haven't called too early."

"I was just finishing up my coffee. I'm on my way out," Iris said.

"Look, I know what I told you yesterday sounds weird, but I'm asking you to trust me and to help me to . . . well, to find some peace of mind. Please have dinner with me tonight and I promise I won't bother you again."

"Can't we speak over the phone?"

"I suppose so, but face-to-face is always better, and now that I found you, my sister, my half sister, I'd like to know you and I'd like you to know about me. How many chances do we get to discover new relatives, new siblings, at this time in our lives?"

There was a pause. Then Iris said: "Call me here at about five. I should be home by then and I'll be able to tell you if we can meet tonight."

"Thanks. I'll call."

Pablo spent most of the day at the Frick, in front of the Rembrandt self-portrait, stunned by the gold and the sepia and the ivory and the red, lost in the light and the shadows playing over the face of the artist, trying to connect with the stern depths in the eyes, cauterized in both pain and joy.

None greater.

He returned to his hotel and called Iris at five. She wasn't in. He called at five after, then ten after. Still no answer.

At five fifteen, she picked up the phone. "I'm sorry, I'm a little late getting home," Iris said. "As for this evening, well, O.K., I'm clear."

"That's great!" Pablo said. "I'll pick you up at about seven, all right?"

"That's fine," she said. "You know where . . . "

"Like I said, you're in the phonebook."

"So I am."

Another doorman on duty called upstairs and Iris met Pablo in the lobby. They took a taxi to a Spanish restaurant near Fourteenth Street that was one of Pablo and Ana's favorites in their New York days. Don Manolo, the owner, greeted Pablo with a hearty *abrazo* and pointed out that one of his paintings, a portrait of Ana, still hung over the bar, despite "monstrous offers" by art collectors. Manolo sent over a bottle of *Finca Valpiedra,* joined them for a toast to everyone's health, then returned to his perch behind the bar.

"You're a well-known artist," said half-sister Iris. "I'm impressed."

Pablo, as usual, grunted at any recognition of his status in the art world.

They shared a magnificent *paella* and Pablo ordered a second bottle of wine. They finished off their meal with Felipe Segundo brandies. Iris matched Pablo drink for drink. She quizzed him about how he had located her at Hunter and he said he was sworn to secrecy, but would tell her if she insisted.

"Who gives a damn?" she decided, then asked him about "things that really mattered," such as his painting, and his likes and dislikes among artists. The phonies were too numerous to mention, he said, and he surprised no one with his admiration and love for Velázquez, Goya and Rembrandt. He told her about sitting in front of a Rembrandt self-portrait in the Amsterdam museum, both mesmerized by and trying to mesmerize the painting, trying to get it to literally speak to him.

"Were you successful?"

Pablo shrugged. "A little."

"What did you two talk about?"

"Inevitability. He told me that to live is to suffer. And that death is no release. I always suspected that. He confirmed it."

Iris' smile disappeared when, looking deeply at Pablo, she seemed to understand he was in earnest, that he was truly serious, sensitive, tormented.

He didn't tell her about the other thing. How what he learned was too much. How the pain almost drove him to the ultimate blasphemy. Or, perhaps, to the most sacred act. An excruciatingly sharp pain stabbed his insides and he flinched. He asked Iris about her work at Hunter College.

"Well," she said with a sigh, about to fall back on an umpteenth confession-explanation, "I began my teaching career in women's studies. Being a lesbian, sexual identity became more important to me than gender identity, so I got into gay and lesbian studies. You know, I was married once, it lasted six months. It wasn't all that terrible, if you want to know the truth. But Jack didn't know what the fuck he wanted, sexually or any other way, so we figured it was better we each go our own way. Well, now I'm a dyke, not because I don't like guys so much as that I like women *mucho mas*. Anyway, I'm really more into lesbian feminism than into what we now call postmodern queer theory, which more or less disses our experiences as lesbians and says there is no such thing as being a dyke *a priori*, that it is society that constructs through language the categories we use to explain ourselves. But I say, bullshit, I say you are what the depth of your being tells you you are, with or without society butting in. Get it?"

"More or less."

"Does that sound like a load of shit?"

"Not if it's what you truly believe."

Iris's bleary green eyes playfully moved up and down Pablo's face. She smiled and winked at him. "Does my sexual orientation bother you?"

"Why should it?"

"It drove Daddy up the wall."

Pablo shrugged. "Daddy was an asshole."

Iris pulled her head back and guffawed. She reached over the table and took Pablo's hand. "You're a cool guy, brother."

"Yeah, well I got to find this fuckin Ferdie before *I* start climbing walls. I have to find out just what happened in Puerto Rico and what that makes the doctor and what it makes me."

"Why should it make you anything other than what you are?"

"I don't know. That's what I got to find out."

Iris raised her eyebrows, explored Pablo's face, went deep into his eyes, and smiled in a sweet empathy that went beyond acceptance.

"Let's go to my apartment," Iris said. "I want to show you something, maybe it will help."

They finished their brandies and caught a cab back to Iris' apartment. The living room was large and well furnished and had high ceilings.

"This was Daddy's apartment," Iris said. "After his death, I eventually got hold of it." She saw Pablo looking at the flat, monochromatic, abstract paintings on the walls. "A friend of mine did them. She's into color fields."

Pablo grunted. Iris gave him a sour smile. "Well, *I* like them," she said. Then she asked: "You want a nightcap? Some cognac?"

"Sure."

Iris went into the kitchen, then came back with two half-filled brandy glasses. They clinked the glasses.

"Come on to my study, bring your drink."

He followed her into a room with wall-to-wall books, a computer setup and a row of wooden file cabinets. "Almost all of these are filled with Daddy's stuff," Iris said, motioning her head to the file cabinets. She went to one of the cabinets and pulled out several manila envelopes. She motioned Pablo to sit next to her on a small green sofa. "There's tons of his stuff here, I haven't gone through it all. You're free to look through them."

Pablo opened the envelopes, whose clasps were mostly rusted off. The envelopes were filled with papers and clippings related to Rhoads' years in the Army Medical Corps. There were citations and commendations and transfer papers to other military posts, as well as newspaper articles about research into poison gas warfare and radiation carried out by Rhoads and others. There were service ribbons and even a gold medal and copies of speeches the doctor had delivered to military groups, medical organizations and Rotary clubs. There were boxes of medical journals. Many of them contained articles by Rhoads.

The title of one of the articles, "The Experimental Use of Plutonium Injections in the Treatment of Some Cancers" sent a shiver through Pablo. The article was close to incomprehensible, but it did mention injecting plutonium into a test group in the Caribbean.

They drank cognac and spent the next few hours going through more files. Finally, Iris found what she believed Pablo would be most interested in. "I knew it was in here some place!" she said, clapping her hands. "I came across this some time ago. It sounded like drunken bullshit, but in light of what you told me . . . "

She handed Pablo a letter, dated Feb. 3, 1958. It was written from the Panama Canal Zone. As Pablo read the letter, his hand shook.

Dear Ferdie:

I don't have much time for small talk. As you know, I will be discharged in another week, and there are many matters pressing on me to complete.

It's all settled: I will be joining the Public Health Service to pursue my cancer research. I also have been appointed to an advisory position at the Atomic Energy Commission's laboratory, which should afford me the opportunity for further experimental findings on our survival in the coming Armageddon. Others have followed my lead. My pioneering work in Puerto Rico appears to be paying off.

One more confession is on the way, my friend. My in-depth experiments on the fallout of human nefariousness will lead to permanent incapacitation and further extermination of scores of "volunteers." I am preparing to send ten more to their Maker, but since they were all either communists or homosexuals, my regret is minimal. In fact, I rejoice at removing further scum from our planet.

Write soon. One hopes that our paths will cross again soon.

Sincerely,

Dusty

"Jesus, Jesus, Jesus! The guy is a fuckin monster."

"Or a monstrous liar."

"No, he's a goddamn murderer," Pablo said.

"Why are you so sure?"

"Because the fuck says so. Why would he write this stuff if it wasn't true?"

Pablo gave Iris a cross look, as though warning her not to dispute such a self-evident point.

"You know, I didn't really know him very well," Iris said, in apparent appeasement. "My parents split up when I was ten, even though they never divorced because my mother was a Catholic, and I was sent to a school in Switzerland. All I remember as a kid is him ignoring me, like I was never there. The next time I saw him I was eighteen years old and I brought my girlfriend along. He kept bugging me about whether I had a boyfriend and I told him I was in love with Kitty and I stuck my tongue down her throat. That was it. I saw him maybe two, three times after that. He was a cold sonovabitch, but whether he would kill all these people, I don't know. He would have to be crazy, right?"

Pablo nodded. "Yeah, he would have to be crazy."

They sat on the sofa sipping their cognac. Iris turned her head to Pablo. Her soft green eyes scrutinized his face. Pablo's eyes, staring into space while he contemplated inherited madness, gradually focused on the here and now. As though magnetized, they locked into Iris' eyes. They held each other's stare, both their faces reddening even more than from the alcohol. Iris rested her fingers on her slacks by the inside of her thighs. Pablo felt the skin under his left eye twitch. Iris looked down.

"Do you want to go through the rest of the stuff in the file cabinets?" Iris asked.

"I can't. I'm starting to see double," Pablo said apologetically.

"O.K.," Iris said. "Let's call it a night. We can continue this later," she said vaguely.

Iris stood, wobbled and steadied herself by putting a hand on the wall. "Wow! I guess I can't drink the way I used to." She smiled self-consciously, then told Pablo: "I'll make you a copy of this letter." She went to a fax machine next to her computer and copied the latest discovered "Dear Ferdie" and gave it to Pablo.

She walked him to the front door. He took her hand and they shook hands. He held on to her hand.

She seemed to be contemplating something, perhaps an offer to him to stay overnight.

"Where are you staying?" she asked.

"At a hotel just a couple of blocks from here."

She nodded, then kissed him softly on the cheek and he hugged her awkwardly. Then, as their bodies collided, they kissed on the lips. Iris moaned and moved her body into Pablo's. They kissed again and their tongues touched and this set off more than sexual passion in Pablo. His hands roamed her body, and his sex stiffened and pushed into her, but in his mind's eye, he saw his hands settling on her throat.

He started shaking and backed away. Iris blinked several times and looked at him uncomprehendingly. They stared at each other, silent, except for their sped-up breathing. Then Pablo turned, opened the front door and left. His legs felt weak and unsteady as he waited for the elevator. He was in a cold sweat and felt nauseous.

Once outside, he breathed the cold night air deeply into his lungs. But that didn't help. He went to the curb and vomited. He threw up everything—paella, wine, cognac, love, hate, desire. Afterwards, his insides felt not so much empty as bereft of being.

Part Two

From the pamphlet, *Heroes and Martyrs of the Puerto Rican Nation*, Liberation Press.

Pedro Albizu Campos, the Nationalist Party leader, spent eighteen of his sixty-seven years in U.S. and Puerto Rican prisons. During his incarceration from 1951 to 1964, Don Pedro was under constant radiation attack, which several times left him unconscious. Because of the intense heat in his body caused by the attacks, he began to protect his head and body with wet towels. The U.S. Government was trying to kill him, Albizu Campos charged, because he had exposed its colonial tyranny. In order to cover up the radiation experiments and discredit Don Pedro as a national leader, the U.S. Government spread the rumor that he was insane.

Albizu Campos' lawyers filed a protest about his health condition in the United Nations, requesting an investigation. They feared he would die in prison. After a series of articles about Don Pedro's condition appeared in the press in Mexico, Argentina and Chile, the U.S. government removed him from federal prison and brought him to a hospital back in his native Puerto Rico. He remained in hospital, under guard. He died one year later, in 1965.

TEN

Three days after speaking with Pablo's mother, Ralph made an appointment by phone to see Dr. García Ríos, who had returned from the conference in Washington. He had told the doctor's secretary it was an emergency. She said the doctor was all booked up until the following week.

"I'm a Vietnam veteran and you could say this is a matter of life and death," Ralph insisted.

The secretary put him on hold. After several minutes, she said the doctor would see him later that afternoon.

When he entered the psychiatrist's office at the VA hospital, Ralph decided that honesty would be the best policy. He told the doctor about his close friendship with Pablo, who was wanted for questioning in the death of Jamie Rosado. The doctor said he had read about the death of his former patient in the press. Ralph told García Ríos that he wanted to find Pablo so that he could convince him to explain to authorities just what happened in his house that night. He said he was looking for information about the victim in the hope that it could shed some light on just what happened and how he could track down Pablo.

"The psychiatrist was polite, but said that he could not violate the patient-doctor relationship.

"Even if the patient is deceased?" Ralph asked.

"Confidentiality does not end when the patient goes to meet his Maker," said the doctor.

"Can I ask you this: Have the police questioned you? What could you tell me that you may have told them?"

"The police have not yet been here," said the doctor, "though I believe my secretary received a call from the authorities while I was out of town. They said they intend to call again."

"Well, what would you be able to tell them of Rosado's problems?"

"I will tell them that which is a matter of hospital records: that the patient suffered paranoid delusions brought on by post-traumatic stress disorder caused by his experiences in Vietnam."

One more Viet vet back in the world with the same diagnosis. There must be something wrong with me, Ralph thought. How did I come out of the war relatively intact upstairs?

Ralph tapped below his nose. "You couldn't elaborate on that?"

The doctor shook his head.

"Look, I'm a Vietnam veteran and I understand what others have been through there. In fact, Pablo Camino, who the police are searching for, is also a Vietnam vet. He's had problems also. I just want to find him so that he doesn't do anything ridiculous. Like harming himself, or others. You understand, I'm sure."

The psychiatrist sighed deeply. "I'll give you one more piece of information, which I will offer the police, if they ask." he said. "The patient's main delusion was that the U.S. government was trying to kill him. How that will help you in trying to find your friend I don't know."

"Well, that could help, if I get further information," said Ralph, trying to figure how it would. "But, it just occurred to me, when I went to Rosado's wake a few days back, there was an American flag above the coffin. And news reports said that Rosado was a decorated soldier."

The doctor nodded. "Yes, he was a war hero. An enlistee. Wanting to defend the American and Puerto Rican ways of life. Yet convinced that the U.S. government had turned against him." The doctor shrugged.

"So what was he doing at the painter Pablo Camino's house the night he was killed?"

Dr. García Ríos rolled an imaginary ball on the globular tip of his nose. Forests of hair gathered in the nostrils. "What was he doing there? I don't know what he was doing there."

"Did he ever mention Pablo, or maybe a Dr. Cornelius Rhoads?"

Who is that, Dr. Rhoads?"

"He was a doctor who was doing research down here in the 1950s. He was involved in a scandal when someone found a letter he wrote saying he had purposely killed some Puerto Ricans while treating them."

The invisible ball now was being rolled on the left nostril. "Yes, yes, I remember that now. I believe I was just entering medical school when that story was in all the newspapers. It all sounded too fantastic to be believed. To answer your question, I don't believe the patient mentioned either that doctor or the artist during our therapy sessions."

"Do you know when Rosado was in Viet Nam, where he might have seen action?"

"One moment." The psychiatrist swiveled around to a file cabinet. He went through the bottom drawer.

"Here he is. He was there from 1971 to 1972. No precise locations."

Those were the years Ralph and Pablo had spent there and met in the hospital in Saigon. Maybe all of their paths had crossed. Maybe, like Ralph, Rosado had been shot up in firefights on the outskirts of Hue, or Rosado and Pablo had cracked up at the same time and were together in the mental ward, or Rosado had sat, as had he and Pablo, on the balcony of the Continental Hotel on Tu Do Street, sipping "33" beers, watching the Vespas and bikes scoot by and admiring the slender beauty of the women in their *ao dais.*

"All right now. You've gotten more out of me than I wanted to give you," said the psychiatrist, suddenly looking betrayed.

Ralph thanked the shrink and left his office.

Outside the Veteran's Hospital gates, on a grassy field beside a busy six-lane highway, a dozen or so men in camouflage fatigues moved in and out of pitched tents or sat under the single tree in the area, eating out of mess kits and smoking. Several white sheets made into a long, red-painted banner and laid out on the grass said: *Vietnam and Gulf War Vets Protest Pension Cuts. Our Mental Wounds Are Real.* The banner apparently had been caught in a downpour. The paint ran down the letters like dripping blood.

Ralph crossed the field to the men under the tree. "Anyone here know a Jaime Rosado? He served in Nam around 1971, 1972."

"Was he a sergeant in the 101st Airborne, up around Khe Sanh? I knew a Rosado there, I don't recall his first name," said a guy with a pinched face and a scraggly beard. "He was a mean motherfucker, a Tex-Mex, I believe he fragged a lieutenant. Oh no, wait. The guy's name was Rosario. Johnny Rosario."

"This guy was Rosado. He was from here. Barrio Obrero. I don't know if you heard about it," Ralph said, "but he was the guy who was found stabbed to death a couple of days ago in the house of an artist in Old San Juan."

Scraggly beard shook his head. "Sorry," he said. "I can't help you on that one."

A short, skinny guy wearing mirrored sunglasses said: "How about the guy who came down here couple of times before he shot his wife and three kids, they put him in the place for locos up in the states? What was his name?"

"That was Rosano. Pete Rosano," said another one of the vets. "A nice guy, didn't take his meds."

"Listen, speak to Sarge," said a fourth vet. "Sarge knows everybody and everyfuckinthing. "Hey, Sarge," he shouted toward one of the tents. The others under the tree joined in, shouting for Sarge. The tent flapped open and a deep sleepy voice came back: "Who the fuck calls?"

"Hey, Sarge, *sir*, get the fuck out here, there's someone to see you."

"I don't have my wheels."

"Fuck it, you don't need your wheels. Just drag your ass over here. No offense, Sarge."

Sarge's face appeared first. It was large and handsome and a wiry black beard matched the full shock of hair covering his head. Two massively muscular, tattoo-covered arms beneath a khaki colored tee shirt over a solidly built torso next made their appearance. Then, with a twist of the upper body, came khaki shorts, and the stumps of two legs protruding from them.

Sarge literally dragged his ass over to the group. He looked up at Ralph with two large, intense, coal-dark eyes. He offered a hand. Ralph felt bones about to give way beneath the handshake.

"How can I help you, my friend?" Sarge asked.

"I'm trying to get some information on a veteran named Jaime Rosado, who was being treated at the VA hospital."

"What's his problem? PTSD? Does he show signs of paranoia, depression, emotional numbing, survivor guilt, flashbacks, fantasies of getting even, negative self-image, rage, self-punishment? Was he exposed to Agent Orange, contaminated by TCDD? Does he have the big C? Do his kids have birth defects? Does he suffer from Gulf War Syndrome? Was he exposed to organophosphates?" Sarge produced a warm white long-tooth smile.

"He has no problems right now," Ralph said. "He's dead. He was killed apparently after he broke into a house in the Old City."

"Oh yeah, yeah," said Sarge, suddenly serious. "I got several e-mails about that. What exactly do you want to know?"

"I'm trying to find out what made Rosado go to that house and what happened there."

"Yeah, I met him a couple of times. Nam vet, right? Sounded off the wall, right? Said he was exposed to Agent Orange, then was radiated in his sleep. Said he was the son of Albizu Campos."

Ralph did an involuntary double take. "The son of . . . ?"

"Yeah, he was also convinced that while he slept, he was being bombarded with radiation, just like Albizu said was done to him, by the U.S. government, when he was in their prisons. He said Albizu was his father, that the U.S. government had murdered Albizu and was going to kill him in the same way. Yeah, real crazy, right? Wait a minute, I want you to see something."

Sarge dragged himself back into his tent, then returned with a computer on his lap. "I want to show you the latest

Vietnam Veterans Of America Agent Orange/Dioxin Committee report."

Sarge pulled up the report on the screen. It said that more than two million Vietnamese veterans had the same psychological and physical problems as U.S. vets and that over 100,000 Vietnamese children born after the war had the same birth defects suffered by kids of stateside veterans. The veterans on both sides were exposed to Agent Orange, according to the report, which also noted that 28 million gallons of herbicide were sprayed in Vietnam between 1962 and 1971.

"I want you to see something else." Sarge accessed several Internet reports on the U.S. government's mind-control and radiation experiments on its own soldiers, dating back to the late 1940s, from exposing them to nuclear explosions to secretly giving them LSD.

"So, all these guys around here, including Rosado, are crazy, right? D'ya think?" Before Ralph could answer, Sarge said: "You know why these guys chose me as their spokesman? Because you can see what's missing from me. They got missing parts too, but you can't see what's missing from them, so the government cuts down on their benefits. Beautiful! So here's what I think about that guy Rosado. If he says he was radiated in his sleep, he was radiated. And poisoned with dioxin. Sometime. Somewhere. And it registered in his subconscious, so he says it happened in his sleep. Also, if he says he was the son of Albizu Campos, that's true too. He carried around scrapbooks of stories and articles and facts about father Albizu. Hey, Christ was the Son of God. Christ is our savior, right? Our Father who art in heaven, right? Like father, like son. George Washington was the father of his country. A wise father knows his own child. Honor thy father and thy mother. Guilty or not, we're all gonna pay for the sins of our fathers, right? Einstein, or maybe it was Teller, or Oppenheimer, or maybe all of them, was the father of The Bomb. Bombs away! Father, why have Thou forsaken me? It's the same thing, you know what I mean? Why did Rosado go to the house where he had his throat cut the other day? Because something inside his head *knew* that he had to go there. He was getting back for being tortured in his mind, you see?"

Ralph tapped the flat space above his lip. "That's something to think about," he said.

"Damn right! But remember this: thinking is what really hurts! That's why these guys have wounds as real as mine. The imagination can give you pain that's even deeper and lasts longer than pieces of metal that rip into your body. You know what I'm saying?"

Ralph nodded and thanked Sarge and got another bone-crushing handshake. While driving home, he kept flexing the fingers of his right hand while thoughts of sinful fathers and errant sons bounced around in his brain.

ELEVEN

Pablo rings the doorbell. As soon as she opens the door, he pushes his way inside the apartment. He grabs her arms. She looks at him defiantly and he throws her against the wall, holds her there with his body as he rips open her blouse and plunges his face into her breasts. His knee is between her legs and her skirt is hoisted to her thighs. She moans and cries and then returns his kisses with a fiery tongue.

Then he feels her on his back, biting into his neck. The blood trickles down his back and he tries to swat her off, but she rips her fingernails across his back and he feels the skin peeling off. He becomes weak and dizzy and tumbles forward. She rips his pants and his underwear off and wriggles out of her panties and penetrates him deep and raw . . .

Pablo woke. He looked down to his shorts. Semen and even some blood. Beautiful dream.

He dozed again. His head was ringing. No, it was the phone. He leaned over to the night table, picked up the receiver and asked groggily: "Who is it?"

"It's me, Iris. I'm sorry."

"What?"

"I want to apologize."

She's apologizing? For raping him in his dream?

"Are you there?"

Yeah, I'm umh . . . I'm here."

"I shouldn't have come on to you last night. I suppose I was drunker than I thought. I'm calling to apologize for last night."

"No. It wasn't . . . "

"In case you're wondering, you told me you were staying a few blocks from my apartment. I checked the hotels in the neighborhood until I got you. I described you to the front desk clerks."

"Oh. O.K."

"So, I put you in a very awkward position last night. And I wanted to tell you that I feel very bad about it."

"No, look, I should be apologizing to *you.*"

"No, don't be silly."

"Yeah, but I . . . "

"No, look, I'm very glad we met. I'm glad you came looking for me. Whatever the reason. I think we should keep the relationship going."

"Yeah, I think that would be great."

"I'd like to help out in your search."

"I appreciate that."

"Anything I can do, let me know."

Awkward silence.

She spoke: "Well, I have a couple of classes now. I have to go. Let's meet up later. Call me and take care, brother."

"You too, *hermana.*"

Pablo hung up. What the fuck did he do now? He wanted her, he wanted her to help him and he wanted to run from her. He turned and buried his being into further dreams. Because no matter how bad they were, it would only hurt while he slept. And maybe just a little after.

Late afternoon. The first thing he thought was that he didn't remember into what further circle of nightmare hell he had been dragged while consciously asleep. *Gracias a Dios.* To show how grateful he was for this post-dream amnesia, he hopped quickly out of bed, showered and dressed. He got a sandwich and coffee sent up to the room. He ate and downed a pot of coffee.

Now what? His pillow beckoned him.

Screw you. You look soft and white, but you play too rough, even for me.

Once outside, he was confronted with a wet, raw slap of gray New York winter. The weather, Pablo understood, was a message from God, replicating Pablo's mood as a sign of cosmic solidarity.

Pablo wandered over to Third Avenue, found the most non-descript bar and spent time nursing a couple of Remys and conversing with himself. He certainly was attracted to his own blood, O.K., half-blood. But that scared the shit out of him. Why did he "see" his hands reaching for her throat, when they were really roaming around her softer, voluptuous parts? Just block out what you "see," asshole, and do what you do. He had to act as he always acted in such situations. A guilt gift was in order. Then he would go off on his own, which he was fated to do.

He exited the bar and set out to fulfill his first mission. The earlier dirty, miserable gray was now tucked under a brownblack cover, as though the sky had been turned inside out. The wind had died down, but the rain had solidified to sleet. Pablo knew enough to navigate carefully through the mean-faced crowds to get to Fifth Avenue without bumping into anyone, which could lead to some sort of confrontation.

He was in and out of Tiffany's in just a couple of minutes. With a gold choker. Anyone wanting to trace him could now do so through American Express. But by the time they got around to it, he'd be out of here. He would leave the gift with her friendly doorman. No card or anything. Just tell the doorman to give it to her.

All the gifts he had gotten for Ana in the past to make up for some idiotic behavior. The jewelry. That antique brooch in Amsterdam.

Twenty years ago. The joy and the sadness of his life then and there.

Pablo opened his eyes and reached for Ana's warmth. She was not in bed; he heard her outside their alcoved bedroom, throwing coals into the little stove in the outer room. He forced himself out of bed and into the frosty room. Ana, wearing only a black slip, was warming her hands over the stove. Pablo, admiring the sweet curve of her behind, put his arms around her and pressed in on her. He kissed her neck and coaxed her back into bed and they made love.

They went downstairs to the dining room for breakfast. Coco ruffled his feathers and his little forehead furrowed as he greeted them multilingually from his cage: "*Goedemorgen, dames en herren. Bonjour, mesdames et messieurs!* Good morning, my ladies and gentlemen. Here's a kiss from Coco. Swack, swack. Here's a kiss for Mama. Swack, swack."

"Mama," the frumpy, no-neck, cigar-smoking, gravelly voiced proprietress of *De Kleine City* bed-and-breakfast on

Reguliersgracht laid out slices of smoked ham and Dutch cheese, butter and chocolate sprinkles, white and black bread and coffee and tea. They ate their fill. Ana loved to sprinkle chocolate on her bread and butter. The phone rang and Coco said: *"Hallo, hallo. De Kleine City. Twee, vier, vijf.* Two, four, five . . ."

They got their bicycles from behind the stairs and rode along the canals, dodging between the small cars that had begun to replace the once almost exclusive bikes on the streets, then pedaled up Museumstraat all the way to the Rijksmuseum.

Ana chose to look at the Delftware and Meissen porcelain; Pablo headed immediately to The Room. He sat on a bench before The Master. Once again they peered into each other's beings. The yellowwhite-turbaned Rembrandt's forehead was furrowed, his eyebrows raised, his black eyes sad, wise, weary, his mouth set resolutely. "This is my life, this is all life," he said to Pablo, giving self and existence their deepest meanings.

Lately, Pablo came to the museum for this painting alone. So far, he only listened. One day he intended to let Rembrandt in on some things also. After awhile, Ana fetched him.

Outside, they stopped at a herring stand and the vendor chopped up onions and stuck toothpicks in the herring and they downed the fish and onions with Amstel. Then they biked to Rembrandtplein and went to their favorite café and drank *jenever* from slim liqueur glasses and lunched on thick pea soup and open-faced sandwiches.

The weather was pretty good, breezy and a bit chilly, while the sun, a bright wafer, slipped in and out of the smudgy clouds. After lunch they decided to bike out to the countryside. First they returned to their room and Pablo picked up his easel and materials and Ana a book of Sean O'Casey plays. Pablo followed Ana, who knew the shortest way out of the city.

They returned to the spot near an octagonal windmill with streamlined sails that Pablo had started painting some days ago. The day had cleared and the late afternoon light sprayed a golden sheen that Pablo brushed into his picture. The windmill stood tall and solid in the forefront of the picture, yet Pablo intimated an immense vault of sky above and an endless flat horizon. Ana smiled and sighed while reading O'Casey, telling Pablo that many Puerto Ricans lived lives parallel to those of the Irish in the playwright's works.

In the evening, as fog rolled off the canals, they returned to the café on Rembrandtplein for more glasses of Dutch gin, then they went to their favorite Indonesian restaurant a few blocks away, then to a movie, then for a nightcap at a cellar club that was crowded and warm and cozy and alive with laughter, conversation and a Count Basie recording of "Jumpin' at the Woodside" coming from a 1940's American-style jukebox.

Ana and Pablo ended their day as it started, making love. Pablo told Ana that he loved her more than life itself, that without her he was *nada*.

That was one of the good days.

He walked a block too far along Fifth, to Fifty-Third Street. He turned up there and passed the MOMA. A long, narrow banner announced a De Kooning exhibit. He reached the Avenue of the Americas, then turned toward Iris' apartment house on Fifty Fourth Street. Puddles were icing up and as he crossed the Avenue of the Americas he slid along one and almost fell on his ass.

Then there were the bad days.

It was about noon. Pablo was not exactly asleep, but he was not fully awake either. Since dawn, he had been sitting up every twenty minutes or so to light a cigarette from a pack on the small bedside table. He smoked the cigarettes down quickly, then stubbed them into an ashtray on the floor by the bed. All morning, he had been cursing Ana for one insignificant thing after another, some minor happening the day before, some exaggerated inconvenience of the moment, some imagined betrayal in the future.

"If you want to know the truth, darling Ana, I hate every fuckin thing and every fuckin person in the world, present company not excluded! The only one I hate worse than you, bitch, is myself." He buried his head into the pillow until the next smoke break.

While he slept fitfully, he dreamed the same dream. He was strangling Ana, now his mother, now Ana, her brownblack eyes swirling in fear and pleading, but it was his mother who was pleading.

Ana no longer sat patiently through these "fits." She was up and dressed and left the apartment as he fell back into another fitful snooze.

She returned some hours later, bringing back some groceries. Pablo woke, looked at her and said in a low, harsh voice: "Get out of my fuckin face."

Ana left again without a word.

Pablo pounded on the wall over their bed. "Bitch! Get the hell back here!"

He tore out of the bed and ran to the window, which overlooked a canal. He struggled with the latch. It seemed frozen in place. He was finally able to creak the window up halfway. He saw Ana moving towards Rembrandtplein. He bent down to get his head halfway out the attic window and a gust of cold wind slapped him in the face. He shouted after her. She gave no clue whether she heard him or not, continuing her brisk walk. He shouted again. Then, when she reached the corner, she did something that infuriated Pablo even more. As she crossed the hump-backed bridge there, she raised an arm straight into the air, turned her hand, curled her fingers and waved them in Pablo's direction without looking back.

"Bitch!" he screamed. "Get the *fuck* back here!"

Pablo pulled his head inside and smashed his fists against the walls. He pounded the front door, like a punching bag, smearing it with blood.

He sat on the small rust-colored sofa across from the stove and surveyed the damage to his crooked, bloody knuckles. He licked off the blood, then went to the washstand to clean the wounds on his knuckles. While he was doing this, a pounding was unleashed on his door, like a very delayed echo of his own attack on the panels. He heard a series of hoarse shouts from the other side of the door, like someone was aping his earlier hysterics, then some truly blood-curdling screams that set the nerves along his arms jumping under his skin.

"Who the fuck . . . ?" Pablo opened the door.

The owner of the hotel stood there with a crowbar held aloft and with Coco on her shoulder. The bird was hopping around, flurrying its feathers, squawking and squealing up a storm. One beady eye looked ready to pop out in frenzied rage. Its little clawed feet moved forward and back on the broad expanse of Mama's left shoulder, its beak jabbed forward, pulled back, then poked out again, while it screeched out threats to Pablo.

"What in de hell think you you doing?" Mama's eyes looked huge behind her thick glasses. The crowbar was still poised over her head, as though Pablo better come up with a good answer.

"Shut that godamn bird up, will you please?" Pablo felt his left eye twitching.

"*You* shaddup! I don't allow no noise like you vas makin' in dis place. If I hear you once more making such a racket, I call the *politie* to kick you by de ass back to from where you come. You got the idea?"

Coco continued to shriek; then the bird leapt off Mama's shoulder into mid-air above her head. It shuddered and flapped its wings; Pablo noticed they were a gold-tinged green, the color of early autumn leaves; then it dive-bombed at Pablo, snapping its beak into his forehead. Pablo swiped at the bird; it screeched and took off down the staircase, and Pablo slammed the door shut.

"Jesus Christ!" He went to the mirror over the washstand, examined the wound on his forehead, washed it with soap and water and stuck a band-aid on it. Maybe the fuckin bird had rabies!

As he headed downstairs, the phone in the dining room rang and he could hear Coco squawking: *"Hallo, hallo, De Kleine City. Twee, vier, vijf.* Two, four, five . . . " In his head, Pablo barged into the room and bit the bird's head off, the feathers sticking with the bird's blood on his chin.

He spent the next hour wandering along the canals, seeing nothing, caring about nothing, realizing that at the age of twenty-six, his life had hit a dead end. The wind had started up again and he was vaguely aware of a sharp stinging on the tip of his nose and the tops of his ears.

What would it be like to be submerged in the canal water? Would the first freezing shock turn into a pleasant warmth once he had dived under, found the willpower to stay under?

Would it be like a return to the womb? Would he be strong enough to prevent his arms and legs from motoring his body to the surface? Could it be done? Could a swimmer purposely drown himself, or would his limbs automatically reflex toward survival? With one foot on the bottom rail he peered deeply into the greenblack canal water, mesmerized by its tiny, wind-rippled waves. Then, he was up and over the higher rail, one outstretched arm holding on.

Would he be strong enough to propel himself to the bottom and stay there until they fished him out? Actually, it wasn't so much that he wanted to end it all. It was something else, more a test of his will. To see if he had the courage to kill himself. So what if he did. Then what?

Stop bullshitting and do it, asshole.

He heard the shouts and looked up. An elderly couple, a young boy and a teenage girl, all Japanese, were about twenty feet to his left. They were pointing at him, then into the canal, and jabbering away. Why didn't they shut up? What was it their fuckin business? They continued to shout and point and he was about to tell them to fuck off. Then he saw the old guy's hat, a fedora with a feather in it, floating on the water. The young boy, about ten, climbed through the railing and leaned over toward the water. The old woman screamed and the teenage girl reached through and grabbed the kid by the hood of his sky blue jacket and yanked him back.

The hat moved slowly along the green brackish water. Two ducks sat silently in the middle of the canal staring at it. One of the ducks tucked its bill under a wing and did something under there that ruffled its feathers. The old man looked forlornly at his hat sailing away, as though a loved one were embarking on a journey of unknown duration.

"Jesus fuckin Christ!" Pablo let go the railing and dived into the canal. The ducks looked at him like he was crazy, made noises and skidded away.

Pablo retrieved the hat and swam a couple of strokes back to the edge of the canal. Two other bystanders leaned over and helped him up. He shook water off the hat and handed it to the old man. There were tears in the old coot's eyes, either from the brisk wind or in gratitude. The old man bowed low to Pablo. So did the old woman. So did the teenage girl and the boy. They continued bowing while Pablo quickly retreated down the street and around the corner.

The wind whipped icily across Pablo's soaked being. He took a quick reading of where he was, on Herrengracht, not too far from the rooming house.

Luckily, there was hot water in the bathroom downstairs and he ripped off his clothes while filling the tub, then eased into it. His muscles loosened, his nerves settled, his whole body slackened. He felt weak in a very relaxing way. He leaned his head back against the edge of the tub and snoozed.

He dressed and walked to the jewelry store in Rembrandtplein and bought the brooch Ana had admired when they were window-shopping some days ago. Then he went to the café where he knew Ana would meet him.

He sipped a yellowish *oude jenever.* After awhile, Ana arrived. She took a seat beside him in the cozy, wood-lacquered café. They greeted one another like old friends ready to spend precious time together after having been forced to take care of inconsequential daily duties.

Ana asked about the band-aid on his forehead. He mumbled something about tripping on the stairs. He took the brooch out of his pocket and presented it to her. She gave him a look that said: "Here we go again, another guilt-driven present." But then she decided to graciously accept the expensive token of forgiveness.

"It's very beautiful," she said. "Thank you so much, Pablo." Ana kissed him on the cheek.

Pablo had pushed his earlier anger, and all other turbulent emotions, into a recess of his soul. The disturbances that had shaped his day eventually would disappear, he told himself. It was just a sporadic madness that was bound to evaporate over time.

He reached Iris' building and was about to speak, but the doorman put up his hand to halt Pablo a moment while he opened the door for someone exiting.

Pablo and Iris looked at each other with alarm and disbelief, though not without a hint of joy. To amend their first brief reaction of looking away from each other, they stared deeply into each other's eyes. Pablo slipped the wrapped gift into his coat pocket.

"I . . . um . . . forgot to tell you how to get in touch with me in Puerto Rico," Pablo said. "I called earlier but there was no answer, so I decided to walk over here and give the information to the doorman for you."

He was grateful that she didn't ask why he didn't leave the information on her answering machine.

"Hey, I was just going to the greengrocer to pick up some artichokes and fruit and wine. I got a huge sirloin steak in the fridge. Come along with me and we'll get the artichokes and stuff and we'll share the steak and I'll make French fries. Whatdya say?"

Pablo remembered that Iris said something important last night that he didn't explore further. He couldn't quite recall what it was. He convinced himself that he should accept her invitation in connection with whatever it was. He nodded and mumbled thanks.

They went to the market, argued over who would pay. Iris forced Pablo's money back into his pocket and touched the gift box and the side of his thigh. He flinched at her touch. She mumbled an apology and he mumbled something back and realized he would have to go out of his way to avoid all physical contact with her.

Upstairs, they both drank Perrier before dinner, then had two glasses of wine with the steak dinner, and no other alcoholic drinks.

"How about a good movie?" Iris asked after they finished dinner. "I took this out of the video club intending to watch it tonight, for the hundredth time. *The 39 Steps*. I love Hitchcock."

"So do I."

"It must be in the genes. Think of it, brother, we share the same genes—on one side of the family at least."

"Not exactly the good side."

"That's true," Iris said, a bit sadly. "But at least we know what to avoid."

Pablo nodded, wondering exactly what that meant.

Pablo dozed intermittently during the film. When it was over, Iris asked: "You want to look in the file cabinets for other stuff about Dusty?"

That's what his stupored mind had registered the night before!

"I have a few things to do on the computer and you won't be bothering me at all," Iris said.

They went into the study and Iris opened the file cabinets. "Be my guest."

Pablo dug in.

More envelopes with rusted away clasps and papers with rubber bands that broke at the touch. Yellowed newspaper articles about military affairs and cancer research, age-spotted commendations from the Army and civic organizations (Lions, Rotary, Shriners), business letters, esoteric scientific research reports, medical journals, and the like. So far, in the first of the three file cabinets, nothing to shed any light on a personal life.

In the second cabinet were tax returns, mountains of receipts for everything from pipes from tobacconists in Sweden to an $8,500 full-length mink coat (for his wife? mistress?) from Saks Fifth Avenue.

Iris did a printout, then turned off the computer. "I have an early class tomorrow, so I'm going to bed. Finish doing what you have to do and let yourself out. Do you have a cell phone where I can reach you?"

"I left it in Puerto Rico."

"Wow. The absent-minded artist." She picked up a slip of paper from her desk and wrote down a number. "This is my cell. Believe it or not, there's even more of these files in Connecticut. If you want . . . Well, call me, soon."

She leaned over as Pablo, on his haunches opening the third file cabinet, looked up. He smelled her perfumeless, soapy smell. She took his head in her hands and kissed him softly on the forehead. "I wish you the best, my brother. Let me hear from you." She slowly slid her fingers down his cheeks and smiled at him with what he interpreted as a mournful regret.

Pablo watched her leave the room, noticing how strong her calves looked beneath the blue skirt she wore. He felt a deep, sad, sexual stirring. He turned and buried his head into the file cabinet.

He placed the gift he had bought for her on top of her computer. Then he returned to the third file cabinet. The private life of Dusty Rhoads started taking on more shape. There were Broadway playbills for, among other productions, "South Pacific" (with the original stars, Enzio Pinza and Mary Martin) and "The Sound of Music" (he seemed to prefer musicals). There were programs from concerts and ballets and scorecards from Yankee baseball games. The scorecards were filled out meticulously, from first to last inning. Mickey Mantle had doubled in the first inning, struck out in the fourth, homered in the sixth, and again in the eighth. Pablo was depressed at seeing the carefully recorded scorecards. They gave Dusty Rhoads a human dimension Pablo would rather not have found.

Then, in the back of the cabinet, inside an orange-brown portfolio tied with a brown ribbon, was the photograph, and the letters.

The photograph was in a cardboard frame with a cover. On the cover were the name of the Latin Quarter nightclub and a head sketch of a tough mustached guy in a beret and his pompon bereted Apache dance partner. In the upper left of the cover was the following: "So this is Gay Paree. Come on along with me. We're stepping out to see the Latin Quarter."

Pablo opened the cover. His mother looked young and beautiful. She had wonderful high cheekbones, a full mouth. But she wore a distressed expression, an unwilling subject of the camera. The guy she was with had to be Dusty, Pablo was sure. He held a pipe in his left hand, wore a bow tie and offered a condescending grin. A smug, self-satisfied motherfucker. The smile was spread above the telltale father-son dimpled chin. Pablo closed the cover and tossed the photo back into the cabinet.

A rubber band limply separated as he pulled it from around a dozen or so letters. The letters were carbons of typed originals. They all seemed to have been sent by Dusty to Dear and Dearest and Darling Julia. There didn't seem to be any in the pile from her to him. Dusty wrote about "the furor over the foolish letter" that got him sent into exile, about the communists taking advantage of it. He professed his love while making a veiled threat that if Julia's father forced him to return to the island, everyone in Puerto Rico would learn of the affair.

What an asshole!

Pablo found Dusty increasingly frustrated in the "love" letters that followed. He had learned about the birth of "my son" and asked to see him. His Mom apparently didn't answer any of the letters, but seemed to get the word to him that he couldn't see the kid. Good move, Julia. Let that sonovabitch rot in his own hell.

Then, right at the bottom of the pile, Pablo found a letter that made his heart race. It was one more "Dear Ferdie" from his pal "Dusty."

The message was brief.

March 8, 1961

Dear Ferdie

I'm overjoyed to learn that the arrangements finally have been made for your trip to Spain. Please let me know soonest about the results of your mission—on both fronts.

You can contact me for the time being at my Connecticut home. I will be working like mad up there on our project.

Sincerely,

Dusty

Pablo understood that Fate had propelled him here, to the home of his half-sister, who not only stirred up the deepest desires and perverted darkness of his own soul, but who also would help him find out just how sullied was the heart and bloodied were the hands of their old man, the despicable Dr. Rhoads.

From "Chapter 17: Findings for the Period 1944 to 1974" of the final 925-page report issued in October, 1995 by the Advisory Committee on Human Radiation Experiments, formed by the U.S. Government to "tell the full story to the American public" about the experiments.

Advisory Committee finds that from 1944 to 1974 the government sponsored (by providing funding, equipment, or radioisotopes) several thousand human radiation experiments . . . These experiments were conducted by researchers affiliated with government agencies, universities, hospitals and other research institutions. Only fragmentary information survives about most experiments.

The Advisory Committee finds that some of the biomedical experiments reviewed by the committee that were ethically troubling were conducted on institutionalized children, seriously ill and sometimes comatose patients, African-Americans and prisoners. The Committee was troubled by the selection of subjects in many of the experiments we reviewed. These subjects often were drawn from relatively powerless, easily exploited groups, and many of them were hospitalized patients. The silence on questions of justice in the conduct of human research was characteristic not only of radiation research but also of the entire research enterprise.

During the 1944-1974 period but especially through the early 1960s, physicians engaged in clinical research generally did not obtain consent from patient-subjects for whom the research was intended to offer a prospect of medical benefit. Even where there was no such prospect, it was common for physicians to conduct research on patients without their consent.

The Advisory Committee finds that the government and government officials are morally responsible in cases in which they did not take effective measures to implement the government's policies and requirements, and the medical profession and biomedical scientists are morally responsible for instances in which they failed to adhere to the professional norms and practices of the time.

The Committee finds that since the end of the Manhattan Project in 1946 human radiation experiments have typically not been classified as secret by the government. Nonetheless, important discussions of human experimentation took place in secret, and information was kept secret out of concern for embarrassment to the government, potential legal liability, and concern that public misunderstanding would jeopardize government programs. In some cases, deception was employed. In the case of the plutonium injection experiments, government officials and government-sponsored researchers continued to keep information secret from the subjects of several human radiation experiments and their families, including the fact that they had been used as subjects of such research . . .

Where records were initially created, important collections have been lost or destroyed over the years. These include the classified records of the Atomic Energy Commission's Intelligence Division; records relating to the secret program of experimentation conducted by the CIA; non-classified records of VA hospitals regarding the thousands of experiments that, the VA told the Advisory Committee, were conducted there; and non-classified files of the AEC's Isotope Distribution Program relating to the many licenses for 'human use' it granted. The AEC denied to the press and citizens that it engaged in human experimentation. We also found that some records documenting the destruction of records have been lost or destroyed.

TWELVE

Spurred on by his talk with Sarge, Ralph wanted to get all the information he could on the radiation experiments carried out by the U.S. government. He had heard about them in general terms and had glanced over the reports that Sarge had pulled up on his computer the other day. But now, closely reading online the Advisory Committee on Human Radiation Experiments report brought home all the nefariousness in the name of national defense. Some irresistible urge seemed to drive governments to use whatever rationalizing technology was at hand to dehumanize. It had to do with more than survival. Must have been something in the primeval slime-water, Ralph thought.

A new message, labeled "*muy importante*" awaited Ralph in his mailbox when he arrived at the University the next day. He was "strongly urged" to report to the head of the department right after class. Tragic revelations encroached upon by chicken-shit concerns. After he gave his class, he decided to go to the University library first.

He looked up the old articles about the Rhoads incident in the microfilm collection of local newspapers. He saw that Albizu Campos was the first to denounce the doctor for the infamous letter. He found a short obit of Rhoads in a Spanish-language paper, which mentioned the incident and the investigation that followed. The obit noted that Rhoads went on to a distinguished medical and military career, which had included research into cancer and chemical warfare.

Ralph decided to again skip the meeting with the department head and drove to the dusty old Puerto Rican Archives across from Muñoz Rivera Park in Puerta de Tierra.

He wanted to read all about the Rhoads investigation. No computer files here. Instead, a smiling young woman wearing slabs of makeup and with her chubby body poured into a tighter than tight short white skirt brought him a faded brown portfolio filled mostly with onion-skinned paper. He read through the investigation transcript. Just about all the witnesses, which seemed to include only the other Rockefeller Institute researchers, swore by Rhoads, who was described as a professional of the highest caliber who at times gave his own blood in transfusions for the patients.

Then Ralph came to the names of the patients who died under the good doctor's care. He sat up in his chair.

The name of one of the deceased was Jesus Rosado Almodóvar. The man found dead in Pablo's house was Jaime Rosado Feliciano. The second last name was the mother's name. Rosado was a common name in Puerto Rico. Still, if he could determine that the family name of the victim's grandmother was Almodóvar, it could mean that Jaime Rosado Feliciano was Jesus Rosado Almodóvar's son. So? *So?*

What did that old guy he bought a beer for after he left the wake call Jaime's father? *Chu!* Chu was the nickname for Jesús!

He was in business. Probably. Maybe.

Ralph parked his car on Calle Buenos Aires and walked around the corner to Calle Caracas. The sound of the noontime soap opera blared from the neighborhood's small wooden homes. Ralph reached the house on the corner of the block, walked up the steps to the porch and knocked on the front door. The woman he had taken at the wake to be Rosado's wife answered. The same baby she had held at the wake squealed and squirmed in her arms. The woman still wore black. Dark circles of grief remained under her eyes.

"*Señora* Rosado?"

"Sí, Señor."

"*Señora*, my name is Ralph Camacho and I was a friend of your husband from the Army. Jaime and I served together in Vietnam. I just heard about the tragedy and I've come to offer my condolences."

The baby let loose a wild cry and Rosado's wife excused herself and disappeared into the house. Ralph stood by the entrance. The door was halfway open. He heard the woman speaking, somewhat hysterically, to someone else in a back room.

Several minutes passed. The woman was shouting, the baby was screaming and someone was answering in a barely audible voice. He waited.

Finally, the woman reappeared. The baby, left in the back room, had stopped howling. *"Perdóneme. Entre, Señor."*

Ralph entered the small front room. Christ of the bleeding heart still hung on the wall, but the crossed Puerto Rican and American flags had been taken down. Beneath the painting, in place of the white coffin that had displayed the body of Jaime Rosado, was a red plastic sofa. Rosado's wife invited Ralph to sit on the sofa. She asked if he wanted some coffee. He accepted and she excused herself again and disappeared into the kitchen.

On the table closest to Ralph, were plastic flowers in a vase. In front of the vase was a framed photo bordered by black cloth. The photo was of a round-faced man in an Army uniform. The man, whose small features gave his face the look of a mischievous, potentially jovial boy, nevertheless stared adult-like and somberly into the camera.

The woman carried on a tray a cup of already sweetened coffee, a plate of crackers and a glass of water.

She put the tray down on the table near Ralph. She looked at Ralph looking at the photo of her husband and started crying.

"I'm very sorry about Jaime. How can something like this have happened?" Ralph asked.

The woman continued to weep. She twisted a handkerchief in her hands. She moved her head several times from side to side, as though it were on springs. She sobbed more loudly and buried her eyes in the handkerchief. As if it had been given the go-ahead by the sobbing mother, the baby started crying again in the back room.

"*Señora*, I'm really sorry. Is there anything I can do?"

The woman put out her hands and shrugged pitifully. Her sobs came louder and so did the baby's crying, showing its mother that she was no match for its tears and howls. Ralph heard someone trying to shush the baby.

"Do you know if Jaime was acquainted with the . . . the killer, why he was in that house in the Old City?"

The woman continued to shake her head from side to side. "No, no." She started beating her ample breast. "*No, no, no!*" She squeezed her eyes shut and her jowly face seemed to become smaller, than wider, her cheeks spreading and drooping to cover the sides of her neck. She let out banshee-like wails.

He was accomplishing a big nothing.

Ralph said one more "I'm sorry." As he exited, he wondered if the neighbors would try to stop him on suspicion of causing the agonizing screams coming from the Rosado home. He put on his sunglasses and could feel the sun beating down on the bald spot on top of his head.

He was about to turn the corner when he heard calls of, "*Señor, Señor.*" He turned. A girl was walking quickly toward him.

"*Señor,* I am the daughter of Jaime Rosado. My mother wishes me to tell you she is very sorry for not being able to control herself. She begs your pardon and wants you to know that she appreciates your visit very much."

It was the pale, beautiful girl with the large soulful eyes whom Ralph had seen at the wake sitting by the coffin. Only she wasn't a girl, but a young woman. Despite her very slim, almost childlike frame, up close she looked to be in her early twenties. She had perfect, miniature features and pale ivory skin untouched by makeup. She wore jeans and a white polo shirt with the maroon University of Puerto Rico logo on it. Her straight black hair hung midway down her back. Her upper lip was dotted with sweat.

Ralph turned momentarily and looked up the street. He spotted a little plaza with a bench beneath a tree in the next block.

"Let's go up there and sit for a minute," he said, motioning with his head. "If you don't mind, I'd like to talk to you."

The young woman nodded reluctantly. Ralph tried to put her at ease with a big smile. "Just for a minute."

They sat on the stone slab of a bench. The young woman, whose name was Laura, nodded when Ralph asked if she were a student at the University. She said that she worked at a day-care center as well as taking classes. She was a history major. She wanted to teach Puerto Rican history. She looked down at the small round watch on her thin wrist. "I have to return to work in fifteen minutes," she said.

Ralph told her he taught a class at the University on the Puerto Rican Diaspora. Laura seemed surprised. A friend of hers was in that class, she said.

"Really? Who's that?"

"Richie Pérez."

Richie, the rat killer, Ralph thought. "He's a good student. A nice guy."

Laura nodded. She colored slightly. Then she pulled out a pack of cigarettes from her jeans. Ralph declined her offer of one and she lit her cigarette with a small black lighter. She noticed Ralph looking at her unpolished, bitten fingernails, and tucked a hand under her arm as she puffed on her cigarette.

"We are a nervous family," she told Ralph between puffs.

Ralph shrugged sympathetically. "I understand Jaime, your father, especially suffered from nerves in the past years, ever since Vietnam."

Laura nodded. Tears filled her eyes. Ralph hoped he hadn't sparked another bout of hysteria.

"Your father wasn't alone," Ralph said. "Many veterans are still suffering from the war."

"My family has been in pain for many years," Jaime Rosado's daughter said almost matter-of-factly.

"I was told by my buddies at the VA Hospital that your father was saying strange things about people experimenting on him with radiation? Did he mention that to you or the family?"

Laura puffed deeply on her cigarette. Behind a smokescreen, she nodded. "Others have had the same happen to them."

"Like the Nationalist leader Albizu Campos."

"That's right."

"I heard that Jaime was telling people that Albizu was his father."

The young woman shook her head. Then, reluctantly, she nodded. "He said that toward the end, when he wasn't thinking right. His real father died when he was very young."

"Jesús Rosado, right?

For the first time, Laura turned to look into Ralph's eyes. "How do you know that?"

"I was speaking with some old man in the neighborhood before I came to your house. I asked him for directions and I got a whole history of your family, which included stories about your father's father who the old man said was a good friend of his. He said he even knew the Almodóvars, your grandfather's mother's family."

"That's right, my great grandmother is an Almodóvar." Laura's face softened. "*Bisabuela* is still alive, living in Jayuya, up in the mountains, where I was born. I love her very much. She's at least ninety now. I'm going to visit her soon."

"Do you know how your grandfather died?"

"Why do you ask me that?"

Is she on to him? Ralph waited.

"I don't know," Laura finally said. "My father hardly spoke about him."

"I want to tell you something, Laura. I can't believe the stories in the papers and on television about your father, that he tried to rob that house. I want to find the truth about what happened there."

Laura again looked deeply into Ralph's eyes. "Don't trick me," her soulful eyes seemed to plead. With the thumb of the hand that held the cigarette between two fingers, she rubbed the palm of her other hand.

"Did your father ever mention the man who lived there, the painter Pablo Camino?"

"I don't know. I don't think so."

"What about a man named Cornelius Rhoads? He was a doctor. Dr. Rhoads?"

Something in her eyes twitched. She shook her head quickly, puffed deeply on her cigarette, then crushed it out on the ground. She stripped the cigarette and rolled the paper into a tiny ball and put it in her jeans pocket.

"Rhoads was the doctor who attended your grandfather when he died. I looked this up. He may have been responsible for your grandfather's death. He was also the father of Pablo Camino, in whose house your father's body was found."

The young woman looked confused and frightened. She lit another cigarette, then looked down at her watch again. "I have to return to the day-care center. I'm sorry."

Ralph stood. "I can give you a ride. I have my car here."

"No, thank you. I prefer to walk. It's only a few blocks." She forced a smile.

"Would you like to sit in on one of my classes? You can hear about Puerto Rican history in the states from the kids who lived it. They'll say things you won't find in the textbooks."

Laura shrugged and put out her hands, as though saying the possibility was minuscule. She excused herself. Ralph watched her small, thin body hurry down the street, her hips no wider than a child's.

He went to his car and took a pad and a pen from the glove compartment, which was stuffed with the copies he had made of the documents from the University library.

"Rosado's daughter confirms her father's father was Jesus Rosado Almodóvar, one of Rhoads' possible victims at Presbyterian Hospital," Ralph wrote. "Did Rosado know about the connection between his father and Rhoads, and Rhoads and Pablo?"

Was nutty Jaime Rosado onto something? Was he, like Albizu, radiated? Maybe we've all been radiated in secret experiments carried out by the military-industrial complex while we dozed in front of the television set.

Something in the back of his brain was trying to push through. He tapped his index finger below his nose. Albizu, Pablo's father . . . something.

Ralph had a headache. He also got an idea for his next class. He would talk about the return of Ulysses to Ithaca and his revenge against Penelope's suitors. Ralph planned to get a discussion going on revenge, ancient and modern, and its timeless roots.

THIRTEEN

The day after the discomforting meeting in her roof garden with Pablo's friend, Julia called Police Superintendent Javier Marrero Delgado.

"Doña Julia, it is indeed a pleasure hearing from you," said the chief of police, whose grandfather, Carlos Marrero Miranda, had been police chief when Julia's father was chief investigator for the Justice Department.

"How is your mother?"

"She is fine, thank you," said the police chief.

"I'm very glad to hear that."

"How can I be of service to you, Doña Julia? "

Julia, who knew that law enforcement blood ran as deep as family ties when it came to special treatment, was fairly sure the police had not yet bothered her about her son after they had learned who her father was. Perhaps they would contact her later, when they could come up with no other leads. But now she had decided to take the initiative, to offer her assistance in finding Pablo, in order to get what she was really after.

She told the young police chief (in his early forties): "I spoke the other day to Detective Miró, who is in charge of investigating that . . . incident that occurred in my son's house. I want to be as helpful as possible, so I'm calling you. Unfortunately, I have nothing to tell you about the disappearance of my son. I'm as mystified as to his whereabouts as you are. While I'm sure my son's role, if any, will be cleared up in due time, I just wanted to tell you that you will, naturally, have my complete cooperation in the investigation. In fact, I'm trying to search my mind for any possible destinations that Pablo may have taken. We haven't been very close in these past years, but if I think of any possibility as to his whereabouts, I certainly will contact you. I also am available for any questions you may have. And I hope you will contact me if you hear anything about his whereabouts. I'm sure you know how concerned I am."

"Certainly, Doña Julia, we'll let you know the earliest when we locate him. If you are able to help us, it would be greatly appreciated."

"Yes, of course," said Julia. "But I have something related to these events that I also would like to discuss with you."

"Yes?"

Was there a hint of suspicion in that question, Julia wondered. No matter.

"I'm calling also about the painting by Pablo that was seized at his house," she told the police chief. "It was taken supposedly as evidence in relation to . . . what happened there. As I'm sure you're aware, my son's work is quite valuable, not only in terms of money, but, more important, in terms of the island's artistic patrimony. The painting, a portrait of Albizu Campos, has been damaged and is in dire need of restoration."

"Yes, I know," said the police chief.

"I'm appealing to you to return the painting to me so that I can get it repaired as soon as possible. It's very important that the damage is minimized.."

"Yes, yes, I understand," said Police Superintendent Marrero. "I understand completely. I, personally, have always admired your son's work. My daughter, Alejandra, who is studying art at the University, has a book of his paintings and drawings. I understand, I understand. Unfortunately, however..."

Julia felt her bile on the rise. "*Yes*?"

"Unfortunately, the evidence cannot be returned at present. The possibility exists that it may have to be presented in court and . . ."

"I can have it restored, then return it."

"I'm afraid . . ."

"It's very important to repair that painting."

"I understand, but . . ."

Julia felt the tension in the pause.

"All right," she said. "Goodbye. Regards to your mother, who was a classmate of mine."

She slammed down the phone. That's what you get, Julia told herself, for not going to the top. Sitting at a desk in her gallery office, this time she telephoned the Justice Department, asking to speak to Justice Secretary Hiram Rivera O'Neill. The Secretary was not available, she was told by one of his secretaries.

"Could you please tell him that Julia Quiñones, the godmother of his sister Vanessa's daughter, called. I can be reached at 723-6805."

"Yes, Doña Julia, I'll tell him," said the secretary.

Julia sat still at the desk, covering her mouth with her hand, as though she were preventing herself from letting loose the frustration boiling inside. She *had* to save that painting! If she could no longer save her son, at least she could rescue one of his best works.

The portrait was a wonder. Pablo had painted the Nationalist leader in a wheel chair just after his release from a federal prison and a couple of months before his death. Her son had captured in that wizened face not only the dignity and the suffering of Albizu, but also his paranoia, false pride, deep disappointment with life and fear of dying. He had captured the old man's humanness. All of humanity's humanness. It was a great painting and she wanted to save it for posterity.

Even if the evening when it was first unveiled ten years ago had brought Julia pain then. And now.

She saw her son standing defensively in a corner near the bar, a drink in his hand. He had managed to put on a clean guayabera for the exhibition at her gallery, but he looked like he hadn't bothered to shave for a week. There were swellings on his forehead and he looked like he was in pain from head to toe.

She saw many of the gallery-goers who might otherwise have engaged him in conversation take one look into his bleary, anguished, accusing, guilt-ridden eyes, or get a whiff of the alcohol coming off him like a repulsive, sour perfume, give him nothing more than a strained greeting and move on. Even some potential collectors veered off when Pablo gave them menacing stares. Those brave enough to attempt a dialogue got intensely quizzical stares, as though Pablo was fervently trying to figure out not what was being said, not even the secret meaning behind the words, but the reason for the speaker's being.

The usual crowd packed the gallery: students, other artists jealously weighing Pablo's latest works, journalists who knew much less about art than they thought they did, free-drink cadgers from the Old Town, notables like art collector-wine importer-drug money launderer Ricardo Rexach, parading in a white dinner jacket and black tie around the gallery with his wife, María del Carmen Bernal de Rexach, her orange-red hair piled in layers of swirls, waves and curlicues atop a horsy face whose skin, from innumerable lifts, was weirdly smooth and tight, like burn tissue.

They looked at Pablo's portrait of Albizu Campos, then spoke about it in low tones and sneaked looks over to him. Julia knew they didn't like the portrait. She also knew that they would. In time.

Julia was accompanied at the opening by her new "friend," Dr. Félix Meléndez, a dignified-looking, white-haired Cuban doctor. They had dined together several times and gone to the movies together and he had always been the gentleman. Extremely considerate and polite. Perhaps too considerate, too polite.

She approached her son. The doctor stood at a discreet distance behind her, patiently waiting for an introduction that would come after some moments of mother-son intimacy.

Julia could tell from Pablo's reaction that she must have had a worried look in her eyes—those sad, half-compassionate, half-stonehard eyes, as her son had once described them to her. She knew she had too many wrinkles around her eyes, even though the rest of her was still taunt and attractive in her iron-gray days.

Pablo looked like he was going to cry!

Julia nodded at him in reluctant greeting. Pablo kissed her. When she went to return the kiss on his cheek, her lips shriveled from the scratch of his beard and her body recoiled from his stink. She couldn't help her reaction.

"Are you all right?" Julia asked.

"Of course. Why shouldn't I be?" He was trying too hard to appear in charge of himself.

She looked deeply, now severely, at him, as though in warning. "Are you in control of yourself?"

"I'm O.K. I had a little to drink, but I'm fine." He managed a warm, easy smile.

Julia kept looking into his eyes, searching out deceit. Then she inhaled deeply and said: "I want you to meet a friend." She turned to the doctor and she too put on an easy smile. "Félix, this is my son, Pablo. Pablo, this is the heart specialist, Dr. Félix Meléndez."

Pablo politely, if somewhat limply, shook the doctor's hand and humbly accepted the doctor's professed admiration for his work.

"It is a pleasure to meet one of the island's leading artists, whose reputation continues to grow throughout the world," said the doctor.

Pablo thanked the doctor, then said to his mother. "You know what today is?"

"No. Yes! The opening of your show."

Then, Pablo blurted out. "Today, mother, is my birthday. Thirty-five years ago today, you brought me into this miserable world."

Then Pablo said to the doctor: "Make sure her lies don't fuck you up and she doesn't desert you."

Julia reddened and tears formed. She looked deeply into her son's eyes. As he blinked several times, her hurt was gradually becoming mirrored in his eyes, and she actually believed that his pain was being inflicted by his unfathomable conscience.

Julia angrily turned and stalked out of the gallery, the doctor following.

Had she hurt him as much in his childhood as he had hurt her in the later years? Probably.

Probably? How self-centered and ignorant could she be? No one can be hurt like a child can be hurt. Oh, forget it, Julia. The son is a grownup now and the mother is beyond guilt. What was, was.

Julia spent the next few hours cataloguing new works acquired by the gallery and caring for the plants on her roof garden. But that feeling of vague anxiety remained. She went down to her office again, picked up the phone and dialed the Justice Secretary's number. He still was not in. Julia said the call was a family emergency (she didn't say which family), couldn't further efforts be made to contact him? The Secretary's secretary said she would again try to reach him.

Several hours later, in the early evening, the Secretary returned her call. Julia apologized for having to bother him and he apologized for not being able to answer earlier. Her connections were not as strong with the Attorney General as they were with the Police Superintendent. Nevertheless, she knew that her father's reputation at the Department earned a callback, at the least. She explained the situation about the confiscated painting.

Secretary of Justice Hiram Rivera O'Neill was, like Police Superintendent Javier Marrero Delgado, very understanding. "Unfortunately . . . "

"There is no way the painting could be returned, repaired, then given back to you?"

"Unfortunately . . . "

"There is absolutely nothing you can do?"

"Unfortunately . . . "

"It is more than unfortunate," said Julia. She hung up the phone. Tears of frustration were gathering. Ridiculous!

It was their loss.

It was the loss of everyone on the island.

Still, Julia knew, the loss she felt was deeper, more painful.

FOURTEEN

After Iris finished her day at Hunter, they took the late afternoon train from Penn Station up to Bridgeport. The latest "Dear Ferdie" had convinced Pablo that, while he was inexorably being driven from within, he was also fatefully being led toward his own reality, as frightening as it may be.

He had called Iris very early, before she had gone to class, and told her about the letter. She needed no convincing to agree to take him to the Connecticut home where she was brought up and her mother still lived so he could look through Dusty's memorabilia and files up there.

They met at the Eighth Avenue entrance to the station and as he saw Iris get out of a cab and walk toward him, wearing a long tight-fitting beige coat with white fur around the collar and sleeves and with a brown wool tam o'shanter on her head, incongruously carrying a beat-up brown briefcase, her green eyes glistening like those of a mischievous cat, he felt an infatuation for his half-sister that he hoped would only last for those few seconds while she approached.

"Papers to mark, undies to change, etc.," she told Pablo, swinging the briefcase out in front of her.

Pablo, who carried no change of clothes, nodded, and they entered the station.

Once on the train Pablo put their coats on the rack above and they sat side by side. Iris' breasts looked full and serious under a green turtleneck sweater. Her skirt was oatmeal color and she wore high brown boots. As he gave her the window seat, she brushed against him and he flinched. Pablo was acutely aware of their arms and hands touching on the shared armrest and of Iris' smell, the same as last night, still perfumeless and soapy fresh.

The train took off through a tunnel, then surfaced into the New York twilight.

"Hey, brother, I want to thank you for that beautiful necklace. I could be hypocritical and say, 'You shouldn't have,' but the truth is, I'm glad you did. Whenever I wear it, I'll think of you."

"Good thoughts I hope," Pablo said.

Iris squeezed Pablo's hand and kissed him on the cheek. He stirred down below; he wanted to put his tongue down her throat right there! Instead, he settled for squeezing her hand back.

Iris gave Pablo a quick small smile, then said: "So I called my mother right after you called me this morning, and told her I was bringing a friend up for a couple of days."

Pablo nodded, as though understanding the need to widen the focus. "She didn't mind?"

"Of course she minded. She's expecting another dyke companion. She'll be surprised when she sees you. But don't worry, she'll find something to complain to me about."

Pablo gave his half-sister a half-smile. "You two don't get along?"

"When I was a kid, I preferred my sonovabitch father. At least most of the time he ignored me."

"I hope we won't have any trouble looking at Dusty's files."

"You'll be sleeping in the guest house. Dad's stuff is on the second floor. You can go through it once my mother goes to sleep at ten o'clock, like always. She likes to start her day early, wheeling and dealing in real estate."

"She still works?"

"Damn tootin'. She's in her late sixties and still has her own business and she ain't givin' it up. She's one tough babe."

"You sound like you admire her."

"Not *her*, per se. Just her ability to keep on going. From what I've been able to pick up, she knew she was on her own after just a few years of her marriage to Dusty. I wouldn't call their marriage a warm and fuzzy thing. He was away more than he was home, and when they were together, even though we had the fireplaces blazing, it was as chilly as winter in the house. I think they stayed together only because . . . well, who the hell knows why?"

The expression in Iris' eyes went from sad to sadder. She took a deep breath, then said: "By the way, how did you find out about him? You know, about your relationship and all the other stuff. I mean, how long did you know?"

"I found out a little at a time. When I was in my first year in college, my mother confessed that the Korean War hero-father she invented for me never existed and that one Dr. Cornelius Rhodes was my real father."

He didn't tell Iris about the article in the newspaper years later. It was just a couple of paragraphs. Twenty-Five Years Ago in History, something like that. There was Rhoads' name, attached to the accusations. After, he went to the University library and dug out the old newspaper articles. He had made copies of the articles and shown them to his mother. She admitted that such charges had been made, but said there was an investigation (without saying it was his grandfather who had conducted it, which he found out later) and no charges were ever brought against his father. She was sure that he could never have done anything so horrible.

He had made further inquiries through the Rockefeller Foundation and found out that the bastard (no, *he* was the bastard) was dead. He had become a big cancer specialist in the states, married, raised a family. He died of cancer. Fitting. He left Pablo with a cancer on his own soul.

Pablo changed the subject. "How do you and your mother get along now?"

"Well, there was a time we weren't talking. It lasted a couple of years, in fact. She could be one mean bitch, that dear mother of mine." Iris shook her head, asserting rather than denying. "Well, *I've* mellowed, anyway."

The train was passing along the Harlem River, moving up to the northern part of the Bronx. The dark, metallic gray of the river mirrored the faded light of the day. Pablo looked over to Iris. He felt a tapping at his heart. His face was reddening. He looked away, and so did Iris.

"I better get some of these papers done, so I can relax when we get up to Connecticut," Iris said. "You don't mind, do you?"

"No, go ahead. I'll read the newspaper."

While Iris pulled out the small table from the back of the seat in front of her and switched on the light there, Pablo swung out of his seat and reached up to his coat on the overhead rack. The *New York Times* was stuffed into one of the pockets. He pulled the paper out and unfolded it.

How long hadn't he and his mother spoken? Ten years, starting after that night at her gallery. His one-man show turned out to be a one-man disaster. He turned off everyone there that night, turned them off from his paintings and from his drunk and mean self.

It was all because of what had happened the night before. Because Ana had taken the kid and left him. Because he had acted like a miserable shit.

It was about three in the morning when he had returned from his usual round of bars. He was as sober as ten or so cognacs could make him. After five, he was drunk, by the tenth, in his mind, he was sober. And where else would he be drunk or sober, if not in his head? He was so sober he was positive that bitch wife of his would still be awake and doing things to fuck him up.

His feet felt like sandbags, but he managed to get up the stairs to the bedroom. Ana was at her desk writing.

"What the fuck are you doing now?"

"I'm writing a letter to a friend in New York."

"Right. I know what you're doing and you sure as shit know what you're doing."

"What's that?"

"Come *on.* You're like everyone else on this fuckin island. Out to get me. What the hell is that towel doing on the bed?"

"I just showered. I got up sweaty. I couldn't sleep."

"Bullshit."

Pablo picked up the towel and threw it at Ana's feet. She stood, retrieved the towel and threw it back into his face. Pablo went to the bed and ripped the sheets off. "They're filthy." He threw them on the floor.

"Put those damn sheets back on the bed!"

Sure." He jumped on the bed, yanked the framed Picasso Minotaur print off the wall and smashed it and the no-glare glass covering it against the bedpost. Then he used a shard of glass to tear a hole in the sheets, which he then ripped to shreds and threw back on the bed. He noticed fresh blood on the sheets. He picked the towel up from the floor and wrapped it around his bleeding finger. Then he said: "I'll fix a few other things around here."

He swept Ana's creams and lotions off her dresser, pulled down a packed bookcase, ripped his recent, unframed drawing of her off the wall and tore it to pieces, then tripped his way downstairs. He emptied the dishes from the kitchen cabinet and smashed them on the floor, methodically, one at a time. While he was doing this, he was thinking: this is really dumb. Every drunk in the world smashes dishes. But he was sober. He should be doing something with imagination.

Ana came down to the kitchen. "You goddamn maniac! *Stop! Stop! Stop! I can't take this any more!*"

She picked up a metal candelabra from the dining room table and threw it at him. It hit him in the back. Big deal. No thrust in her throw. He went into the dining room and picked up a chair. He smashed it against the chandelier hanging over the table. The chair's two front legs got caught up in the chandelier, which didn't break. That really pissed him off. He stood on the table and swung on the chandelier until he and it came crashing down.

Pablo was lying on the floor on his back, tying his handkerchief around his bloody finger, while Ana swatted him with a dishtowel. A limp weapon, to say the least. He looked up and saw his daughter shivering silently behind her mother. Emmy's eyes were huge and liquid, like in a crummy Keane painting.

Pablo let Ana swat away. Ana was saying something about not being able to take any more. Then he heard top-of-the lungs screaming. But it was not Ana or Emmy. It was coming through the open window in the kitchen. It was a curdling scream. His mind flashed back to a huge bird, vulture, condor, albatross, screeching out a portent of doom.

"Shut the hell up! You woke my three babies, *cabrón!*"

It was Alma, the bitch who lived next door. A single mother, she worked at the bakery down the street.

"Mind your own fuckin business," Pablo shouted back.

"I'll show you whose business. I already called the police."

"Fuck you and them."

A couple of minutes later, two cops knocked on the front door. Ana opened it. Pablo was still lying on the floor. He felt relatively peaceful and calm. The cops stood over him. One of them had a nose like a swollen prick that curves off to the left. The other had a pumpkin head with two-dimensional, drawn-on features.

The cops spoke to Ana, then told Pablo to stand up.

"Why should I?"

"Because we want to talk to you," said prick-nose.

"This is my house, you know? I can do whatever the fuck I want here. I can talk from any position I want. In fact, I don't feel like talking. In fact, both of you get the fuck out of here. Get the *fuck* out of my house, assholes!"

The cops looked at each other, then both bent down and each took an arm and yanked Pablo to his feet. Teardrops, icicles and drop-earrings of glass fell off his body and tinkled onto the floor. An incredibly sharp pain sliced like the jagged edge of a broken windowpane into his lumbar, just above the tailbone. He let out a whooping roar and tried to pull free to put soothing hands on his pain. The cops took this for resistance and twisted both his arms up behind his back and this produced even greater agony. He kicked at shins and the cops looked at each other again, then started kicking and clubbing him and dragged him across the apartment's tiled floors and out into the street. Prick-nose let go for a minute and Pablo punched him in the mouth and clubs didn't stop whacking his legs and body and the back of his head all the way to the police station, as each cop took a turn sitting in the back with him.

After a couple of more cops at the precinct joyfully joined in the beating, Pablo was tossed into a piss-puddled cell for the rest of the night.

In the morning, he was brought to the judicial center, where he was charged with assaulting two officers. But after a rambling argument by Pablo that didn't even make sense to himself, the judge angrily threw the charges out.

"I know this man," said the judge. "That is, I know of your work, *Don* Pablo. I own two of your paintings, a self-portrait and a wonderful seascape that includes the shacks of La Perla in the Old City, which I proudly display, both of them, in my home. You are a great artist, our Rembrandt, our Picasso, our Van Gogh, and you must be free to continue your magnificent work. There is no case here."

Pablo mumbled his thanks, glancing poker-faced at the two cops, who gave each other the same looks as they did when they started beating him last night. The cops creased their brows at the judge and Pablo left the courtroom.

When he got home with a pair of gold earrings and a family of teddy bears, he learned that Ana had packed and taken their daughter to the airport for an early morning flight to New York.

Cunt!

He felt incredibly embarrassed. Embarrassed and pained, as though he was suffering from an incurable, self-inflicted ailment. They had had ten beautiful years together. After Amsterdam, New York. Then those first years in Puerto Rico, the feeling of finally coming home, his senses opening like never before, his heart happy, his soul, for the first time, at ease. The soft morning light, the delicate slant of shadows, the changing colors of the day. Life had been like a pastel dream, for Chrissake.

O.K., it wasn't always beautiful. There were plenty around with hearts as black as tar. And the tar seeped into other hearts, other minds and places so that sometimes it seemed as though it covered everyone and everything.

But he had loved her. And his daughter, she took his daughter. They left him.

He deserved it. He had been despicable.

Emmy, ten months old, sitting on his shoulders, slapping the top of his head and laughing gleefully as he lifted her way up, then brought her down to his chest and hugged her. He would die, or kill, for her, for them. He hated himself.

Now he remembered what it was that got him going that night. He had brought up questions about his father again, and Ana had said: "It's time to accept the past, whatever happened. There's not a thing you can do about it.

You're a grown man. How many more years are you going to agonize about this? His life is not your life. Live your own life."

Why did that piss him off? Because he was a goddamn idiot! *Was*? Still is!

They got a cab from the Bridgeport station to take them to Newtown. Pablo knew that Connecticut was supposed to be the richest state in the world's richest nation, but you couldn't tell that from the seedy look of downtown Bridgeport. Soon they were on a highway, then onto country roads, rolling alongside evergreen trees and occasionally there were glimpses of dark shining lakes. Houses were no longer along the roadside, but set back, mansion-like, off driveways. Under Iris' direction, they drove along several dark hilly roads under bare, wiry branched trees. Finally, they pulled off the road onto a short driveway. A Lincoln Continental was parked at the end of the driveway.

Iris' former home was no mansion, but it was large enough, two stories, surrounded by plenty of land. In the back of the house was a gazebo on top of a small hill, and beyond that, a pond. Off to the side were a lawn and a pool and a smaller two-story guesthouse, where Iris told Pablo he would be staying.

"But before we get you settled in," she said, "let's meet Moms."

Pablo nodded at the unsought inevitable and Iris pushed the button in the center of the front door. The button gave off an angry buzz.

No answer. Iris buzzed again. Still no answer. She shook her head and this time kept her finger on the button, looking as angry as the sound it gave off. The buzzing went on for some minutes.

Finally, the door unlocked from the inside, then opened.

"Well, I'm glad you're home," said Iris.

"I was watching television," said her mother. "I got so involved in my show, I didn't hear the bell."

Mother and daughter embraced like they didn't mean it.

Iris said: "This is my friend Pablo Camino. Pablo, my mother Dorothy Rhoads."

"Call me Dottie," said mother Rhoads.

They shook hands. The mother's hand was moist, possibly from recently applied hand cream. For an older woman, she had a solid grip. Her face was somewhat lined, but her skin seemed still pretty firm (face lift?) and there was something tense and alert in the blue eyes behind her rimless glasses. Iris had her mother's high cheekbones. Dottie's hair was dyed a reddish brown and wrapped in a tight bun. As she led them into the house, Pablo saw one sure sign of age: Dottie's legs moved stiffly. Hip problems, Pablo figured.

Iris' mother led them into a sitting room, where pillow-covered, slightly worn sofas and easy chairs pointed toward a huge TV screen. She motioned to a large, multi-pillowed blue sofa for Iris and Pablo to sit on and eased herself into a blue-covered easy chair off to the side of the sofa. Between the sofa and the chair was a glass-topped table, which held the day's newspaper, a half-filled glass with melting ice in it and a bottle of Chivas Regal.

"Iris, go get yourself and your guest glasses with ice from the kitchen, so we can have a welcome drink," said Dottie.

"Do you want a drink?" Iris asked Pablo.

"Sure."

As Iris went to the kitchen, Dottie drained her glass, then shouted to her daughter, "And bring me in some more ice, sweetheart."

"Excuse me," said Dottie, gluing her eyes to the TV screen, "but I have to watch the end of my show."

Her show, and the show of millions of others, Pablo knew, was the hospital drama, "E.R." Interns and nurses were supra-realistically working over a severely suffering individual.

Iris carried in a tray with two tall glasses and a plastic container of ice cubes.

"Refresh my drink, sweetheart," Dottie said without taking her eyes off the TV screen.

Iris gave Pablo the sourest of smiles as she dropped some ice cubes in her mother's glass, then filled it halfway with scotch. She did the same for Pablo and herself.

Iris and Pablo sat on opposite ends of the sofa, sipping their drinks, smiling apologetically at each other, as though they blamed themselves for assenting to Dottie's unspoken demand for silence until the program ended.

The emergencies were finally taken care of, or left to be taken up again the next week, and Dottie shut off the TV. She picked up her drink and took a healthy gulp. "I love that show," she said. "It's so real that it gets right into you." She pointed with her thumb below her heart and above her stomach.

"When did you start hitting the bottle, mother dearest?" asked Iris.

"Oh, I've been taking a nip or two before bed for the past several years," Dottie said, as though she were under doctor's orders. "It helps me sleep."

She turned to Pablo, suddenly very interested in him. "So what do you do for a living?"

"I paint."

"Oh, I see," said Dottie. She took another hefty gulp of her drink.

"Pablo is a well-known artist, mom," Iris said, hoping that would block her mother from coming up with something snide.

Pablo shifted uncomfortably in his seat. He too took a deep gulp of his drink. He hoped this would be a short get-together. He wanted to get over to the guesthouse and go through Dusty's papers and get the hell out of there.

"So you're a painter. Well, you know, I sell real estate, usually beautiful homes to wealthy people who buy expensive furnishings. Maybe I can ask them if they would like you to do some paintings to decorate their homes. Perhaps we can do some business."

"Je-sus!" said Iris. Then realizing she was reverting to her anguished teenage years, she covered over her dredged-up anger with a loud guffaw. "Pablo is an *artist,* not an interior decorator."

"I know, sweetheart," Dottie said, humoring her daughter. "I know that artists *never* think of making money." Her head was starting to weave. She sipped her drink. Then she said: "Pablo? Are you Spanish?"

"I'm Puerto Rican."

"Really?" A sour smile started to creep across Dottie's face. She freshened up her drink. "I spent some time in Puerto Rico, many years ago, when I was young and stupid. When I let people lead me around by the nose." She rubbed her nose, then took another healthy swallow.

Iris gave Pablo a surprised look. Dottie had never mentioned that to her daughter before. She wondered if her mother knew about her father's escapades down there, and the trouble he got himself into.

Pablo also poured himself another drink. When was she down there? Did she know Ferdie? He felt his heart beating very fast.

Dottie's eyes seemed to be retreating in their orbs in self-protection. "I was there for several weeks, visiting your father, who was working there," Dottie told Iris.

"It was before we were married."

"You never . . . "

"It was none of your business, sweetheart. It still isn't."

All three drank. Then Pablo asked: "Didn't you like Puerto Rico?"

"Why shouldn't I have liked it?" Dottie seemed defensive.

"The way you looked, Mom," Iris said. "The expression on your face."

"I *loved* Puerto Rico," Dottie said. "The weather, the beaches, *most* of the people."

"But something happened down there, right?" Iris coaxed.

"What are you talking about, sweetheart?"

"Did Dad have any problems down there?"

Dottie looked long and hard at her daughter. She took another gulp of her drink and sat back in her chair, suddenly looking very tired. Then she smiled, then mumbled something to herself. Then she said:

"As a matter of fact, he did have a problem there. Some foolishness about a letter criticizing the natives. He left because of it and yours truly returned to Connecticut. Things were quite tense for a while and your father and I only got to see each other intermittently. Then one day, after several months, he proposed, I accepted, we married and nine months later, practically to the day, you were born."

"Did you ever meet Ferdie?" Pablo asked.

"Excuse me?"

"Ferdie. The fellow your husband wrote that letter to that got him in trouble."

Dottie sat up. "How do you know about that?" She appeared indignant, but not quite sure why she was. She poured herself another drink.

"People from Puerto Rico remember the incident," Pablo said.

"Oh, such nonsense!" Dottie steadily downed her drink, stood, wobbled, sat again. "My God, I certainly drank more than I'm used to! I usually take one or two nips before bedtime. Well, it's time for beddy-bye. Help me up sweetheart," she told Iris.

Both Iris and Pablo got Dottie to her feet and she hugged her daughter, this time with feeling, and then she hugged Pablo. "Very nice meeting you, Pedro."

"Pablo," Iris said.

Dottie ignored her daughter's correction. "Take me up to my room, sweetheart," she said. Iris helped her mother upstairs.

Pablo finished his drink. He began pacing the room. He walked into a good-sized dining room furnished in dark mahogany, then returned to the sitting room, then went to the staircase and anxiously looked upstairs. Iris came down. "I just accomplished a first," she said. "I actually put my mother to bed!"

"Let's go to Dusty's files."

"How about tomorrow?" Iris said. "I'll go with my mother to see her sister, my aunt Ruth, she lives two towns over. I'll say you don't feel well. I'll call you before we start back. You'll have three or four hours."

"I want to start looking at the files now," Pablo said.

Iris gave Pablo a look, then shrugged.

They went to the two-story guesthouse. A pool between the two buildings was covered with tarpaulin. Iris showed Pablo where he was to sleep, on a sofabed in the downstairs room. The bed was already made up (by Dottie in an earlier show of consideration?). There were floats, summer chairs, chaise lounges, a large table umbrella and a folded-up round white metal table stored in the corners of the room.

"Let's go upstairs," Pablo said.

The upstairs room, long and low, was used to store furniture. The furniture looked in good shape but apparently did not conform to the latest sets in the living and dining rooms in the main house. Also stored there was an old-fashioned rolltop desk, swivel chairs, many cartons containing what Iris said were her old school books and old LPs and forty-fives, and several more file cabinets, which held, hopefully, other secrets to Dusty's unsavory past.

Pablo went to the file cabinets. They were locked. He let out an angry growl.

"Not to worry—yet," Iris said. She went to the roll-top desk. The top was down. It too was locked. So were the side drawers. "Wait, wait," Iris said. "Now I remember. Stay put, I'll be right back."

She ran out of the house. Pablo looked over to the file cabinets. His anger at the inanimate was rising. He was ready to try to rip the drawers open, somehow, or to kick the cabinet, punch it. Then Iris returned. With a hairpin.

"Watch this," she said, inserting the hairpin into the rolltop desk lock. She moved it around. Nothing happened. "Hmm," said Iris.

She took the hairpin out of the lock, closed it further together, inserted it again, twisted–and the lock clicked. She rolled the top back. She fetched a box that once held paper clips from a compartment in the desk. Inside the box was a set of small keys. Iris tossed the keys to Pablo. "They should open the cabinets."

Five slim silver keys were held together by a twisted wire. The third key opened the first file cabinet. Iris helped Pablo go through the contents of all the cabinets. One-by-one, they emptied the cabinets, putting the papers and folders and envelopes on a dinette table, reading them, then returning them before going through the next drawer. None of these files dealt with Dusty's medical career. There were no military citations, no publications by or about Dusty and his work, nothing relevant to his personal life. The files, instead, were filled with political material, mostly writings about Communism, mostly Cold War blather.

Once again, it was not until going through the last drawer of the last file cabinet that Pablo reached pay dirt. There he found several carbon copies and original letters clipped together by paper clips that left rust-colored imprints on the top sheets when he unclipped them. Several of the letters were addressed to such U.S. agencies as the Justice Department, the CIA, the FBI, the Department of the Interior and to individual members of Congress. They were similar inquiries on whether funding was available to supplement clandestine operations by a private organization composed of "former U.S. military officers, exiles from the totalitarian communistic regimes of Cuba and Hungary and American patriots, banded together to fight communism throughout the world." All the letters were signed by Cornelius P. Rhoads, Colonel (retired), U.S. Army.

Among the answers was one from the FBI, dated April 5, 1961. The letter praised the efforts of Col. Rhoads and his patriotic cohorts in efforts "to launch a counter-attack against the most menacing threat yet posed against the Democratic ideals and beliefs of our Nation." It suggested that Col. Rhoads contact the FBI agent-in-chief in his state, "who will forward further information to me." The letter was signed: J. Edgar Hoover, Director.

There did not seem to be any other FBI-Rhoads correspondence in the file. But then, like the hand of God lifting Pablo's hand and putting it in the right place, Pablo picked from the pile another letter attached to an envelope by a rusty paper clip that made his heart race and his hand shake.

The return address on the envelope was of a hotel in Madrid, on La Gran Via. The name written above the hotel was Fernando Alberto Méndez y del Río. The ink on the two pages of the letter was faded to purple (or maybe that was the original color), the script was small, yet with flourishes on the capitals. The letterhead was that of the same Madrid hotel as on the envelope.

This letter was signed: "Ferdie."

FIFTEEN

Ralph's twelve-year-old Plymouth Caravelle climbed the outer lane of the precariously twisting road, into the *cordillera central*, the mountain chain that rose like a spine through the center of the island. Just off the side was a drop of several hundred feet and a dizzying view of steep ravines and houses cemented on the sides of rolling hills, a scene from a tropical Switzerland. A refreshing morning breeze blew through the open windows.

He came into the town a little past noon. The plaza was bordered on one end by a non-descript City Hall and on the other by a gray stone Spanish-style church. Ralph followed a car with a loudspeaker on its roof announcing a sale at the local dry goods store. Behind City Hall he found the police station, where he got directions to the home of Doña Clarita Almodóvar. She lived in a one-story, sprawling white house at the upper end of one of the town's sloping streets. Beyond were lush green fields and hills that had long, thin shades drawn over them as the sun rested behind passing clouds.

There was no doorbell, but a large cowbell hung down on a rope from the flat roof. Ralph tugged at the rope. Dogs barked. He shook the bell again.

"How can I help you?"

Ralph looked around.

"I'm up here."

Four dog paws and a large straw hat shadowing a barely discernable face protruded over the ledge of the roof.

"*Señora* Almodóvar?"

"*Sí.* At your service. How can I help you?"

"I'm here about your grandson, Jaime Rosado. We were in the Army, in Vietnam, together. Can we speak?"

"*Momentito.*" The straw hat, the shadowy face and the dog paws disappeared. The barking soon resumed behind the front door. After several minutes, the door opened.

Clarita Almodóvar was a short, thin woman in a long, flowered yellow dress whose hem partly covered her bare feet. She stood straight and gave Ralph a wide, sparkling smile, looking decades younger than her ninety years. Her eyes crinkled. Two shorthaired beige-colored mutts made a racket. Doña Clarita ushered Ralph in. The look-alike mutts reluctantly allowed him to enter into a bright, spacious room filled with wicker and straw furniture. They sniffed around Ralph, growled at his intruding feet, then got bored and pattered into another room.

The whitewashed walls were hung with colorful tapestries and the hardwood floors had dulled to a whitish color. All sorts of potted tropical plants stood around the room. A large wooden fan clicked overhead as it whirred warm air around the room. Some of the wicker and straw furniture was unraveling, paint was chipping from the walls and there was mold in the corners of the ceiling. But, despite its age, the house, like Clarita Almodóvar, seemed comfortable and in good condition.

The straw hat was gone. Doña Clarita's graywhite hair was braided and hung over one shoulder. Her skin, while freckled, creased and creviced with age, was an almost translucent ivory. Her probably once blue eyes were faded within narrowing slits to a watery gray, but they were still lively, and her lips, now colorless and chapped, were still full.

"I was working in the garden on the roof," she said, shooing a cat curled up on her rocker and lowering herself with minimum effort into the straw-backed seat. She indicated that Ralph should sit across from her in a twin rocker, also occupied by a curled-up furry bundle. The cats hissed at one another, as though each blamed the other for interrupting its nap. Then they too crept out to another room, as perturbed as the dogs at Doña Clarita for inviting a stranger into their home.

"I grow tomatoes and squash on the roof," Clarita Almodóvar said.

Ralph nodded, as though all ninety-year-olds had this hobby.

"Would you like some lemonade?"

"That would be nice."

Doña Clarita started to get up, then decided to reach over to an upended wicker basket used as a table and to extract a slim brown cigarillo from a pack sitting there. She offered Ralph one. He declined, but reached over for the lighter on the table. She beat him to it. "Sit down," she said, lighting her cigarillo. She took a deep puff, slowly let out the smoke through her nostrils and her eyelids fluttered. Then she asked once again: "How can I help you?"

"Well, when I heard about Jaime . . . "

"Oh, excuse me. I forgot about the lemonade."

Ralph was about to say it was O.K., he could do without it, but she lifted herself from the chair and shuffled off barefoot into the kitchen at the back of the house.

"Can I help you?" Ralph shouted after her.

"Just stay there. I'll be back."

Ralph saw something dart across the floor, then stop in front of a potted plant. It was a small green lizard. It stood stock-still and seemed to be looking with its bulging eyes sideways at Ralph. Then it ballooned the skin under its chin, flicked its tongue at the air, shot up into the plant and disappeared.

None of the animals in the house seemed overjoyed by his visit.

After a few minutes, Doña Clarita returned with two tall glasses of lemonade with lemon wedges floating on top. The cigarillo was hanging from her mouth. She held out one glass to Ralph and he took it. He was about to take her glass to put it on the table next to her rocker but she waved him away. She drank standing, puffed on her cigarillo, then sat in the rocker.

"Why are you here?" she asked. "Do you want to sell me something? You'll have to speak up because I'm a little hard of hearing."

She apparently didn't hear what he had said when she was on the roof. He repeated loudly that he had come to talk to her concerning the tragic death of her grandson, Jaime Rosado, and that he and Jaime had served together in Vietnam.

"Where are you from?" Doña Clarita asked.

"I'm from San Juan, by way of New Jersey."

"I recognized that your Spanish had an accent." She switched from Spanish to English. "I lived many years in New York, you know?"

Ralph smiled, waiting.

"Yes," Doña Clarita said, rocking in her chair and puffing on her cigarillo. "I worked for many years at Tropical Casuals, two fifty-five, West Forty-First Street. I belonged to the ILGWU. I was a shop foreman and I organized for the union in other places, in the Bronx and New Jersey." She pronounced Jersey as though it began with a Y.

Ralph nodded. "Were you in New York with your family?"

"What did you say?"

"When were you in New York?"

"Oh, I was there for many years. I lived in Brooklyn, then the Bronx, then Queens. I came back to *la isla* about ten years ago. I longed for my island, you know? I couldn't stand those New York winters no more."

"When you were in the states, your grandson Jaime and I were in Vietnam and . . . "

"The ILGWU became my savior. I got a living salary, thanks to God, and was able to support myself during all those years in New York. I still get a pension check from them now along with my Social Security. God bless America and God bless David Dubinsky and the ILGWU." She puffed on her cigarillo, coughed, let out the smoke through her nostrils and smiled warmly.

"Were you living with your family in New York?"

"*Sí, hombre!* The union was my family."

"Yes, but your husband and your children, did they . . . ?"

"Mr. Max Bernstein, he owned Tropical Casuals. He always told me he wasn't crazy about the union, but he was crazy for me. He was a widower and he said he wanted to marry me. Maybe he was kidding, maybe not. But I only kidded him back, you know? He was a very nice man, Mr. Max Bernstein. But then I went to work fulltime for the union, so I didn't see him no more. I heard he moved with his business to Puerto Rico. He got himself a Puerto Rican wife, after all. Then he got a heart attack and died."

Doña Clarita exhaled smoke from her cigarillo and stared through the smoke. She shook her head back and forth, then she smiled warmly, remembering other things.

Ralph was wondering how to get Doña Clarita on his track when she suddenly switched rails. Her smile disappeared.

"I went to New York, you know, after what happened here. The same thing happened to my grandson that happened to my son." Her lips flinched and her jaw shook. She angrily crushed the cigarillo into the ashtray on the arm of the rocking chair.

Ralph put an inquisitive look on his face. Doña Clarita lit another cigarillo. She puffed hard and blew out a lot of smoke and rocked faster in her chair.

"My son was killed by an *americano* doctor, who confessed that he gave him cancer. My grandson was also killed by the *americanos*. They took him in the Army and God knows what they did to him there, they made him crazy. I love the *americanos* but I hate them too."

Ralph nodded, recognizing the reasonableness of Dona Clarita's ambivalence. "What happened to your son?"

"He was sick, but the *americano* doctor made him worse and killed him. We tried to get them to investigate. Then the doctor said so himself. He wrote it in a letter. He killed others too, the same way. But then they told us there was nothing they could do, because the doctor said later he really didn't do it and the government said he didn't do it too. So there was nothing we could do. He was my only one and his father left a long time ago and when my son died I left too, to New York, where I began my life again. I don't cry now about all that like I used to. I don't know why. It still breaks my heart when I think of what happened to my only boy, but I don't cry no more. He's one part of my life, which is made up of a lot of parts when you've lived as long as me, you know?"

The light in Doña Clarita's eyes, which had dimmed, sparked up again. She kept rocking and puffing on her cigarillo.

"Do you think your grandson knew how his father died?"

"Sí, Señor! Everybody knew, it was in all the newspapers, and although he was very young, you know, eventually he knew. I think he tried to forget what happened but when I saw him last year when I took a *público* into San Juan because the ILGWU they gave a banquet for me and some others and we got plaques for being members of the union for fifty years, I went over to see him and his family, they were surprised that I was still moving around so well. But Jaimito, my grandson, he was acting funny, because he was very nervous, and he kept telling me that he was going to get even because they killed his father, my son."

"Did he say how he was going to get even?"

"No, he just said he was going to revenge himself for who killed his father. He talked very quiet, but his eyes scared all of us. Everyone looked at him, no one said anything, then we all looked away. Then I had to go to get my *público* back home."

Ralph took a very deep breath. How the hell did Jaime Rosado, who, according to Sarge, claimed in his psychotic state to be the son of Pedro Albizu Campos, manage to find out about Pablo's connection to Dusty Rhodes? Did he? He must have. Why else would he have been at the house that night? Do madmen have some special intuition into the lives of murderers, and their offspring?

"When Jaime said he was going to revenge his father's death, did he mention anyone by name?"

"No. When I saw how he was, looking so strange in his eyes, my heart went out to my grandson. What did they do to him in the Army?"

Ralph shook his head, raised his eyebrows and opened one hand palm up, acknowledging that he shared her bewilderment.

Ralph stood and thanked Doña Clarita. She looked at him, puzzled. "Why did you come here?" she asked. "Were you going to sell me something?"

"I just wanted to talk a little about Jaime, your grandson. We were in the Army together."

"Did the Army make you sick too?"

Ralph said he didn't think so, but you never could be sure. The two mutts, sensing he was leaving, came out into the room again. They looked at him, one of them licking his shoes, the other snarling.

What did that snarling dog sense about him?

Maybe he wasn't all that well, Ralph reflected as he climbed into his car and began the long, winding ride back down to San Juan.

A week later, Laura Rosado, Doña Clarita's great granddaughter, showed up for Ralph's class. Richie Pérez gave her his seat and went to bring back a chair for himself from another room. After the class, she asked Ralph if she could talk to him. They walked together toward the faculty parking lot. The girl lit a cigarette.

"When we talked last, were you implying that my father was killed because he went to this artist's home to kill him? That he wanted revenge because of what the artist's father did to my grandfather?" She looked nervous and confused.

Ralph knew he had to be truthful with the daughter, as far as he knew the truth. He nodded. "And your father may have been killed by the son of the man responsible for the death of your grandfather."

The girl looked deeply into Ralph's eyes. He saw dread and tears, which, he understood, was what truth sometimes spawned. He felt a cramp in his stomach and a quick throbbing in his chest, as though some crucial part of him suddenly was caught in a tightening web of need to fathom the heart's dark corners.

May 3, 1961

Dear Dusty:

So far, I have met with both Rivera and Gavira-Cruz and they assure me that those closest to the Generalísimo confirm he would look kindly on us establishing the European headquarters of our organization in Madrid. I am told that he agrees with our premise that as the bulwark of anti-Communism in West Europe, and especially in light of recent events in Cuba, Spain must play an even larger role in U.S. defense policy.

The Generalísimo, I have learned, will both ideologically, and to some extent materially, support extra-official organizations such as ours, so long as we stay away from local politics. I have given assurances that our one and only interest lies in preventing the advance of Godless International Communism and that we regard the Generalísimo's regime as congenial with our interests.

Tomorrow I am off to further our contacts in South and Central America and the Caribbean. In view of last month's Cuban debacle, brought about by Mr. Kennedy's inexplicable decision to pull out our air cover, I'm sure we are both agreed that we must solidify and broaden these contacts. Cuba falls to godless Communism today, Santo Domingo, or even Puerto Rico tomorrow! I'm sure you agree that we must do our utmost to prevent this from happening.

Now, as to the other matter, I have made several visits to the woman in question. With sorrow I report that she remains as adamant as ever in her opposition to renew any personal communications with you. I found her quite charming and I can well understand your feelings for her after all these years, despite your other attachments.

The young man in question seems quite intelligent, if somewhat sad-eyed. You can, of course, contact me, as usual, through Seguros Hispanoamericanos, at the Miami office.

Any correspondence there will be forwarded to me at whichever branch office I will be at the time on "insurance" business.

You will hear from me next from Buenos Aires, si Dios quiere. *Until then, old friend, I remain*

Affectionately,

Ferdie

SIXTEEN

The information operator couldn't find a listing in Miami and all of Dade and Broward counties for *Seguros Hispanoamericanos*, or for Hispanic-American Insurance Company, or Hispanic Insurance or Spanish-American Insurance, but there was a Latin-American Insurance Company in downtown Miami.

Pablo dialed the number and asked to speak to Fernando Alberto Méndez y del Río. The switchboard operator put him on hold. Some minutes later a deep, smooth voice came on the line.

"Can I help you, sir? Would you prefer that I speak in English or Spanish?"

"Are you Fernando Alberto Méndez y del Río?" Pablo asked in English.

"This is Mr. Méndez. Can I help you?"

"Do you go by the name of Ferdie?"

Silence. Then: "I'm sorry?"

"Ferdie. Ferdie. Is that your nickname?"

"Freddie."

"What?"

"Freddie."

"Not Ferdie?"

"I'm sorry, Ferdie?"

"Do people call you that?"

"They call me by my name, sir. Federico. When I was a small boy in Argentina, I was called Freddie. My full name is Federico José Méndez Ypres. Before coming to the States, I spent several years in London, where I was called . . . "

"O.K., sorry."

Despite the air-conditioning in the airport, Pablo was sweating heavily in his flannel shirt and corduroy pants. He carried his parka on his arm. When he left his New York hotel to take the train to Connecticut with Iris he had forgotten to pick up the warm-weather clothes he had worn up from San Juan and put into the hotel laundry.

On the flight down, he had reread the letter. He remembered the sonovabitch with the little beard who sometimes came to their rented apartment in Madrid. How he used to look at his mother, take stock from head to toe when she wasn't looking. He always feigned cheerfulness, but Pablo knew even then that there was something weird and mean about that sonovabitch.

Despite the age of the letter, written over thirty years ago, Pablo was sure that Fate had provided him with a personal map. "You can, of course, contact me, as usual, through Hispanoamericano Seguros, at the Miami office . . . " He would track the fucker down starting from here, no matter where it took him.

He had insisted on going to Miami right away, as though Ferdie was down there and ready to take off at any minute. Pablo was able to make a reservation on a noon flight and pay at the counter in cash. Iris had borrowed her mother's car to drive him to Kennedy Airport.

Iris made sure that Pablo had her cell phone number and made him promise to call her from Miami.

"You're going to keep in touch, right?"

"Yeah, O.K."

"You'd better!"

"All right."

She had hugged him and kissed him lightly on the lips.

Pablo called the information operator again. This time he seemed to have hit the jackpot. There was a residence listing for an F. A. Méndez y del Río in Coral Gables. He excitedly wrote down that phone number and address. He grabbed a quick shot of Cuban coffee at a counter, then rushed out of the airport and got into a waiting taxi.

After a few minutes of swerving around underpasses and overpasses, they moved down a long, broad avenue, passed a dog track, then turned into tree-lined streets of large private houses, not unlike those in the more affluent suburbs of San Juan.

The houses gradually became more modest-looking and the taxi pulled up in front of a one-story cement home with a small porch fronted by a small lawn behind an iron gate. Unlike the other houses on the street, there were no flowerbeds near the front door. Heavy grillwork surrounded the porch, which was occupied by one potted rubber tree, one small glass-topped table and one metal-framed chair. The carport was devoid of vehicles, which must have meant that F. Méndez y del Río was not home. Pablo decided to try anyway.

He unlatched the gate and went to the front door. It too was covered with grillwork. He rang the bell several times. No response.

A car pulled up in the driveway next door. A tall man in a short-sleeved guayabera and with an iron-gray crew cut got out of the car. Pablo went up to him.

"Excuse me, I'm looking for *Señor* Méndez."

The man narrowed his eyes. He looked Pablo up and down. "Are you one of his religious friends?"

"I've never met him. I'm here on a business-related matter."

The man's long, creased face seemed to doubt Pablo. "Méndez is no longer in business," he said. "He used to be, but now he's not."

"Well, I have to see him about something that happened when he was in business."

The man shrugged. "He's a Jew."

"Excuse me?"

"He's a Jew. He became one a couple of years ago. He's got a beard. He's usually not home during the day. Not until late at night. Then he leaves early in the morning."

"Do you know where I might find him?"

The man's eyes narrowed again. "Is your visit here related to the days when he was one of us, in the struggle to free Cuba from Castro?"

"I don't give a fuck about Castro. I'm just looking for your neighbor on a business matter." Pablo smiled.

The man's face tightened. He was about to angrily say something, then decided not to. He shrugged. "I hear he hangs out all day in the Jewish churches in Miami Beach. If you want my opinion, I think he's *loco.*"

Pablo grunted and left.

He walked several same-looking streets, searching for a main avenue where he could get a cab. The sun slipped in and out of clouds, but the humidity was high and he sweated and itched like mad under his flannel shirt. Finally, he landed on a busy thoroughfare and got a cab. Pablo, who was last in Miami about ten years ago, remembered the Bass Museum. He told the driver to take him there.

They followed the sun logos on the traffic signs, were held up on a drawbridge, then crossed the bay into Miami Beach. Pablo got out by the museum, then found a room at a nearby Holiday Inn on Collins Avenue. He immediately went to the telephone book under the nightstand.

There were dozens of synagogues listed in Miami Beach. Pablo looked at a map provided in the tourist brochures in his room. The closest one, Temple Emanu-el, was on Washington Avenue, a couple of blocks away. He tore out the page from the phone book and pocketed it and the map.

The main doors to the synagogue were locked. So were all the doors to the other synagogues Pablo tried in the next few hours. Apparently Jews didn't drop in for prayers in the middle of the afternoon.

Pablo found himself at the far end of the Lincoln Road pedestrian mall. He bought underpants, a couple of short-sleeve shirts, white tennis sneakers and a pair of seersucker pants. He dumped his espadrilles, whose rope soles had started unraveling, then hurried back toward his hotel, intending to rip off the heavy clothes and shower and change.

Then Destiny, Fate, whatthefuckever, took over.

As he passed Wolfie's delicatessen on Collins Avenue, he realized he hadn't eaten all day. He decided to get a pastrami sandwich to go. The Early Bird crowd took up most of the pickle-laden tables, under blowup stills of Clark Gable and Judy Garland and Myrna Loy.

As Pablo waited at the counter for his sandwich, a senior citizen came up to him. *"Shalom."*

Pablo nodded at the man.

"I saw you was looking to get into the synagogue over dere." The man cocked his head to somewhere outside. "I was out walking."

"I was looking for someone," Pablo said.

"Yeah? Who was dat?" The man asked as though he could mentally scroll down a full list of synagogue regulars.

"A man by the name of Méndez. His full name is Méndez y del Río. His first name, I think, is Fernando."

"He's a Jew? Sephardic?"

Pablo shrugged, then nodded. "I suppose so."

The old man, who had surprisingly muscular arms, said: "Méndez? A Sephardic Jew? I don't know nobody like that."

"I understand he spends a lot of time in one of the synagogues around here, but to tell you the truth, I don't know which one."

"You was expecting to find him over at Temple Emanu-el in the afternoon?"

Pablo shrugged again.

"Dere's only one place around here where the Jews spend their afternoons *dovening* instead of playing pinochle. If you want to come wit' me, I'll show you where."

"That's very kind of you."

"You don't have to give me no compliments. We'll go as soon as you eat."

"I was going to take out the sandwich."

"No, eat it here."

"What?"

"Here it comes. Don't bother wrapping it," the man told the waitress behind the counter. "He's going to eat it here."

He told Pablo: "Look, I'm finishing up my meal at the table over dere with my wife. Eat your sandwich and I'll take you over to the place. Go ahead, eat. Another fifteen minutes, the Jews will still be there talking to God."

Pablo sat at the counter and ate his sandwich, washing it down with a black cherry soda. His self-appointed guide came over to him while he was finishing up a piece of cheesecake and coffee.

"O.K., you ready?"

"Ready."

Pablo paid his bill at the cashier and the man threw a kiss to his wife, who was still at a table, drinking a cup of tea under a blowup photo of a youthful, extremely handsome Gary Cooper. She waved him off. "Go, go," she said with a sour expression, then smiled warmly at Pablo.

The two men crossed Collins onto Ocean Drive, to the restored pastel-and-neon South Beach area. The older man introduced himself. "Sam Roth."

Pablo gave his traveling name and took a surprisingly strong hand.

"Gillespie don't sound Jewish," Sam Roth said. "But nowadays, who knows, right?"

Pablo nodded and grunted.

"I was in millinery—feathers, flowers, novelties—till the women stopped wearing hats. Then I went into bridal gowns. Now I do pushups and other workouts in the morning, take a dip in the pool before lunch, read a book, take a nap, eat an Early Bird dinner, play pinochle, watch the TV news, then hug my wife good night and maybe, occasionally, you know, I don't have to spell it out."

They passed violet and flamingo pink, lemon and lime-colored hotels and bars. Two young women with their nipples tight against the men's undershirts they wore skated by. A bare-chested, copper-brown guy with spiked yellow hair sashayed past, his pecs bulging and his behind sticking out of tiny shorts. The street was crowded and the colors sparkled in the bright tropical light.

"We're almost there," said Sam Roth. "Where the Jews pray and talk and talk and pray all day and all night."

In the middle of this? Pablo wondered.

They entered an old, decrepit, mustard-colored building that the Art Deco revival had passed by with a vengeance. The building was sitting between two glitzy boutiques on a narrow street between Ocean Drive and Collins Avenue.

They climbed one flight of stairs, and went through an open door into a long, narrow, dark room. The sweltering heat was occasionally stirred by a couple of noisy window fans. The only furnishings in the low-ceiling room were several rows of benches and, up front, a long table and folding chairs. About a dozen men sat around the table and on the first row of benches, some rocking back and forth, mumbling to themselves, others rocking and reading, still others conversing in low voices. Pablo's heartbeat sped up as he realized that F. (Ferdie?) A. Méndez y del Río could be behind one of the bearded faces in the group.

Sam Roth said: "I ain't crazy about these guys. They remind me too much of what I escaped from the old country. They study the Kabala and all that mystical mishmash day and night, which if every Jew would be doing, there wouldn't be no Israel, you know what I mean? I wish you luck, my friend." Sam Roth gave Pablo another crunching handshake and left.

Pablo moved slowly down the side of the room. No one seemed to notice him. He decided to sit on the end of the bench in the first row, waiting for a break in the praying. He tried to catch an eye, but no one looked towards him. He waited. And waited.

He watched the men rocking and mumbling and pointing out things to each other in the books they were reading. They were all ages. The beards ranged from coalblack and curly to chest-length, Father Time-white. Pablo, who still carried a shopping bag with his newly bought light clothes inside, was sweating like a pig. But he couldn't be as uncomfortable, he figured, as these men with their long, unkempt beards, several of whom were wearing, incredibly, long black coats and broad brimmed black hats. The others wore long-sleeve white shirts buttoned at the wrists and black skullcaps.

Pablo decided he had waited long enough. He stood and, above the metal blade-scraping sound of the fans, and the mumbling and the murmuring, said in a booming voice: "I'm looking for Méndez. Mr. F.A. Méndez y del Río. Are you here?"

The murmuring and the mumbling stopped. Only the fans kept scraping. All eyes—large, sad, soulful, startled—looked up, as though Pablo's presence was a complete surprise. Then the eyes turned to a man at the far end of the rectangular table. He was tall, wiry and looked to be in his late sixties, with a full nicotine-brown-and-gray beard. Behind tinted, aviator-style glasses, his eyes locked into Pablo's, then skittered away. He looked scared as hell.

"Are you *Señor* Méndez?" A fist tightened inside Pablo's stomach.

The man said nothing. He stared down into the book in his lap.

"Méndez, I have to speak to you, in private," Pablo said.

The man continued to study his book and nodded slowly, as though continuing in prayer.

Is he nodding yes? Instead of following his impulse to grab the guy by his scrawny, chicken neck and pull him out of his chair and into the street, Pablo said: "I'm sorry to disturb you. But there's something important I have to talk to you about. Can we do it as soon as possible?"

The man looked up from his book. With thumb and forefinger on each side of the frame, he carefully, almost daintily, took off his glasses, wiped them along the front of his white shirt, blinked several times and stared woefully again at Pablo.

Pablo saw in the man's eyes a familiar expression of anxiety, weariness, suffering. He knew that look only too well. Because, he realized with a tightening in his chest, he had recently seen, and painted, that same haunted look in his own eyes.

"Please wait for me outside," the man said. "I'll meet with you in a short time. I must finish here first."

"O.K." Pablo nodded to the others as he took his leave. They already were back in their other world of holiness, in which Pablo did not exist.

Pablo waited in front of the eyesore of a building on the narrow street of boutiques. Would F. A. Méndez y del Río reveal all he knew about his late good friend, Cornelius P. "Dusty" Rhoads? He'd better.

There was a gnawing inside Pablo's stomach. He had to know the murderous depths of the man who had sired him, whether his father intentionally wreaked suffering on so many. He *had* to know, even if those hard truths toppled him into a mad dark pit!

Sweat was pouring from his body. Where the *fuck* was that guy?

The bearded men started coming down the stairs. Pablo closely searched each face for Méndez. They averted his eyes and quickly dispersed in different directions.

Two more worshipers exited. Then no one.

Pablo dashed into the building and up the stairs. The door to the long, low-ceilinged room was locked.

Pablo wrapped hard against the door. He shouted: "Méndez? Méndez!"

No answer. He thrust his body against the heavy wooden door. It didn't budge. He rushed back down the stairs and circled the block to the back of the building, which gave off on an alley filled with large dumpsters. There was a metal door at the back of the building. He tried it. Unexpectedly, it opened.

He climbed a metal staircase. The back door leading to the makeshift synagogue was also locked. Its upper half was composed of a glass window. He looked around, rushed downstairs again and found a two-by-four in one of the dumpsters. He went back up and smashed the glass half of the door, reached over and unlocked it from the inside. His hand was a bloody mess. He was sure he hadn't cut it on the glass. He looked at the slab of wood, which was bloodied around a nail sticking up from it.

He reached into the bag containing the clothes he bought on the mall and ripped up one of the shirts to wipe away the blood and tie around the wound. He opened the door.

There were two doors across from one another in a small alcove. The fans in the long room were shut off. The room was even more sweltering. No one was there.

He went to one of the doors at the back and opened it. A water closet. Méndez was not crouched between the filthy commode and the cracked and rusted sink. He went to the other door. It was locked. Pablo knocked. "Méndez? Open up. I know you're in there. Look, I just have a few questions, then I'll leave you in peace. Open the door."

Silence.

The door looked flimsy and he crashed his shoulder against it several times, backed up and pounded into it with all his strength. It flew open and he stumbled inside.

The windowless room—crowded with shabby furniture, busted suitcases, rusty file cabinets and Hebrew books, newspapers and religious items—was as hot as a steam bath. It stank of mildew and body odor. Méndez sat on a footlocker in a far corner, his face glistening with sweat.

Again with thumb and forefinger, he removed his glasses and wiped them on his shirtfront. He let the glasses dangle in one hand.

Pablo walked over to him and looked down into Méndez's eyes. There was real fear there. Not the fear of someone crazy. Pablo knew how that fear looked. A madman was aware on some level that his fear was a means to defend himself, so there was usually a glimmer of defiance in the eyes. But this was unadulterated fear, a purely cringing, helpless look.

"Which side are you?" Méndez asked. He put his glasses back on, then tried to control his shaking hands, moving them across his stomach, then into his lap, then finger-locked across his stomach again.

"What?"

"I'd like to know who is going to assassinate me." Méndez tried hard to instill a note of defiance in his cracking voice. "Were you sent by Fidel, or do my former anti-Castro *compañeros* think it's time to eliminate me? If neither, then it's she who sent you. Her jealousy knows no bounds. Is it her?"

Pablo felt sorry for the guy. But there was too much at stake now. He'd start off like a diplomat.

"Let's talk, Ferdie. You tell me what's bothering you and I'll tell you what's bugging me."

The man flinched, then sent out a wobbly, yet relieved, smile. He exhaled audibly. "Ferdie? I'm sorry, but you have the wrong brother."

"What the hell are you talking about? You're Fernando Alberto Méndez y del Río, also known as Ferdie."

"I'm Felipe Alfonzo Méndez y del Río. Ferdie is my older brother."

"Bullshit."

Méndez pulled an old, bulging wallet from his back pants pocket and showed Pablo his driver's license. His photo was accompanied by the name, Felipe Alonzo Méndez y del Río.

"You're looking for my brother," said Méndez.

Pablo eyed Méndez suspiciously. "Ferdie is your brother?"

"That's right. He's my older brother, by seven years. And he left Cuba as soon as Castro marched into Havana. I haven't spoken to that *sinverguenza* since the day he used his connections at the American Embassy to get on a plane for the United States and left the rest of us, his family, in Havana."

"Where is your brother now?"

"I don't know where that sonovabitch is and I don't care."

"Do you know how I can find him?"

Brother Felipe shrugged. "Maybe . . . "

"Maybe what?"

"Well, possibly. We might be able to make the connections. Let me explain certain things."

"First let me ask you something else. Have you ever heard of an American doctor named Cornelius 'Dusty' Rhoads? He was a friend of your brother's back in the fifties."

"My brother had many American friends. He went to university in America, and even before Castro, he traveled often to the states. Yes, my parents were able to send their favorite son to study in the United States. The rest of his brothers, we're four in all, had to make do ourselves in order to get an education. I graduated from the University of Havana. That shameless one said nothing to us when he went to the states after the revolution and left his family behind to struggle. I think he was a spy for the Americans.

"But we had to survive and I went to work for Fidel in Cuba while Ferdie worked against him in the United States. Ten years ago, I lost my faith in the revolution. I was sent on a diplomatic mission to Mexico and I went to the U.S. Embassy and asked for political asylum. They didn't believe me, they thought I was a Cuban spy, which I won't say I never was. So they kept me in a locked room. But I climbed out of a window. It was two stories down and I broke my ankle, but I dragged myself away. I can still feel the pain in my ankle when it rains. I stayed with some people I knew in Ciudad de Mexico for some weeks, then I was smuggled into the United States in the back of a truck carrying cases of tequila across the border. I went from Texas, to New Orleans, then to Miami, where I met up, of course, with other exiles. Soon the groups plotting to overthrow Fidel got in touch with me. I was very valuable to them. I knew the insides of the Castro regime, how it worked, its most important people, etc.

"Then, one day, I had this revelation that made me understand that politics and revolution would never solve anything. The answer to man's many woes, I understood, was not to look to governments or politicians, not to look to dictators or presidents, not to capitalism, socialism, democracy or communism. The answer, I realized, was to look to God."

Pablo took a deep breath. What the fuck was going on? This sounded like some kind of prepared testimonial.

Felipe Méndez continued: "How did I know what the answer was? Well, one day I was passing a synagogue, the big one on Washington Avenue. I looked up at the Star of David on the front of the synagogue, and in the center of the Star, appeared an eye. It was not literally the eye of God, of course, because that eye would cover the entire sky, but I felt it did emanate from His power, and that that eye looked straight into my heart and transmitted on a ray a message from Him. The message was that the only thing that had any meaning for man was to worship Him. The rest of this worldly life means absolutely nothing. All the rest is sound and fury. Signifying *nada!*"

"So what does this have to do with . . . ?" Pablo was starting to feel angry, and uncomfortable.

"Please," the brother said, putting up a hand. "It is very important that you get a full explanation. You see, the Zohar, which we are studying now, teaches that what we see of this world is only the visible tip of the iceberg, you know, outward manifestations of those things that come from God, which, of course, means all of existence. Everything we see before our eyes has an inner life. Nothing is static, everything vibrates with God's essence. Every single thing in the world, in fact, comes from *Eyn Sof*. That, my friend, is the hidden, infinite aspect of God. What we get comes to us in vessels, spiritual ones like the Torah, or in material things, like the human body. You see, since every object contains divinity in one form or another, you can retrace the steps of existence back to the source, which is God, blessed by His glory. As for the *Sefirot*, the ten aspects of the hidden God . . . "

Pablo's temples were pulsing. "Cut it! O.K.? All this stuff is your business and I don't want to hear about it. What I want to know, is where I can find Ferdie. Are there any other relatives in the states who might know where he is?"

"My other brothers are still in Cuba. There is one sister, Angelica, who married an *americano* businessman. She is now widowed, living in New Jersey. She was close to Fernando, but now she is old and senile. I don't know if she even remembers anyone in her family."

"Is there a way that I can contact her?"

"She is in a nursing home. I have the address in a book at my home. If you want, I will give you the address. But be patient, my friend. I'm explaining to you how we will make the connections that will lead to my brother."

"Make it quick." Pablo opened his shirt to his navel and blew down to his chest and stomach. He was feeling light-headed. He flopped into a swivel chair. It was broken and Pablo just caught himself before tumbling backwards. He sat gingerly on the edge of the chair.

Felipe Méndez assumed a professorial air. He seemed sure that he would be able to draw Pablo into what would be a wonderfully convoluted, Talmudic scholar-like explanation.

"The Sefirot, as we will see, are the bridge across the abyss, the link between the infinite God and the finite world. They are God's attributes, the objects of our prayers, the God of the Bible. In other words, they are *not Eyn Sof*, the incorporeal, immaterial and unchangeable nature of God, blessed be His glory, but the God who, for instance, spoke at Sinai . . . "

Sweat burned Pablo's eyes. This guy was pulling his chain. The nerves along his arms were jumping.

"O.K., here's what this means," Felipe Méndez said, as though now ready to get down to business. "The term *Shekhinah* comes from the verb root *shakhan*, which means 'to dwell.' Since the *Shekhinah* is the symbol of God's presence in the world, this is the one we aim at in prayer. In other words, I will pray to the *Shekhinah*, which is another name for God when He is present in the world, to know the dwelling place of my brother."

Felipe Méndez, who seemed taken by his own brilliant reasoning, flashed Pablo a somewhat condescending smile. Pablo returned the self-satisfied smile with a very intense, narrow-eyed stare. Felipe made a slight motion with his hands, coaxing Pablo to understand his brilliance and accept his point of view.

Sweat was gathering beneath Pablo's flannel shirt, by the waist, just above where the shirt was tucked into his corduroy pants. Pablo pulled at his lower lip and stared at the ceiling. It was crusted with dirt. Cobwebs laced a corner. He looked back to Méndez, whose smile had lost none of its confidence.

"I'll get in touch with you." Pablo hurried down the back stairs and out the emergency exit.

The early evening Miami air, still warm, was a relief from that stinking sauna. Pablo walked back up to Ocean Drive and crossed the street onto the beach. He tore off his flannel shirt and tossed it into a trash barrel. The sand cooled and hardened at the water's edge. He toed himself out of his tennis shoes, held them in one hand and let the ocean foam sizzle refreshingly between his toes. He trotted back to the beach, dropped the tennis shoes and the package of clothes and ran back to the ocean, diving through a breaking wave, and he felt a fundamental joy, all the sweeter because he had forgotten the sensation.

He put on the second short-sleeved shirt he had bought and the seersucker pants and tennis shoes. Even though his undershorts were soaked beneath the pants, he felt relieved to have shed his corduroys. He went toward the dark green barrel where he had dumped his flannel shirt, intending to toss in the pants. Panic hit. Where was his passport? In the pocket of his flannel shirt. And the shirt was no longer in the top of the trash barrel! He upended the barrel. It wasn't there!

Then he spied a man about fifty yards ahead, a shirt—*the* shirt—slung over his shoulder. Pablo took off after him. He caught up and tapped him on the shoulder.

"Excuse me, sir, that shirt, I tossed it away, but I left something in the pocket."

The man turned. His features looked out-of-focus. "You looking for trouble?" he said in a slurry voice.

"No, no, I just want something in the pocket of the shirt." He reached out for the shirt and the guy pulled it back. Then, incredibly, the guy bundled the shirt in his arms and started running down the beach, weaving and stumbling.

Pablo took off after the guy. He soon caught up and tackled him. He ripped the shirt out of the guy's hands and dug into the pocket. He got his passport and tossed the shirt back to the guy, who stared up with open mouth.

Pablo recrossed Ocean Drive to return to his hotel. Then he saw someone else who looked drunk staggering along the sidewalk. People jumped out of the way.

This guy's hands were folded across his stomach, as though he was trying to hold in some swelling sea animal spreading crimson tentacles under his white shirt. His glasses hung on one ear. The guy stumbled down the street, his face above his beard as white as that dwindling part of his shirt not covered by blood.

Felipe Albert Méndez y del Río stopped suddenly and wove from side to side like a weighted doll. Then he collapsed into Pablo's arms.

Part Three

SEVENTEEN

The moon, high endurance light globe for the world, slanted luminescence off the whitewashed wall of the San Juan Cathedral and onto the street's blue bricks. Julia Quiñones, walking down the street, passed scores of young people out for a night of fun in the Old City. She was on her way to El Convento, the Seventeenth Century nun's convent converted into a tourist hotel, far from sure what the warm night would hold for her.

His letter was respectful and correct, civilized and self-deprecatingly humorous, even if a little strange for its familiarity, as though she and he had been closer than they actually were those many years ago. He said he had gotten her address from an art dealer in Madrid, who had done some business with her gallery. He seemed much more cultured and intelligent than she had remembered. Still, she sensed some strange undercurrent in the letter. He appeared to imply that both had played some significant role in each other's life. She was not aware of any such significance. He seemed to hint that he wanted something from her. What that was, she wasn't sure.

He wrote that he was passing through the island. It would be just a short stay, before his return home. Could she please, please meet with him at the hotel where he was staying, just one night, for dinner and conversation? He knew how she felt about some things of the past, the difficulties she had been put through. He promised no unpleasantness would be allowed to surface in their conversation. More than anything, he wanted her enriched by their meeting, after all these years.

Her first inclination was to ignore the letter, or to turn him down with a short, curt note. He represented unpleasantness to her, even though he, himself, was not to blame. He did what he did out of loyalty.

Then this thing with Pablo and those questions from Pablo's friend digging up the past. She certainly didn't need that.

But then again, she figured, he does have her address. What if he pops in unexpectedly? She certainly didn't want that.

Finally, she decided, what the hell? She was seventy-one years old—and still curious! A dinner, some conversation, then she would be on her way. See you in another forty years. What did she have to lose?

She went through the hotel's massive wooden front doors into the small lobby and to the sofa beneath the tapestry of Columbus embarking for the New World. He was seated there, as he said he would be, beneath the women weeping and the priest blessing the ships setting sail.

As soon as he saw her heading toward him, he pushed himself to his feet with a silver-tipped black walking stick. He took her hand and kissed it. "I recognized you immediately," he said. "Almost forty years, and you are beautiful still."

"You're very kind," Julia said.

"Truthful." He raised his index finger and smiled in soft correction. "I will try to prove my kindness in other ways."

The goatee was gone. Instead, a thin silvery mustache. His hair was still full and wavy, but gone completely white. He must be in his mid-seventies. He was handsomer now than all those years ago. His face was no longer thin and non-descript. His fleshed-out features were more expressive. His face gave signs that over the years he had become aware of what he might have denied in a stodgy youth: the emotional fervor of life, his own and others. He had a rich man's—or *faux* rich man's—suntan.

He wore a light blue silk ascot under the open-collared white shirt beneath his double-breasted, gold-buttoned navy blazer. She wore a beautiful green chiffon scarf threaded with gold inside her yellow linen dress. The ascot, the scarf, brought out the color of their eyes, but, more importantly, partially hid the telltale signs of age between chin and collar bone.

"I am tempted to say that judging by your beauty, the years have been very kind to you," he said. "But the difficulties and . . . and suffering that one experiences in life do not always etch themselves in the skin. Sometimes they reflect in the eyes." He looked deeply in Julia's eyes. She returned his gaze. Then he said: "What I do see there is an understanding of life's vagaries and your own strength and sensitivity."

Julia felt her face flushing. She looked away.

He backed off. "Would you like a cocktail before dinner?"

"Yes, that would be nice."

He led her to an umbrella-covered table in the hotel patio, limping slightly and leaning on his walking stick. He got into the chair with some difficulty, explaining that an old wound from a hunting accident had recently begun acting up again. She ordered a daiquiri and he had a vodka martini with three olives.

He told her he had just come from an art auction in New York, where he represented a Japanese client who made a successful bid on an early Monet. She asked him if he was an art dealer. She didn't remember, if she ever knew, what his profession had been those years before.

"No, I did this as a favor for the Japanese. He is a client of the insurance company I am still connected with, in an advisory capacity."

He gave her a card: *Seguros Hispanoamericanos*. Oficinas: Madrid, Buenos Aires, Miami. His name appeared in raised letters on the side of the card, without a title.

She remembered something. "Weren't you living in Havana when we first met, when you came to see me?"

"Yes, you have a good memory. The company had an office there. But it closed operations there soon after the revolution and moved to Miami. You know, I was born in Spain, in El Ferrol, the hometown of the Generalísimo, Francisco Franco"–he gave Julia what seemed an apologetic smile–"and when I was eight years old the family moved to Cuba, a country I truly loved until that . . . that *sinverguenza* turned it over to the communists." For the first time, his features hardened. But then he smiled broadly and somewhat apologetically again. "Let's leave politics to those with limited imaginations," he said.

"And where do you live now?" Julia asked with a quizzical half-smile.

"Everywhere and nowhere." He flashed another warm smile, then, with a very slight nod of the head, indicated that he preferred to leave it at that.

Julia changed the subject. They spoke about the inflation of the art market, which he called "incredible and in many cases ridiculous." She agreed in general, but said no price too high could be put on some masterpieces. He was about to make another point on prices, but then decided to nod. "Certainly there are priceless masterpieces," he said.

They went from the patio into the hotel restaurant, a high-ceilinged, cavernous room that was overly air-conditioned. He saw her shivering slightly and insisted that she drape his blazer over her shoulders.

They shared a so-so *paella* and were serenaded with the other diners by a flamenco guitarist whose nasal voice reached stratospheric levels via the sound system. After the main course, they escaped back to the outdoor patio for coffee and brandy. They had had a bottle of wine with dinner and Julia was feeling tipsy. She slowly sipped her cognac.

He had, so far, been true to his word, avoiding "unpleasantness." Meaning, of course, avoiding any mention of Dusty Rhoads. They did talk about Spain, however, how it had become part of modern Europe with a vengeance. Julia, who now tried to make a trip a year to Madre España, spoke about how the sensuality that had been bottled up during the Franco years was now bursting forth. He agreed whole-heartedly.

There was a pause in the conversation. They ordered another cognac. They drank and smiled at one another. They spoke some more about Spain, then about Puerto Rico–he said he couldn't understand why the island had not yet become a state, Julia answered that it would be a tragedy for the uniqueness of Puerto Rican culture, which would be seen under statehood as a form of U.S. regionalism. He nodded in sympathetic understanding. Then he said: "I want you to have something. Would you accompany me for a brief moment to my room?"

Julia gave him a questioning look. His smile was warm, sincere. "Please, it's very important to me, and I believe, I hope, you too will understand its importance."

What would he do, try to seduce her? "I'll wait for you down here," she said.

"Please, you will understand once we are in the room why it is necessary to accompany me there."

Ridiculous. "I don't see . . . "

"You will, once you accompany me upstairs."

Julia gave him a long, sideways look.

"Please trust me." He gave her the softest of smiles.

Jesus! What the hell is going on? All right, let's see what he has up his sleeve.

They took the elevator to the fourth floor. The doors to all the rooms gave out on the corridors that surrounded the patio below.

He had difficulty opening the door to his room. His hand holding the key shook and Julia wondered if he were older than he appeared, and perhaps somewhat palsied. Finally, he steadied his hand and opened the door.

They entered the room and he closed the door. Julia sat on the edge of an easy chair in the corner. He sat on the side of the bed facing her.

"First," he said, "I have a confession. I know many things about you, about your life since we last met those many years ago, though, honestly, to me our meetings seem like yesterday. Please excuse me for enquiring and finding out about you from my 'sources' here in San Juan. And please understand that in enquiring I have had only your interests at heart. I wanted to ease my mind by knowing that your life has been on a comparably even keel."

Julia was confused. Maybe it was the drinks. As far as she remembered, their previous contact, so many years ago, held no great import, in so far as establishing a relationship between them. He had made three or four visits and she had treated him, and his exhortations on behalf of Rhoads, with nothing more than politeness. Why this keen interest in her and her later life?

As if reading her thoughts, he said: "I know those meetings so many years ago meant little to you, Julia." He gave another of his warm, confidence-inspiring smiles. His teeth were very white. Were they his?

He continued: "I must explain something to you. Although our meetings were of little account to you, to me they had a precious meaning. After the first few minutes of our first meeting, I understood what a jewel of a Julia you were. I understood what made him plead with me to plead with you. He truly loved you, dear Julia, and I understood why. He was a selfish man—aren't all we men selfish? — but he truly loved you."

Julia took a deep breath. "Please, I'd prefer not to . . . "

"Certainly, certainly," he said quickly. She noticed that his hands, which were resting on his walking stick that stood between his legs, were trembling slightly again. Something went out of the smile that remained plastered on his face. Rather than warm and winning, it was now . . . something else.

"Julia, dear," he said, "I asked you up here to give you something. What I want to offer you is a pledge. A pledge of my eternal loyalty to you. Since that first day I visited you, up until our meeting this evening, over these many years, through the days and nights, my thoughts have been filled with you." He nodded his head slightly to the side, to tell her he was confident that she was following the drift and would be prepared for what he'd say next.

"You see, Julia dearest, I fell in love with you immediately upon meeting you and I've sustained that love, and it has sustained me, all this time. Now that we meet again, it's so wonderful to have confirmed for me that I have not been living a fantasy all these years, that you are as beautiful and as magnificent, as sweet and as intelligent, insightful, understanding and compassionate as I remembered you to be. You know, I never married, just as I understand you never have also. I believe we both know."

Julia's stomach tightened. "*Know?* Know what? What are you talking about?" She felt light-headed.

"*You* know. *I* know. We both know."

He's mad as a hatter!

He pushed down on his walking stick, stood and took the few steps toward her. He laid the stick down, bent over and reached out his arms to her. Julia tried to shrink in her chair.

"Darling Julia, love of my life, love that has conspired to bring us together again–finally–to consummate this passion that has burned in me for forty years and now has burst into flames that are licking at my heart. You, darling, are my heart, and my soul–*mi corazon! mi alma!*" His breath smelled of garlic and liquor and old-aged minty.

He took her by the arms and attempted to pull her out of the chair. When that failed, he sunk to the floor and wrapped his arms around her legs and buried his head in her lap. He looked up. All his features were quivering. "My old body disguises the eternal youth of my heart," he said. "In my heart, I'm still young. My love for you has kept me that way. Please come to bed with me. We will make love and then you may beat me, if you wish. I will be your love slave."

Despite her mounting panic, Julia tried a placating smile. "No thank you. I think I should . . ."

"I believe, darling Julia, that you don't fully understand. I will subjugate myself *completely* to your every whim. You command, I obey. That is what love means to me."

She discerned beneath the lust in his eyes a wrenching sadness. Which didn't lessen her greatest desire–to get out of there!

"All right," she said. "Let go of my legs so I can get up."

He dropped his arms and as he was about to push himself to his feet, Julia jumped up and shoved him onto his back. He looked up startled. She went to step over him and he grabbed a leg and pulled her down on top of him.

They began struggling on the floor. He apologized as he got on top of her, put a hand on her breast and attempted to kiss her on the mouth.

She bit down hard on his upper lip. He rolled off her, tapping his mouth with his trembling hands. He looked at the blood on his hands and moaned over and over: "*Ay, Dios mio!* Oh, my God! My God!"

She was up and out of there, walking quickly, then running along the corridor outside the doors, to an emergency staircase. The stairs led to the far side of the patio, near an empty swimming pool. She hurried across the patio. The wavering voice of the flamenco singer echoed out of the restaurant and into the lobby. Once outside, she found herself gasping for breath.

It wasn't until she was back home, sipping a glass of iced tea on her roof garden, when she was able to calmly assess what had happened. She laughed at the ridiculousness of the evening, two senior citizens actually rolling on the floor like teenagers. Why had she reacted like a young girl protecting her virginity? Why didn't she lend her old body to his old body? She had found him fairly attractive—until he began pleading.

He was mad. Or maybe he wasn't. Maybe this was his seduction method. He surely would have caused future problems. He still may. This both scared her and angered her. She wanted his existence buried. Figuratively, of course.

She drank the tea and the ice cubes clinked against the glass. She giggled to herself again, but also felt one of those nagging discontents whose cause lies just below the surface. She was too tired to give the evening any further thought. As she undressed and got ready for bed, she realized this was the funniest, saddest, most disconcerting thing that had happened to her in a long time.

EIGHTEEN

Ralph opened his eyes. As usual during the past few nights, he had slept uneasily, spending the hours waking, dozing, waking, dozing. He was more pissed off in his half sleep than he had thought during full consciousness about the meeting at the University.

He had finally gone to see Herr Doctor Hiram Rodríguez del Valle, who had told him that appearing at staff meetings was as important—no, actually more so—than showing up to teach class. The meetings set the parameters for successful instruction in the classroom, Rodríguez del Valle said. As long as *he* chaired the department, attending staff meetings would be required. Could he make it any clearer? Ralph said he took the job to share his experiences with young people and found the staff meetings mostly boring and unnecessary. The department head said if that was the way Ralph felt about it, he didn't think it would be possible to renew his contract for the next year. Ralph told him what to do with the job. Rodríguez del Valle said he was afraid he would not be able to give Ralph any recommendation for a similar position at any other institute of higher learning. Ralph said he would really miss the students, and that he, Rodríguez del Valle, was an idiotic bureaucratic academic asshole.

But that was not what was *really* keeping Ralph from a decent night's sleep. What kept him tossing and turning was trying to figure the connection. How did Jaime Rosado wind up at Pablo's house with his throat cut? Even if he knew that his father was one of the victims of Dr. Dusty Rhoads, how did he link up Pablo with Rhoads? Rosado thought he was the son of

Pedro Albizu Campos. So what did that have to do, if anything, with Pablo? And even if he figured all that out, how would this lead him to Pablo?

Was he, Ralph, now more obsessed with making the connections than actually finding his friend?

If he did find Pablo, what would he tell him? Give yourself up? To whom and for what? Just have him explain what had happened that night and they would both figure out the next move.

He remembered Pablo's "confession" to him after they had met in the hospital mess hall in Saigon. A cast covered Ralph's left arm and shoulder and he was having a problem carrying both his overloaded food tray and a pint carton of milk that didn't fit on the tray. Pablo took his own and Ralph's tray, one in each hand, to a table. Ralph thanked him and Pablo said, *"de nada."*

"You speak Spanish?"

"What I remember of it. I'm still not too clear upstairs."

Pablo wrinkled up his nose as he looked down at the khaki-colored gravy soaking the nondescript slices of meat and puddling the mashed potatoes. "Even the fuckin gravy is in Army colors, Pablo said. "Nothing like Army hospital chow. Besides forgetting almost everything else, I don't even remember what rice and beans tastes like anymore."

A compatriota, Ralph realized.

After the meal—Pablo could only manage the salad and milk—they went outside on the hospital grounds for a smoke. Pablo had a blue pack of Gauloise cigarettes and Ralph accepted one and they lit up with Pablo's Zippo and the burning tobacco had that dark heavy distinctive odor.

They spoke about the past—Pablo born in New York and raised there and in San Juan, Ralph born in

San Juan and raised in New York—each with two hometowns, two allegiances, two flags. Two Ricans caught in this fuckin horror show sparked by colonialists and communists and capitalists and assorted other assholes.

Then the wounds.

"You know, I had it made as a combat artist," Pablo said, "until we ran into that ambush, or whatever the fuck it was, outside of Khe San. There I was, cross-legged on the ground, sketching my grunt buddies, Campos was leveling the bubbles when the first incoming exploded, then a second and a third blew everything to hell, I looked down at my sketchbook, there was blood running down the page, I wasn't sure if it was coming from me or Campos or Brown or all of us, and I looked over there and arms and legs were detached and wriggling on the ground, and the heads were popped open, then rolling on the grass, so I looked down again to my sketchbook and with the blood on the page I drew arms reaching out for heads, then I crawled into the brush and tried to become a ball, I wanted to tuck my arms and legs and my head into a body pocket which I couldn't locate. See, I definitely remember all that, but nothing for days and weeks after, and I keep forgetting things, though some are starting to come back, but not enough."

Ralph looked into Pablo's eyes, earth-colored, turned inside himself, not so much with fear or pain or anxiety as incredible sorrow.

Then Pablo flinched and Ralph reached out his good arm to steady him, but Pablo backed away.

"Don't worry, I'm O.K.," he said. He smiled gently at Ralph. "You got shot up in the shoulder," he said, "I got decapitated. It's getting better because I'm growing a new head. I'll be discharged as soon as my new head grows in."

Ralph looked deeply at Pablo, who nodded, then broke into another smile. Ralph returned the smile and felt an endearment for his new friend.

They spent the next few months together at the hospital and at a convalescent center, getting passes to go into Saigon and drink beer and share a hotel room and pick up hookers, then Pablo got transferred to Japan and was given his discharge. They kept in contact and when Ralph got out he found an apartment on the Lower East Side near Pablo. Over the years, each moved back and forth between New York and San Juan, usually at different times, either in the same or in opposite directions. Then marriage and parenthood, friendship occasionally tested, but never severed.

Now this. Pablo was the one true friend Ralph had. He felt helpless . . . and guilty He had to keep trying to find him.

Ralph showered, dressed and on his way out picked up the newspaper lying outside his front door and carried it with him. He was going for a usual Sunday breakfast at La Bombonera, letting his wife and kid sleep as late as they wanted.

Rosado, Rhoads, Pablo, Albizu. Where were the connections? And did they matter? Maybe he needed to grow a new head also.

NINETEEN

A highly dramatic photo of blood-splattered Cuban exile Felipe A. Méndez y del Río grasping the arms of an unidentified man on Ocean Drive in South Beach appeared on page one of *The Miami Herald.* The accompanying story said the photo was taken by a tourist and that the man holding the victim, who was knifed to death, disappeared before police arrived on the scene. The unidentified man, whom police were searching for, was the prime suspect in the slaying, the newspaper quoted authorities as saying.

The story said that several members of a group of religious Jews, who met daily in a nearby building for study and prayer, identified the man in the photo as the same man who earlier had barged into their meeting room looking for the victim, a recent convert to Judaism.

Méndez, according to the eyewitnesses, displayed great fear when he was approached by the man. The devout Jews said that as they left the building after the meeting they saw the unidentified man waiting outside. "He had a murderous look on his face," said one of the eyewitnesses, who refused to give his name out of fear of reprisal.

The writer noted that the devout Jews, who described Méndez as a "brilliant scholar" of Kabala, or Jewish mysticism, argued that the unidentified man may have been "an emanation of *kelippah*," or the shell of Evil.

But, the writer added, the killing may have more earthly, political overtones. It was learned that Méndez was a former spy for Castro who was debriefed by the CIA after he defected to the United States in 1988 and subsequently might have been targeted by Cuban communists for assassination.

The slaying took place less than two blocks from where world-famous designer Gianni Versace was murdered outside his South Beach home in July 1997, the story said.

Police said a bloodied two-by-four had been found outside the room where the religious Jews had met earlier in the day. But police could not say if the wood was connected to the killing. Fingerprints on the wood were being checked.

The photo showed a side view of the victim, eyes half-closed and shirtfront darkened with blood, desperately clinging to his possible killer, and an opposing profile of the suspect, apparently struggling frantically to free himself from the victim's grasp. Copies of the photo were being disseminated to authorities at the greater Miami area's airports, piers, train stations and highways.

Pablo viewed the photo and read the story while sipping coffee on the balcony of his hotel room. A room service waiter, who evidently didn't recognize the half of Pablo's face shown in the photo—if he had glanced at it at all—had brought coffee, a plate of fruit and the newspaper, which had been left, *gratis*, at the door to the room.

Pablo decided he needed a drink. He could call down for one.

No, not now. He had to act.

Going to the police to tell them that he hadn't stabbed Méndez was, of course, out of the question. They would check on his background and find he was wanted, or was at least a suspect, in another stabbing murder in Puerto Rico.

There was one more chance to find Ferdie, to get the definitive explanation, as far as it would go, for his father's thoughts and actions. It was a long shot, but he had to reach the sister. He had to find that address book.

He showered and put on the seersucker pants, white short-sleeved shirt and tennis shoes, all of which were splotched brown with Méndez's blood. Nervously, he checked out of the hotel, hurried to the nearest clothing store on Collins Avenue and bought another outfit, changing into it in the store's dressing room. He dumped the blood-stained clothes into a trashcan outside the store. No one seemed to have noticed him or his earlier predicament and he felt a relief. He went to an Avis nearby and rented a Buick Le Sabre. His credit card was accepted. So far, no problem. He searched the phone book at Avis and found the address of a Home Depot in a North Miami mall. He drove there and bought an acetylene torch, the only way to cut through iron grillwork, as well as a flashlight. But he realized he had to wait until the depths of night to make the break-in. He bought still another outfit in the mall: a dark tee shirt, dark chinos and black loafers, and this time changed his clothes in the car. He put his passport in the glove compartment.

Before leaving the mall, he bought a pair of wraparound sunglasses, then drove to Vizcaya and spent the afternoon wandering around the gardens, avoiding the other visitors before they got a good look at him. He drove up to Hollywood, checked into a motel as John B. Gillespie. The young woman at the front desk was too engrossed in a Spanish-language soap opera on a TV by the desk to look closely at him. After going out for a couple of big Macs at a drive-in, Pablo spent the evening watching TV and napping. Finally, night set in and he drove back down to Coral Gables.

He parked a block away from the house. He was about to get out of the car when he spotted a small, elderly man shuffling quickly down the street, carrying a Chihuahua in his arms and twisting his head from side to side. The man disappeared into a house on the corner. Pablo decided to reconnoiter. He hoped there was a way to break-in through the back, or the side windows.

The Miami windows along the sides of the modest, one-story house were all shut tight, but a wrought-iron door protecting the regular back door was hanging off its hinges and a glass window on the door had been broken. Pablo walked very slowly up to the door. He tried it. It was locked, but he realized he didn't need the torch. It was just a matter of reaching his arm inside the broken glass window to open it.

Had someone laid a trap for him? Who the fuck knew? He'd find what he had to find, then get the hell out of there.

He opened the door, relocked it and stepped into the kitchen. The lights were all off, but the moon cast a half-light through the kitchen window. He switched on his flashlight.

The kitchen was in in an incredible mess. Smashed dishes littered the floor and the sink, the refrigerator door hung open and its contents were strewn all over the floor. Canned goods rolled around the floor as Pablo tried to tiptoe through the chaos.

The living room was minimally furnished. But the one sofa and two easy chairs had been ripped open and white filling and spongy foam spewed from the arms and cushions. The TV set lay on its face, the back pulled off, the wiring ripped out.

Pablo checked the two bedrooms. In one of the rooms, old cartons had been torn open. Papers and clothes were thrown everywhere. In the other bedroom, the sheets were pulled off the bed and the mattress ripped open, a dresser overturned and a closet emptied of hangered clothes, shoes and a couple of suitcases. The bottles in the medicine cabinet in the bathroom were all open and their contents were spilled into the sink and onto the floor. Rusty red liquid ran down the middle of the sink and pills and capsules were scattered on the bath rug.

Off to the side of one of the bedrooms was an alcoved office. The space was occupied by a large wooden desk, a swivel chair, a metal file cabinet, a tall narrow bookcase and a small safe. A bent-necked lamp splayed light across the desk. The books had been ripped down from their shelves and tossed helter-skelter. The drawers of the desk and file cabinet had been pulled out and turned upside down and papers and other materials were strewn all over the desk and the floor. The safe was still closed.

What the hell was going on? Pablo rifled the papers, the desk and the file cabinet looking for a Rolodex or an address book, for the name of Angelica something-or-other living in a Jersey nursing home.

He heard them enter the kitchen, whispering as they crossed the living room. He pocketed his flashlight and ducked back into the nearest bedroom, leaving the door open as it had been. He fitted himself behind the door, pushed it forward just enough so he could see through the crack into the alcove.

There were two of them. One was the tall, iron gray crew-cut neighbor Pablo had spoken to when he first came to the house looking for the brother he thought was Ferdie. The other was short and muscular in a dark tank top. They went right to the safe and continued to speak softly. The shorter one took clanking metal objects out of a plastic bag he had set down, sat on his haunches and appeared to be attaching something to the safe. "We better find what we're looking for in the safe," said tank top. "I don't want to have to make a third visit."

The tall one looked down at him, then glanced around. He seemed to see something in the mess of papers on top of the desk. He went to the desk, looked for something but didn't find it. "I left those phone numbers up here," he said as much to himself as to his companion. He looked on the floor and picked up a sheet of paper tucked beneath several other sheets. He put it back on the desk and told his companion to stop working on the safe. He whispered something.

The other stood and cautiously moved into the second bedroom off the alcove. The tall one headed for the room where Pablo was standing behind the door.

As soon as the tall guy got within reach Pablo slammed the door into him. The man let out a howl and staggered back and out the room. Pablo headed toward the living room, but the guy, lying on his back, managed to grab him by an ankle. The other one rushed into the alcove and made a flying tackle.

They pummeled Pablo. The shorter one reached into his many pocketed khakis and came out with a long-barreled black pistol. Back on his haunches, he pushed the barrel into Pablo's left nostril. "You move one muscle, *cabrón,* I shoot out your brains."

Pablo remained still. The gun was withdrawn. He sat up partially, resting his back against the desk. The other two were standing over him.

"What the fuck are you doing here?" the neighbor asked.

"Just like you, I came by for something." Pablo's nose was bleeding and he could barely see. They had landed several punches around his eyes. The warm blood dripped over his mouth and chin and onto his shirtfront.

The neighbor made a face. He reached into his back pocket and tossed a neatly folded white handkerchief into Pablo's lap. "Wipe your nose."

Pablo held the handkerchief to the wound. The taller one shook his head derisively. "What the fuck are you butting in for? You're not Cuban, I can tell. Are you one of Fidel's communist *compañeros* from outside the island? What are you–

Venezuelan, Dominican, Puerto Rican? Are you working for that pig of a dictator?"

"I'm not working for anyone," Pablo said. "I'm here looking for a phone number of the sister of the guy you killed. It's a personal matter that has to do with family. I don't give a fuck about Cuba or Castro or you assholes killing each other in Miami."

"Who the *fuck* are you calling an asshole, you motherfucker!" The muscular man smashed the pistol against the side of Pablo's head, just above the ear. Blood trickled into his ear.

"O.K., no problem," said the neighbor, grabbing his companion's arm. "Not a problem, O.K.?"

"Yeah, right," the other one said. His breath was coming short as he stared murderously at Pablo, who wanted to stare back the same way except he couldn't pry open his swollen eyelids. His features and his head felt numb, but he knew they were going to hurt like hell in a few minutes.

"We killed no one," said the neighbor. "That man died because of his own sins."

Pablo said nothing. He started to get up. The muscular man pushed him down again. Pablo rolled on the floor toward the entrance to the living room, managed to get to his haunches and sprung into the living room. The short man dove at Pablo's legs and tackled him again. Then both were hit by sudden blinding light.

"Don't move. Stand up slowly and show me your hands."

From behind the blinding light, a hand wrenched the pistol from the short, muscular man. Someone else with a flashlight rushed into the alcove and shouted: "Police! Show me your fuckin hands!"

The cops had their pistols drawn. Pablo and the other two were led outside, pushed against the patrol car, told to put their hands on the hood and were patted down. One of the policemen said something into the car radio and got a static-filled response.

The three men, hands cuffed behind their backs, were ushered into the back seat of the patrol car and taken to a police station in Little Havana where they were fingerprinted, mug-shot and locked into individual cells.

At a press conference the next morning, police spokesman Jorge Castro said Miami-Dade police had arrested last night three members of a radical anti-Castro exile group, who had broken into the Coral Gables home of Felipe A. Méndez del Río, the Orthodox Jew who was killed in South Beach the other day. Castro, the police spokesman, said the arrested men belonged to *Commandante Zeta* (Commander Z), the group suspected in the killings in the past year of at least four of the Cuban dictator Castro's agents."

"We got a confession from them that they broke into the victim's home to search for documents tying the victim to pro-Castro activities here," spokesman Castro said.

He spelled out the names of the arresting officers—patrolmen Felipe García and Bobby Ray Jamison, who, he said, were called to the scene by a neighbor who was out walking his dog and noticed the back door to the kitchen hanging off its hinges. In answer to questions from reporters, Castro said the neighbor declined to give his name to police.

Castro identified the perpetrators as Raul Godoy, Segundo Méndez Ríos (no relation to the South Beach victim) and Pablo Camino.

He told the reporters, "on background, don't use my name," that police were investigating whether Camino was the man Méndez y Del Río was holding onto in the photo published in the papers.

Later he told *The Miami Herald* reporter, "It looks like we got our guy in the Ocean Drive killing. Don't quote me, but murder charges should be filed against this Camino guy in the next day or so."

TWENTY

Julia couldn't remember where any of her classrooms were located. She was about to miss still another class. The doors would be locked after the second bell, which had just rung. Her parents had pushed so hard for her to be accepted at the prestigious University of Puerto Rico High School, where applications always far outnumbered places. She would surely fail all her subjects and bring disgrace on the family. Then a third bell rang and a fourth and tears came to her eyes and her chest felt heavy. She had let down her parents, which was only the beginning, she knew that later in life she would let down so many others . . .

She picked up the phone. "Yes?" she asked groggily.

"Good morning, Julia. I hope I didn't wake you."

Oh, shit. It was *him!*

"How are you this morning?"

"Umh."

"I dreamed about you last night."

Pause. "Oh, really?"

"Yes. It was a *wonderful* dream. Do you want to hear about it?"

"No!"

"Sweet Julia, in my dream we passionately, yet tenderly, consummated our love."

She said nothing.

"Julia, my darling, let us spend one glorious day together. I'll hire a limousine to take us to Palmas del Mar, to the villa of an acquaintance of mine who is on a business trip in Hong Kong, and we can eat just-caught red snapper in a wonderful little restaurant I know of in a nearby quaint fishing village. Say the word, and the time, *mi vida*, and I will pick you up at your gallery."

Just as though nothing happened last night. Incredible.

"I appreciate your invitation, but I have a *terrible* headache. I don't think I'll be able to go anywhere today."

"Oh, I'm very sorry to hear that. Perhaps if I let you sleep another hour or so, you'll feel better."

"Perhaps." She hung up and buried her head under the pillow.

Her head still beneath her pillow, she heard the constant jangling, and let it continue until her answering machine switched on. There was a muffled message. The talking stopped, the machine clicked and Julia willed herself back to sleep once more.

She awoke at the precise moment that the telephone started ringing still again, as though her mind were wired into the transmission lines.

She had the very strong feeling that he would call forever, until she picked up the phone. Once and for all, she would tell him to stop bothering her.

"Yes?"

"*Corazón,* I hope you are . . . "

"I'm not well. Please don't call again. I can't, I won't go anywhere with you. Now please leave me alone."

She hung up. He rang again.

"Will you stop! Do I have to leave the phone off the hook, or make a complaint somewhere? Just leave me alone, please." Her headache was now real. Her stomach was quaking. Her nerves were jabbing at her skin.

"Please, precious Julia, don't threaten me. I couldn't abide by your refusal to see me anymore. I don't know what I would do if you refused to see me again. Allow me to come over to the gallery. I promise I will cure you of what ails you."

"I won't see you today or any other time and I *definitely* do not want you coming to the gallery. I hope I've made myself very clear. I don't want to see you again. Now please leave me alone."

She hung up and braced herself for the next call. It didn't come, which was more frightening. She pulled herself up from the bed, quickly brushed her teeth and threw some water on her face. As she put on a pair of black slacks and a silky green blouse and slipped into her sandals and tied the green scarf she wore last night into a bandanna around her head, the beating of her heart sped up. She expected at any minute to hear the ringing of the doorbell or the pounding of the large brass knocker on the front door.

She hurried downstairs to the gallery, then carefully opened the front door. She peered down both sides of Calle San Francisco. There were a few Sunday late morning strollers and churchgoers on the sun-splattered street. She hurried down the several blocks toward La Bombonera.

Then she saw him, coming down the street. He was dressed in an open-collared shirt and a maroon-colored ascot and white pants and white shoes and his double-breasted Navy blue blazer. He was limping along with the help of his walking stick. Large dark sunglasses covered his eyes. There was a determined expression on his face.

Julia quickly turned down a side street, praying that he had not seen her. She ducked into a doorway. He was on the way to her gallery home. He was a clown and obviously had emotional problems. What should she do?

She waited a few minutes, until she was sure he was out of sight, then continued to the bakery-restaurant. All the booths and tables as well as the counter seats were taken up by the regulars or families spending the day in the Old City. She looked down at her hands. They were shaking. She knew her face was extremely pale. She needed a cup of coffee very badly.

She moved halfway into the restaurant to the stairs leading to a second level. If she were lucky, there may be an empty table, although it took forever to be served up there.

As she was about to mount the stairs, their eyes met. Julia started to look away, then brought her gaze back to him and smiled. Pablo's friend, Ralph, smiled back. He was seated near the back of the restaurant, alone in a booth, eating a Spanish omelet and sipping a cup of coffee, the Sunday newspaper spread out on the table. She went over to him.

"Good morning, or is it good afternoon?" she said. Then she said: "Do you mind if I join you?"

"No, not at all." Ralph quickly folded up the newspaper and partially stood while she slid into the other side of the booth.

The elderly men arguing about politics at a table in the rear spied Julia. They bowed their heads toward her.

"So many years they've been coming here," said Julia. "They stay for hours. It's their second, or perhaps for the ones who live alone, their first home."

"A sort-of fairly clean, almost well-lighted place," Ralph said, looking up at a row of fluorescent lights flickering on and off overhead.

Julia smiled and nodded absentmindedly.

"I let my family sleep late on Sundays so I can come down here and read the paper and watch the passing show," Ralph said.

The waiter appeared and Julia ordered a *café con leche* and a *mallorca tostada.* Ralph also ordered a *mallorca* and another coffee. Julia gave Ralph a quick, tense smile, then looked up front. She kept looking there, frowning. Then she looked back and smiled nervously again.

"Have you found out anything further about the whereabouts of Pablo?"

"Nothing," Ralph said.

"Nothing," Julia repeated.

"I spoke to relatives of the man who was found dead in Pablo's house. I'm trying to figure the connection between that man and Pablo."

Julia nodded, but said nothing further.

The waiter brought the coffee and sweet rolls. They ate in silence, parentheses of white sugar from the pastry forming around their mouths, Julia often glancing to the front of the restaurant. Then, suddenly, her eyes widened in fear and dismay. She grabbed the newspaper lying on the side of the table near Ralph and opened it to cover her face.

"Please look by the door up front," Julia said.

Ralph turned and saw several people milling near the entrance, either waiting to pay their checks at the cash register or for seats.

"Is the white-haired man in the blue jacket with the walking stick still there?" Julia asked from behind the newspaper.

Ralph spotted the man right away. He was peering from booth-to-booth and table-to-table, an anxious look on his face.

"He's there."

"What is he doing?"

"Looking around. He's coming back. No, he stopped. No, he's coming this way. He stopped again. He's turning around. He's leaving."

"Is he gone?"

"He's going out the door. He's turning around again. Starting back. No, he's heading for the door. He's gone."

Julia put the newspaper down. She tried another smile. It quivered on the edges. "I'm sorry, this is so . . . silly, really. It's absurd."

Ralph gave a little questioning nod.

"That man is, was, an old friend. Well, not really a friend, an acquaintance from many years ago. We had dinner last night and, well, some unpleasantness followed, and I no longer want to see him, but he called me this morning and insisted we meet. So I'm trying to escape him. I imagine he is now searching for me in the few restaurants open today in the Old City. The whole thing seems ridiculous, doesn't it?"

"No, not if you feel . . . "

"There's just something about him. Something desperate and a little scary." She exhaled audibly. "I just hope he's not waiting for me in the street."

"If you like, I'll walk with you to wherever you're going next."

"That's very kind of you. Perhaps if you could accompany me back to my house. I'll lock myself in for the day and won't answer phone or doorbell, which I should have done, or not done, in the first place. It's just that . . . well . . . I suppose I panicked somewhat, and felt I had to leave the house."

They finished their coffee and sweet rolls and Ralph shrugged off Julia's protests and picked up her check.

They walked the four blocks down Calle San Francisco to her home. They were on the sunny side of the street, where her gallery was located. The sun was shivering in the sky and Julia was sweating like mad. At least her stalker was not in sight. At the front door, she thanked Ralph again and asked if he wanted to come in for another cup of coffee or something cold to drink. Ralph declined. He told her he had to get home to prepare a test for his class at the University the next day.

He wrote his phone number down on the top of the newspaper and tore it off and gave it to her. "I'm sure everything will be all right, but just in case."

She thanked him and shook his hand. As she put the key into the door lock, she heard her name called out. He emerged from the doorway of a three-story apartment house across the street.

"Oh, my God, *Dios mio!* " She looked helplessly at Ralph as the other crossed toward them, limping, his walking stick knocking against the blue bricks that paved the street.

"Julia, my dear, I hope you are feeling better." He smiled shakily at her, then bowed slightly to Ralph. His deep suntan seemed to have faded to a greenish beige and the creases in his face appeared to have deepened. His skin was damp.

Julia noticed the swelling above his lip where she had bitten him. He seemed to have aged considerably overnight.

Julia introduced the two men. Julia's acquaintance from many years ago reached into the inside of his jacket pocket and produced for Ralph a business card. "Fernando Alfredo Méndez y del Río," he said with a little bow, then turned to Julia.

"If the gentleman will please excuse us, I must speak to you privately." He gestured to a spot a few feet away.

Julia inhaled deeply. "Excuse me a minute," she said to Ralph. "Please wait for me."

She accompanied the now elderly looking man halfway down the street. Bells from churches around the Old City tolled out the hour.

"I am in crisis, Julia. Only you can bring me out of this."

"Out of *what*?" Julia felt her face coloring.

"I believe I had a mini-stroke last night. I've had one before, which is really why I use this walking stick. The feeling was the same, the lightness in the head, the numbing of the limbs."

"What can I do? Do you want to see a doctor?" Why the hell did she now feel guilty?

"No, no doctor. I'm scheduled to leave early tomorrow. I have a flight to Miami. If you would just spend the day with me. A quiet, relaxing day I'm sure will improve my well-being. If you don't, I won't be able to control my agitation. *Please,* Julia, I'm pleading with you to show me kindness and mercy."

Tears of anger, frustration and, yes, pity came to Julia's eyes. "I'm very sorry, I can't.

I . . . "

His face dropped, then took on a perplexed look. "Why? Just one day. Is that too much to ask of an old friend?"

"I . . . I . . . "

With one hand, He slowly took off his large sunglasses and squinted watery eyes at her. His eyes got smaller, then mean, and with the other hand he pounded his walking stick on the sidewalk three times. "You must!" he said in a high, cracking voice. "You must!"

Julia shrunk back and looked quickly over to Ralph, who was standing awkwardly by the door to the gallery. He started over.

Fernando Alfredo Méndez y del Río eyed Ralph coming toward them and he backed off into the street. He swung his walking stick over his head, turning with it on the third swing. He stumbled backwards, then forward, then collapsed onto the Old City's blue bricks.

TWENTY-ONE

"Your honor, I certainly don't have to tell *you* about the long and honorable fight to free our beloved Cuba from the dictator Fidel Castro. My clients, your honor, are part of that noble struggle. They have entered a guilty plea for breaking and entering into the home of the deceased, who, let the record show, was a known collaborator of the corrupt government that now rules in Havana. Your honor, my clients, certainly over-zealous and impatient, have admitted their guilt, which is the guilt of those frustrated by complicity and deceit on the highest levels, the guilt of those intending to follow the noblest of ideals, the guilt of those who have broken man's law to obey God's command to set their people free, the guilt of . . . "

"Enough, counselor," said Dade County Superior Court Judge Armando Salazar. "I quite understand your plea. I sentence your three clients to six months apiece on each of the three counts to which they have pled guilty, the sentences to be served concurrently. I further suspend the sentences and put the men under the supervision of a parole officer, to be assigned to each at a further date. Next case."

Attorney Félix de Jesús, put a hand through his double-breasted, dark-blue, pinstriped suit jacket and contentedly patted himself on the stomach. He turned his large, wavy-gray-haired head to his clients, fixing on them his sad, canine-like brown eyes, and winked.

Two of the clients winked back. The third, Pablo Camino, looked morosely at the lawyer.

The tall man with the crew cut had told Pablo when they were being taken to court that if he said nothing, allowed the Cubans' lawyer to represent all of them at the hearing and did not complicate the situation in any way, they would all be quickly released. He would be free to go on his own, no hard feelings. The Cuban indicated that the fix was in.

Pablo signed some papers, was returned his wallet, keys and belt and took a taxi right back to the neighborhood where he had been arrested. Thank God his rental car was still there. He drove by Méndez y del Río's house. Police cars were parked out front and men were moving furniture, desks, papers, a computer and other stuff from the house to a van with a Metro-Dade government insignia on it.

Pablo spent the day driving up the coast, from Fort Lauderdale to West Palm Beach to Fort Pierce and all the way up to Daytona Beach, then back down, trying to decide on his next move. That night, he slept in his car outside West Palm Beach.

Breakfasting the next morning in a roadside diner, he picked up a *Miami Herald* and learnt that he had again made page one.

The story pointed to "still another serious foul-up" in the Metro-Dade judicial system, noting that possible murder suspect Pablo Camino was allowed to walk free after pleading guilty on charges of breaking and entering. An unnamed police source said that charges were about to be brought against Camino in the Ocean Drive knife slaying, but the court had set him free and his whereabouts currently were not known.

Another source, however, from the county attorney's office, insisted that while Camino may be wanted for questioning in the slaying, no charges were pending against him "as of this time." The police source, meanwhile, said the source in the county attorney's office was trying to cover the court's "appalling mistake."

To add to the confusion and the sensationalism, the reporter noted that he had called down to Puerto Rico, Camino's place of residence according to documents police had found in his wallet, and learned that Camino, a well-known artist, was wanted in Puerto Rico for questioning in another stabbing death, which had taken place in the suspect's own home.

The story was accompanied by a mug shot taken by police after Pablo was arrested. His eyes were puffed and bruised in the photo. He looked barely human.

Pablo put his wraparound sunglasses back on, wolfed down his scrambled eggs, toast and coffee and kept his head lowered as he exited the diner. He returned to his rented car. What the fuck should he do next? He tugged on his lower lip. His back felt as though something was forcefully pulling at it from his insides, his neck was stiff, as though a metal splint were placed under his skin. Pain darted up to the top of his head.

This is what he would do: He would return to the scene of the crime. He would ask around. Certainly someone must have seen something before that man fell dead into his arms. He would go back to the Jews in that building off Ocean Drive and make them give him names and addresses of the man's relatives, friends, enemies, wives, lovers. He would track down the real killer and clear himself.

Then he would return to Puerto Rico. He would turn himself in and explain to the police what had happened. Self-defense. Obvious. Why else would he be fighting an intruder in his own home? He would confess why he had to leave the island. He would clear himself of that killing also.

Then he would pick up the pieces and try, once more, to get it—life, painting, conscience, soul, spirit—together. Fuck

Ferdie, fuck Dusty, fuck the killer within. Fuck whatever the hell he was looking for out there. His atonement for his sins, and for the sins of others, would be the way he would live the rest of his life. It was the only way.

He sat in his rented car, paralyzed.

TWENTY-TWO

He was lying on the brown leather couch in the office storage room. Julia and Ralph had helped him to his feet and brought him into the house. He was having trouble breathing and his face was scarlet. They loosened the sweat-damp ascot around his neck. His neck was old man's scrawny.

He pleaded with them not to call an ambulance. He said he would be all right, after a few minutes rest and a tall glass of ice water. Julia went to the refrigerator upstairs to bring him the water.

"I . . . I'm so sorry. I . . . I feel very ashamed for my actions just moments ago. Too often as of late I've had problems controlling my emotions, which I had been so good at almost all of my life. I don't know what it is, but now, once I start talking, I just go on and on. That too is quite a change from those years I was sworn to secrecy on so many important matters. I don't quite understand. I'm very ashamed."

Julia and Ralph, sitting on two swivel chairs, assured him there was no offense taken. He kept blinking his eyes. Then he said:

"Much water under the bridge since our last meeting, Julia. I don't mean last night, our wonderful evening together. I'm referring to all those years since Madrid."

Julia nodded and said nothing, seeming to sense that the conversation could take an embarrassing turn.

"What we've all been through, eh? You and I, and of course Dusty, who seemed to have come out the best. When he was alive, of course." His head rested on a green throw pillow and he stared up at the ceiling.

"Well," he continued, "at the risk of just babbling on again, I suppose I should tell you certain things so that you will be able to put all our lives in perspective. You might call it a 'death bed' confession." He gave a self-deprecating grin, as though he wanted everyone to smile warmly at his exaggeration.

Julia shot Ralph a cautionary glance, as if to say, "Take what this man says with a grain of salt."

"You know, my mission to Madrid had been two-fold: to see you on behalf of my great friend, of course, but also to meet with Spanish government officials on a project that Dusty and I had been working on. You see, my dear," he went on, seeming unaware that Ralph also was in the room, "from our earliest days at Yale, where we met, each recognized the uncompromising idealism in the other. We both realized even then, even before the United States entered World War II, that the true enemy, which surely we would have to confront one day, was godless Communism. Were we wrong? Certainly not. Hitler was just a brief intrusion, a homicidal maniac. His Third Reich had no real staying power compared to the communist government in the Soviet Union. Do you know why? Because the Nazi ideology was really an empty shell. There was nothing there. They attracted sadists, misfits and perverts and ruled by power and fear, not by philosophical brilliance.

"But Dusty, I, and others, saw the brilliance in the communist ideology, the appeal to the downtrodden and to the intellectual class. Unfortunately, the humanism of those brilliant thinkers caused a blockage in their understanding of the most fundamental need in man: his spiritual development. For so many years that was our goal: to restore the world to its senses by exposing to it the true nature of Communism. Your one-time lover, Julia dear, was a great man. Along with his many accomplishments in the field of medicine and preventive chemical warfare, he was a true giant in the fight against Communism.

"We worked long and hard, within and outside governments and, I like to think in all modesty, my dear, that we contributed our little grain of sand to the eventual defeat of perhaps the most seductive and the cruelest menace ever devised to the spiritual side, to the very soul, of man. Of course, there remain challenges ahead, certainly in my beloved Cuba. I *know* if Dusty were still alive he would be in the forefront of a renewed fight to defeat Communism in my adopted homeland. And I would gladly follow him in whatever plans he would devise to free the spirit of man on that godforsaken island.

"Unfortunately, however, since our European victory, *my* spirit has been laid low. These last years have been . . . well there are times when I question whether I should go on. I suppose, in all honesty, I should look to no one or nothing for my current despondency, only to myself alone, for these dark days. Dark days? Dark *years!* When you are in the midst of battle, you feel the surge, the rush, you feel compelled to continue the good fight against the Dark Forces of Evil. And then, after it's over, after you've been triumphant, after you suddenly witness a victory you thought was still so far in the future, then . . . I know that only I'm to blame for not preparing for anything to nurture the spirit after the struggle has been won. No family, no fortune, no real home, fewer and fewer friends. On the horizon: only old age and loneliness."

His eyes were filling, his colorless, barely discernable lips trembling. He looked over to Julia and smiled in brave self-pity. The tears started rolling down his now yellowish cheeks.

He picked up the glass of ice water from the floor and gulped it down. Julia took his hand. He grasped it like a lifeline.

"I talk too much," he said. "Sometimes, I just can't control myself."

No one spoke for several minutes. Ralph tapped the space above his upper lip. Then he dug into his shirt pocket and took out the card he had been given by the prone man on the couch. He looked at the card, then turned to the man.

"Are you Ferdie?" Ralph asked.

"Ferdie?" The man smiled. "Yes, Ferdie. My friends have called me that."

Ralph looked over to Julia. She started to look away, then decided there was no need to. She gave Ralph a warm, guileless smile.

"You're the Ferdie who was supposed to have received that letter from Dr. Rhoads all those years ago that forced Rhoads to leave the island?"

Ferdie looked at Julia. She closed her eyes and nodded. Ferdie, in turn, nodded at Ralph.

"I never received such a letter. Other letters, yes, but that particular letter, no. As he so often insisted, my friend never sent it. It was all an incredible misunderstanding. Just some *yanqui* humor that we Latinos did not understand. There is much that we Latinos do not understand about *yanqui* culture, and about the world in general. Unfortunately, many of us do not understand reason. Or logic. All many of us understand is the heart, the stomach and . . ." He touched his heart, his stomach and his groin.

"Excuse me, Julia dear," he said.

"Anyway," he continued, "the whole thing was ridiculous. Dusty Rhoads was a man of honor, vertical, self-sacrificing, willing and wanting to help the less fortunate. Why do you think he came down here? Because he wanted to fight disease. Why do you think he joined in the battle to rid the world of Communism? Because it was another disease that afflicted mankind. The man was a true healer."

"Could he ever have done what he said he did in the letter?" Ralph asked.

"Of course not. That's ridiculous! That letter . . . It was a *yanqui* joke. He often said or wrote seemingly outrageous things that were nothing more than displays of his sense of humor."

"Had Dr. Rhoads done any work with radiation?"

"The man was a physician, a cancer specialist, an expert in many things, one of the most respected doctors in his field," Ferdie said. "I don't know what radiation has to do with anything. Dusty was a wonderful, selfless man and the best friend anyone could have had." Tears again balanced on Ferdie's eyelashes, and he blinked them down his cheeks.

Ralph said: "Julia's son, Pablo Camino, the artist, is looking for you. We don't know where he is, but he believes that you can tell him something that might be connected with a killing in his house. We have to find him to help clear up what happened. If Pablo were to find out where you lived and was looking for you there, where would that be?"

"Where? Here. There. Everywhere. I have no home to speak of. I live from time to time, in several locations. I can't really give you a 'home' address."

Ralph looked again at the card Ferdie had given him. *Seguros Hispanoamericanos*. Oficinas: Madrid, Buenos Aires, Miami. "What about Madrid, Buenos Aires or Miami?"

Yes? I've lived in those cities."

"Where have you lived last? Where do you live now?"

"I told you: I don't *live* anywhere. I travel from city to city."

"Where do you intend to go next?"

"I . . . umh . . . have business appointments in several cities in the next few days. Look, I fail to see the importance . . . "

Ralph took a note from his wallet, unfolded it and handed it to Ferdie. "Before Pablo left, he wrote this."

Ferdie took out a pair of half glasses from his inside jacket pocket, put them on and slowly read the note aloud." The chickens have come home to roost. What are you going to do about it? Be prepared. Because I'm coming to get you . . . "

Ferdie's face turned red again, then pale gray.

"Chickens coming home to roost? That was said about Kennedy after his assassination, yes? Is this man, who I have never met, except when he was a young boy in Spain, is he a spy for Fidel Castro? Does he intend to assassinate me? What is this all about?" He looked over his glasses to Ralph. There seemed to be a pleading in his eyes.

"The man who was killed in Pablo's house was the son of one of the eight persons who died under Rhoads' care down here fifty years ago. One of the eight Rhodes 'joked' about killing. Pablo is looking for you to tell him whether his father was a killer or not."

"What is all this?" Ferdie was agitated again. His hands started shaking. He began mumbling to himself and closed his eyes.

"Listen! In the letter Rhoads wrote to you, he said something about the 'Georgetown group' and some guy who got a job that Rhoads seemed to want. What was that all about?"

Ferdie looked over to Ralph again. "Georgetown group?"

"That's right."

Ferdie exhaled loudly. "I suppose he was referring to CIA, when it was still in its—how shall I say? —formative stages. Dusty, of course, was quite qualified to head the OSI, but . . . "

"The OSI?"

"Office of Scientific Intelligence, which at the time was doing the Agency's scientific research. Later, sometime in the 1960s I believe, the OSI became part of the DDS&T, Directorate for Science and Technology. Don't ask me how I remember all those initials and what they stand for. Well, it's true, I do have some knowledge of the Company, which I suppose I can share with you since it is all ancient history now."

Ferdie seemed to have come back to life. He vigorously nodded his head as he took off on another talking jag.

"You see, the DDS&T not only hired the true geniuses of science and industry, but it also relied on expertise and advice from outside CIA. People moved between the DDS&T and private industry all the time. Let me put it this way: Dusty and I worked in both official and non-official capacities in scientific and technical intelligence gathering. We formed groups, the nature of which I won't go into now, and the DDS&T contracted us out on a number of projects. Dusty also did some key work in the Army that aided immeasurably in providing scientific and technological tools in our war against godless Communism."

"When did you form these groups?" Ralph asked.

"Oh, let me see. Sometime in the mid-1950s."

"But Rhoads was in the Army then," Ralph said, remembering the obit he had read in the University library.

"Maybe it was in the 1960s. It was all so long ago. Ancient history."

"I believe Dr. Rhoads was at Sloan Kettering in the 1960s," Ralph said.

"Oh, for *God's* sake!" said a suddenly angry Ferdie. "Do you mind telling me what is the difference? It's ancient history. It's finished! *Everything* is finished!" Still on his back, he turned his head away from Ralph. Then he turned his eyes to Julia. The dark gray sacs beneath them were swollen, as if with stored-up tears.

"Do you mind, my dear, if I sleep some? I'm feeling quite exhausted."

Julia acquiesced with the nod of one who accepts the inevitable. "You can rest here for a while."

Ferdie's eyes already were closed. Ralph looked over to Julia. She stood and motioned him out of the room and into the art gallery.

"What do you think happened at my son's house that evening?"

Ralph looked at a painting of an old man on one of the gallery walls. Then it came to him: what he was trying to think of that day he was told all that stuff about Rosado thinking Albizu was his father. The slashed painting Ralph had seen on the floor of Pablo's house was his portrait of Albizu.

"I think Pablo acted out of self-defense," Ralph said. "The guy who went there was obviously mentally unbalanced. He thought the Nationalist Albizu Campos was his father. Somehow, he found out that an Albizu painting was in the house and he tried to destroy it."

"He succeeded very well," Julia said. "The police are holding it as evidence, but it is in dire need of repair. There was a newspaper article about the painting a few days before that the man might have seen," Julia said. "Many felt my son had insulted that great patriot with his portrait."

"If the man went to destroy the painting that insulted his 'father,' was it just a coincidence that Pablo also was the son of Rhoads? Did the guy somehow know on some level that Pablo was the son of his father's possible murderer? Was there a connection there?"

Julia said nothing. Fear of the uncanny flickered across her face. Then she smiled. "Thank you so much for helping me," she said.

"Is there anything else I can do?" Ralph motioned with his head to the back room.

Julia put her cold hand on Ralph's arm. "Everything will be all right. When he wakes I'll send him back to his hotel. He has a plane to catch for Miami tomorrow morning. If I run into any problems, I have your phone number. Do you mind if I call you?"

"No, not at all."

As they walked to the front door, Ralph noticed another painting, a portrait by Pablo of his wife Ana. Ana was young and beautiful and her smile was at the same time tender and shrewd and vulnerable, as though she were on to the heartbreak of the world. In the background was a landscape, like in Renaissance portraits. The landscape was flat, the sky was enormous and there were windmills in the background.

Pablo had often spoken about his years in Amsterdam with Ana. Ralph thought, maybe he should visit Ana again. Maybe seeing her again and tapping into her intelligence and sensitivity would give him another clue about Pablo, where he may have gone to search out whatever the hell he was really looking for.

TWENTY-THREE

When Ralph called that night, Ana said she had classes at the University the following day, but she could see him at noon. They agreed to meet in the Faculty Lounge.

As Ralph drove down Ponce de León Avenue toward the campus he heard the shouts and the chanting. An unusual number of police cars were parked on the side streets. Cops were patrolling outside the campus gates. For the first time, Ralph was stopped by a security guard at the vehicle gate. The guard asked for identification.

"What's happening?" Ralph showed his faculty card.

The guard, who, like most middle-aged security guards, looked as though he was moonlighting to pay off deep debts, shrugged. "The usual. The *independentistas* and communists are disrupting classes."

Ralph parked his car in a space reserved for faculty in front of the University Tower. A few hundred students gathered down by the corner gate were listening to a speech by a young guy in a black beret. Ralph made his way to the Faculty Lounge. There was another demonstration going on in the quadrangle in front of the University Theater. The students marched around the quadrangle, chanting, clapping, raising fists and blowing whistles. Campus police stood in front of the quad buildings, being heckled good-naturedly by the demonstrators. The air was more festive than threatening.

A young guy with a scraggly beard and wearing a black tee shirt with a "Navy Out Of Vieques!" message and a red bandana around his head handed Ralph a leaflet. Ralph read: "We are protesting in the name of the oppressed peoples of the world, and the insulted and injured residents of Vieques. We are protesting against the worldwide military imperialism of the United States, as demonstrated in the Navy bombing of the Puerto Rican island of Vieques. We are protesting the bombing and the shelling and the firing of uranium ammunition on Vieques, which is destroying the environment, the economy and causing our people great physical and mental suffering, including the highest rate of cancer in Puerto Rico. We blame the Navy for causing the cancer by poisoning the air, the water, the land and the lungs of the inhabitants. We intend to keep protesting until our government makes the Navy leave the island. Navy out of Vieques! Vieques, sí! Navy, no!"

More cancer-causing charges against the U.S. colonialist-imperialists. Either colonialism caused cancer, or cancer-paranoia overtook the colonialized, who felt their condition had metastasized into a slow, malignant, agonizing death, Ralph figured, mustering as much sardonic detachment as he could.

Ralph saw several students in his class among the demonstrators. One of them was Richie Pérez. Richie had one fist raised and one hand holding the hand of a female companion. She was pale, slight and beautiful with large dark eyes. It was Laura Rosado. Evidently, they were pretty close friends. The daughter of the guy who was sure he was being bombarded with death rays, the daughter of the guy whose father was one of the purported "cancer" victims of Pablo's father, was out there demonstrating.

Small, interconnected, paranoid-like world.

Ralph made his way to the Faculty Lounge down a hill from the University Theater. Students stood around discussing whether to go to classes or not. There were no demonstrators in front of the faculty building.

As soon as he entered, he saw Ana sitting by herself at a long table in the back of the cafeteria, sipping coffee and reading a book. She smiled, enjoying the sentences she was reading. She wore half glasses tipped to the edge of her small, somewhat snubbed nose. Sensing that Ralph had arrived, her large and deep brown eyes rose over the lenses, and her rounded forehead creased. Despite their previously arranged meeting, she looked as though she were questioning, not unkindly, Ralph's presence at that moment. "How's it going?"

"Great."

Ana smiled. "Quite a bit of excitement going on outside."

"Yeah," Ralph said. "Have you had any trouble teaching your classes?"

"Not yet. But I understand that the demonstrators are going to try to disrupt classes in the afternoon. They want to force the University to shut down."

"What will you do?"

"Do? I don't know. I wish this country had enough courage to just declare its independence and kick the damn Navy out."

"Until then?"

"Until then—I guess I'll invite the protesters to take part in the class. We're studying the plays of O'Casey, who knew all about the ridiculousness and the rage of the colonialized."

"Good luck," said Ralph not unkindly. Then he said: "You know, I'm still trying to track down Pablo. You haven't heard from him in the last couple of days by any chance? Or maybe thought of where he might be?"

"No," Ana said, "I haven't. If he's no longer on the island he could be anywhere."

"Amsterdam?"

Ana pulled her head back, then smiled. "Amsterdam? Sure. Why not? But what made you think he might have gone there?"

"I don't know . . . It's just that I was in his mother's art gallery yesterday and I saw a portrait he did of you there. There were windmills in the background."

Ana closed her eyes and nodded, continuing to smile. "Actually, it was in the countryside, at Kinderdijk, where we spent several days in a little room we rented to get out of the city. I sat on the second-floor balcony outside our room every morning, with the windmills behind me. I remember some mornings it was *freezing* out there."

"Pablo told me a lot about his time in Amsterdam with you. I take it from what he said that those were happy times. And when his mother mentioned something about Pablo going to search for his humanity, I thought maybe that's the best place to look for him."

Ana nodded. "We had some wonderful times there. After awhile, we met some great people—poets, policemen, jazz musicians. But there were other times too." She smiled again, but this time with a profound sadness.

"Do you know about the incident with the Rembrandt portrait?" Ana asked.

"Pablo told me there was one Rembrandt in the museum there that he would always go to see. That he constantly thought about it and dreamt about it. That it 'spoke' to him. I think he meant that literally."

"He did," Ana said. "Except the conversations started getting too personal for Pablo. Just before we left Amsterdam, he, we, went through some very . . . umh, trying times.

"The portrait haunted Pablo. He obsessed on it. He kept saying that there was too much truth in it, that what he saw in it terrified him, but he had to keep going back to it. Rembrandt told him, he said, that after he, Pablo, died his torment in the after-life would be much worse than what he believed he was now suffering and that it would last for eternity. Wonderful news, eh?"

Ana seemed slightly embarrassed as she related Pablo's Rembrandt woes. She looked into her coffee cup, and seemed dismayed that it was empty.

"I'll get you more coffee," Ralph said. Ana smiled gratefully.

He went to the coffee machine and poured out two steaming cups of black coffee. Ana nodded her thanks. She took a long sip, then continued:

"By the time we were ready to leave for New York, Pablo was acting weirder than I had ever seen him act before. I mean, by that time I was a nervous wreck, and now I got *really* scared. He wasn't his usual screaming paranoid self. He wasn't even drinking his Remys. Something else was taking hold. He was walking around like a zombie. His flesh looked gray. He didn't answer me when I spoke to him. We were in our little room and the stove was glowing hot and I touched his hand and it was like ice. His eyes looked glazed over, except for some tiny points of light that definitely looked ready to burn holes into whatever they concentrated on. He scared the hell out of me. Then, in the middle of packing—we were going to fly out that night—he rushed over to the rubber mat next to the sink where our plates and stuff were drying and he picked up the sharpest knife there and ran out of the room and down the stairs and out of the house. It was the middle of the day but he was still in his bathrobe and slippers and he ran out into the freezing cold dressed like that.

"I ran after him. I saw him coming out the front door with his bicycle, we stored them behind the steps. I asked him where the hell he was going and he pushed me away and started pedaling down the street. I got my bike and started going after him. He had hair down to his shoulders then and it was blowing in the wind and there he was pedaling like a maniac in his bathrobe and slippers and even though I lost him several times, I knew where he was going, so we got to the Rijkesmuseum not too many minutes apart."

Ana sipped her coffee. There was a painful expression on her face. She looked into the cup, as though she were deciding whether to continue the story. She took a deep breath, then said:

"He was getting looks from everybody, but no one stopped him from entering the museum. People were doing all sorts of weird things in Amsterdam in those days. Maybe they still are. So the people at the door were reluctant to stop some guy in his pajamas and bathrobe from coming into the museum. But I saw them put their heads together and one of them made a phone call.

"I followed Pablo to the room where the Rembrandt portrait was hanging and my heart was in my mouth. It was a weekday in winter and the room was empty, except for a guard standing at the far end and looking the other way, into the next room. I sort of hid by the entrance to the room and watched Pablo. Both his hands were in his bathrobe pockets, and the knife was in one of the pockets.

"He went up very close to the painting and I held my breath, then I started breathing really heavy and I thought I was going to faint. I was about to yell at him or for the guard, but he backed away and sat on the marble bench in front of the portrait and crossed his arms and legs. That was the way he usually looked at the Rembrandt, sitting on the bench with his arms and legs crossed, so I began to feel better. But then he suddenly stood up again and started moving toward the painting and his hands went back into his pockets and just then the guard disappeared into the other room, so I jumped out and ran up to Pablo and put my arms around him and tried like mad to pull him back across the room.

"He looked at me like I was even crazier than he was and pushed me on the floor and then, *gracias a Dios*, guards came running from all over, and they separated us. They thought we were having some sort of marital spat and they forcefully but politely led us out of the museum.

"Pablo asked me if I was crazy and I asked him the same thing. He denied that he was going to do anything to the painting and when I asked him if he had the knife in his pocket, he told me what I should do to myself and pedaled back to our guesthouse on the frozen canal. I didn't know what to expect but I went back there too and when I went back up to our room he acted as though nothing had happened. He even greeted me with a smile. The day after we got to New York, he bought me jade earrings and a jade necklace.

"So that's Pablo. That's how our stay in Amsterdam ended. We had some wonderful times—and other times. I know, I put up with such incredible things that no woman in her right mind would have. I'm five years older than Pablo. I felt that I had to be the mature one, and I put up with more than I should have. When we got to New York, I gave him an ultimatum: he goes to a psychiatrist to get some help, or we split up. He went for a couple of years. It helped for a while. Until we got back to Puerto Rico."

She slowly shook her head, as though trying to dispel the worst of the past with Pablo, including her own timidity. Then she said: "I'm not sure if, or why, he would go back to Amsterdam."

"To tell you the truth, neither am I," Ralph said. "It's just a hunch. Maybe he'll go back to speak to his buddy on the museum wall. To talk over things and try to get more answers from him."

Ana shrugged. She seemed peeved, either at Ralph's presumption or at the possibility that Pablo would make such an irrational move. "I don't know what to tell you," she said. "I just hope you find him soon, in one piece." She took another very deep breath. "Well, I have a one o'clock class that I might try to teach if any students show up."

"I'll walk you over there."

As soon as they went outside, Ralph sensed that the situation had gotten worse. Groups of students were running back and forth calling out to each other. The sun had slid behind thick, dark clouds, as though it were ducking unpleasant things-to-come.

When they got to the quadrangle near the Humanities Building, they saw that the situation was rapidly deteriorating. The protesters had grown five-fold. The students' heckling of the University guards was no longer good-natured. This time insults were coming from angry, red faces. The protesters began hurling rocks at the guards, who ducked inside the porticos and behind the columns of the surrounding buildings.

A rock smashed through the window of a small truck parked in front of the University Theater and students cheered. The crowd in the quadrangle was multiplying by the minute as some students ran shouting into the Humanities Building, apparently to disrupt whatever classes were going on there. Ralph took Ana's arm and started across the quad.

"It looks like your class is going to be postponed," Ralph said. "I think we should get out of this area."

Ana did not disagree. But as they moved toward the far end near the administration offices, the students there began running toward them, shouting and screaming. Ralph and Ana froze; then Ralph took Ana by the arm and they rushed to another side of the quad, under the portico of the Natural Sciences Building. Chasing on the heels of the students were state police. They wore helmeted visors and bulletproof vests and some wielded shields and clubs while others carried shotguns. The administration had called in the Riot Squad.

The students now grouped together by the University Theater, running around, looking for rocks. They let go a first salvo that banged off the advancing cops' shields and helmets. Then the police shot tear gas canisters into the protesters who panicked and ran in all directions. The cops with the clubs ran after them and brought down some of the students with blows to the front and back of the knees and bloodied the heads of others.

Ralph saw Richie Pérez and the daughter of Jaime Rosado, still hand-in-hand, running past with two cops right behind them. One of the cops smashed his club across Richie's shoulders and Richie let go the girl's hand and flew forward, staggering, trying to stay on his feet. The other cop, who was fat and looked out of breath, put his club around the girl's neck and pulled her backwards. He was three times the girl's size. Richie was on the ground with his hands in front of his face while the other cop smashed his body with the club, then, as Richie went to cover his body, the cop clubbed him on the head.

Ralph ran over and grabbed the cop's club. "That's enough!"

The cop pulled his club out of Ralph's hand. "M*aricón!*" He lifted the club toward Ralph, then decided to scoot after a student.

The small truck in front of the University Theater suddenly burst into flames after a Molotov cocktail was thrown through the windshield. Several gunshots snapped through the air and the cops ducked behind their shields. The shots seemed to be coming from the roof of one of the buildings. The police returned the fire. Some of the shots toward the police were now coming from the ground level of the same building. The police pulled back toward the University Theater, firing their pistols and shotguns and the students ran for cover toward the surrounding buildings. The center of the quad was cleared, except for some students holding their heads while walking around dazed and moaning. People were screaming at them to seek shelter from the continuing gunfire. They ran and crawled away.

Except for one student, whose body did not move from one of the stone walks crossing the grassy quad. Blood ran like dark water from beneath the body onto the stone and down into the grassy area.

Lying there with one arm twisted beneath her body and one leg half bent and touching the other, was Jaime Rosado's daughter. Laura Rosado looked like a broken, life-sized doll.

TWENTY-FOUR

The vehicles crawled up to the top of a steep street at the entrance to the Old City and passed Fort San Cristobal. They wound around to Boulevard del Valle, bordered on one side by pastel-colored colonial homes, on the other by the Sixteenth Century Spanish-built city wall. Below the wall was La Perla, the slum by the sea. The vehicles twisted down the narrowest of roads and went through a short tunnel before arriving at the seaside cemetery. The cemetery was packed tight with graves, many guarded over by stone-carved angels gazing in frozen innocence and fierceness at the ocean and the sky.

The cars were parked along the road and on small hillsides and scores of mourners exited the vehicles and moved toward the cemetery. Just outside the cemetery gates, the mourners passed two young men standing at parade rest positions beside an easel. A floral wreath was placed against the legs of the easel, which held a white cardboard poster. On the poster was an eight-by-ten photograph of a very pretty young woman walking across the University campus and waving to the camera. Black calligraphy below the photo read, first in Spanish: "*Laura Rosado: Una mártir para el pueblo sufriendo de Vieques;* then, for the English-language media: Laura Rosado: A martyr for the suffering on Vieques because of the U.S. military bombing. She was assassinated by the police."

Many of those moving toward the gravesite were University students. Others were not students and did not know the young woman, but sympathized with the cause for which she died. Also present were politicians who knew that the young woman's funeral would get full media coverage. Photographers and TV cameras snapped and rolled on the poster and on the young men standing beside it in quasi-military dress—boots, fatigue pants, black tee shirts and black berets—and on the politicos who grabbed at the chance to mourn before the cameras and give a short anti-U.S. Navy interview. Laura Rosado was being buried in the cemetery reserved for the country's patriots.

Laura's family sat in wooden chairs at the gravesite. The mother cried hysterically while holding her squealing infant son in her lap. The circles under her eyes were black as coal. Laura's teenage brother's face jumped with tics and his body shook, as though he were palsied. Just behind them sat aunts, uncles and cousins, most of them with brown and wrinkled country faces. Also sitting back there, staring straight ahead and dry eyed was 90-year-old great grandmother Clara Almodóvar.

Ralph and his wife, Tere, and Richie Pérez and his mother, Yolanda, stood at the edge of the grave, across from the seated family. Richie wore a dark, heavy, too-tight suit, a worn-out survivor of New York winters. Mercifully, the day was cloudy and a breeze blew off the nearby ocean; still, sweat dripped from Richie's heavy eyebrows, his bushy mustache and curly sideburns. His round, boyish face was suffused with both grief and confusion, as though he was not yet ready for the depth of his feelings.

Richie's mother, a tall ample woman, wore a plain black dress and, surprisingly for the time and place, a black hat with a veil down over her face. All through the ceremony, she dabbed pink-colored Kleenex under the veil, at her eyes and across her forehead and around her neck.

While the Spanish priest lisped prayers, Ralph tried not to look at Laura's mother, who wailed along with the baby in her lap. Her uncontrollable grief was too hard to take. Ralph's eyes met those of Doña Clarita. She stared through him. She probably did not recognize him, he thought, because of her own private grief, because of some self-protecting numbness to her surroundings. Or maybe she intuited his feelings of guilt for her great granddaughter's death. Although she was stone-faced, every now and then her lips would move uncontrollably, as though she were rapidly talking to herself.

Ralph felt that by speaking to Laura about her family's troubles, he had instilled in her his own belief that her father had gone to Pablo's house that night on a mission of revenge, that he might have gone there to kill Pablo—because his own father was killed by Pablo's father.

Because Puerto Ricans were required to fight in U.S. wars, Jaime Rosado had cracked up in Vietnam and saw his father as Albizu Campos, who tried to free the island from colonial rule. If Rosado had not visited Pablo that night and Pablo had not disappeared and Ralph had not gotten involved trying to find his friend and had not gone to the Rosado family home and not met Laura and not sparked in her the need to demonstrate against the colonialism that allows the U.S. Navy to bomb a small island populated by thousands of Puerto Ricans, Laura might not have been out there marching hand-in-hand with Richie Pérez and her little body wouldn't have wound up lifeless and contorted on the ground.

Then again, maybe there was no cause and effect.

Everything connects and nothing connects. Both the paranoia and the randomness are true.

Ralph felt heartsick.

To top off everything, while having breakfast, he had read about Pablo's plight. The Associated Press had picked up the latest story from *The Miami Herald* and it had run in the Puerto Rican newspapers. Famous Local Artist Now Sought in Miami Murder.

The story said that Pablo was mistakenly released from custody in Miami two days before and was now being sought in connection with killings both in San Juan and Miami. It said that Pablo and "two other members of a Cuban exile group" had been charged with breaking and entering into the home of the Miami murder victim. The man murdered in Miami was identified as F. A. Méndez y del Río, the patriarchal and matriarchal names on the card Ferdie had given him. But Ferdie was in San Juan, at least up until Sunday, and the murder was committed some days before that. Cuban exile group member Pablo killing a guy in Miami who at that time was in San Juan? What the hell was going on?

If nothing else, he at least knew where Pablo was. That is, if Pablo were still somewhere in or around Miami. And on Sunday Julia mentioned that Ferdie was leaving for Miami the next morning. Ralph figured he could take a flight up to Miami and start by looking for Ferdie and talking to those religious Jews who had seen Pablo and had known the victim. Continue investigating. Find the connections. The intrigue of the mystery was turning to obsession. Do it! Before his own guilt paralyzed him.

After the burial, as Ralph and Tere came out of the cemetery, he saw a reporter approaching Doña Clarita. Ralph overheard her say: "Three generations of my family, all martyrs, all sacrificed so that the American government can continue to dominate the world."

Later that afternoon, Ralph was able to make reservations for an early morning flight to Miami.

Pablo was slashing the Albizu painting. No, it was the other guy who was stabbing into the eyes of the painting. Only it wasn't the Albizu portrait. It was the Rembrandt, the one that spoke to Pablo. Pablo and the guy were locked in the knife fight again. Circling one another. Then, locked . . . in an embrace!

Each asked the other: "Why?"

"Because we love each other," said the guy. Or had the guy become Iris?

"Bullshit!" said Pablo.

Pablo cut the other's throat. He saw the eyeless Rembrandt shaking and chortling in his frame. "What the fuck did I do?" Pablo felt terrible. Pressure pushed behind his eyes and the tears flowed. He cried for what seemed like hours. "Please forgive me," he pleaded to the man with the cut throat lying on the black-and-white tiled floor, then to Rembrandt in his frame. "I've made you martyrs. Please, I beg of you, forgive me."

Rembrandt continued to laugh.

Maybe he should cut out his own eyes. No, then he would never be able to paint again. So what? Painting was his life. So what? He killed the guy—and the death meant something more. Wasn't it bad enough just to kill? Yes. No. There was something more. "Oh, God, please forgive me!"

Then he and Iris were on a train, in Puerto Rico, which he knew no longer has trains. The train was running along the oceanfront. An incredible red balloon of a sun was setting. He asked Iris to forgive him. "We're family," he said. She laughed too, just like Rembrandt.

Iris was now beneath him, her strong, muscular legs around his back, her heels digging in while he churned the tingling softness below—he couldn't believe the sweetness! —but wait, it wasn't Iris beneath him, it was—oh, God! — it was Julia. No, it wasn't Julia, it was Ana. No, it wasn't Ana, it was Iris . . . She wore the choker. Julia stood by, watching with a critical eye. She too wore the choker. So did Ana. What the fuck . . .

Forget that fuckin dream was Pablo's first command when he awoke. At least, he thought he awoke, but soon realized he was still dreaming. Wake the fuck up!

Which he soon did. No, he was still . . .

Forget that fuckin dream was the first thing he told himself when he sat up in his rented car. He had spent the last two days and nights in the car, parked alongside an empty lot. He was far enough away from the closest neighborhoods. During the day, when he skulked around to fast food restaurants getting takeout meals and using the bathrooms, all he saw were poor blacks and Latinos and no patrol cars. Now, on awakening, he was aware of a new biting in his heart. That guy didn't want to kill him. He wanted to cut up the Albizu painting. He could have dropped his knife and told the guy to leave.

What if the guy had stabbed and killed him?

Good, then he wouldn't have this sick feeling in his heart and soul.

Who did he kill? Why did he know in his gut that he had to make it up to someone? The dream had awoken him to the full horror of what he had done.

He drove back down to Miami Beach, stopped in Wolfie's for a take-out container of coffee and to use the rest room. The public library was right up the street. It was nine a.m., but already the sleepy eyed elderly were moving through the stacks and sitting at tables reading newspapers. He was able to use a computer and got on the Internet.

He typed in his own name on a search. There were a couple pages on his art, including two scurrilous articles written for island newspapers ten years ago criticizing his supposed insulting, ignoble portrait of the great patriot Albizu Campos.

Nothing more. Then he typed in the search box "dead body found house Pablo Camino." A story from the island English-language newspaper came up. It identified the victim as Jaime Rosado, 49, of Barrio Obrero. When he read that Rosario was a Vietnam veteran his heart twisted and his stomach tightened.

Still, there was something more.

His fingers typed in two Spanish words: *familia, mártires.* Where the hell did that come from? He hit "Search the Web."

It came right up in the first reference, then the second and the third: *Una Familia de Mártires.* A Family of Martyrs. His heart was coming through his chest.

It was an article by the Spanish news agency, EFE, appearing in today's newspapers in Colombia, Panama and Venezuela. Outside the cemetery in Old San Juan, a white-haired woman told a reporter about the death of her great granddaughter in a demonstration against the U.S. military on the Puerto Rico island of Vieques. She said that the young student's father, her grandson, who was mentally unbalanced because of his service in the Vietnam War, also had been killed recently. Then she said that her own son had been a victim of an *americano* doctor who confessed to killing him and others on the island almost fifty years ago.

"Three generations of my family, all martyrs, all sacrificed so that the American government can continue to dominate the world," said the aged, white-haired woman.

The car radio! The two *words—familia, martires—* yesterday on the radio, as he was flipping past a Spanish-language news broadcast. Just those two words. He was driven by a dream to a technological unearthing of what he had intuited in a flash from hearing those words.

He had killed the son. The murderous father begat the murderous son, who killed the son of one of the father's helpless victims. How could he live with that?

The enormity of what he had actually done flat-lined everything else.

The portrait of the great artist materialized in his mind's eye. That wrinkled brow, those damning eyes. When it spoke to him, he had never understood enough. When he looked, he had never seen enough. The radiance of the light wasn't enough. Even then, he had wanted to know more. That's why, those many years ago, he was ready to plunge both of them into the deepest part of night. To see what lay in the true darkness of the act.

Pablo left the library, crossed Collins Avenue and walked between two hotels and onto a boardwalk. He sat on a bench. It was a murky morning. Only now and then did the sun manage to slip through the smudgy clouds. The lead-colored ocean was calm, heaving little waves along the shore.

The great artist had told him that suffering continued beyond the grave, that misery is for eternity. No need to walk into the ocean, Pablo knew.

He didn't like the way the people passing looked at him. He wore his wraparound sunglasses; still, the old buzzards out for their morning walks seemed to peer deeply into his face, as though not quite placing someone familiar. One of them was bound to recognize he was the one wanted for the murder only a few blocks away.

He got up and rushed back to his car parked down the street from the library. He drove back to the expressway to North Miami, getting off at One Hundred and Third Street and finding that weedy lot he had parked alongside in the past days. He pulled the car in and cut the motor.

In deepest depression, but also with a certain satisfaction, Pablo realized that he had reached the deadest of ends.

TWENTY-FIVE

He lay on his side, his breathing coming more easily now. He was in deep sleep and Julia decided not to wake him. He could stay on the couch indefinitely—as long as he did not regain consciousness. When he did awaken she would get him out of her house, out of her life, *pronto.*

She went to the small bar in the large and airy sitting room of her second floor living quarters and mixed a gin and tonic, cut up a lime and squeezed half of it into the drink. She took the drink up the staircase, and stepped into the cool tangle of her roof garden. She sat in the huge round-backed wicker chair beneath the light green plastic awning. The mid-afternoon sun slid wafer-thin behind smudgy clouds that had gathered in abundance since the morning, a possible prelude to rain showers, which Julia would gladly welcome. She was sure her bruised-looking plants would also salute a downpour. She knew she should keep the gallery open on Sundays, when people were strolling the Old City streets, but she detested doing business on that particular day, not out of any religious feeling, but because she preferred to mostly sleep the day away. She had always hated Sundays, especially when the sun glared down, bringing into barbed relief the emptiness and solitude of the world.

Julia picked up yesterday's newspaper from the rattan side table. Politics and crime, crime and politics. She tossed the paper back onto the table and finished her drink. She may as well make herself another. A couple of drinks would help her deal with the man on the couch when he awoke. In fact, she was starting to feel antsy about him. Perhaps it was time to wake him and send him on his way. First another gin and tonic.

She went back down to the bar, squeezed the other half of the lime into her drink and sat at the bar drinking it.

She heard an appalling sound. Something between a howl and a cry. She froze, then went to the top of the stairs.

"Hello? Is everything all right down there?"

No answer. She started down the stairs.

"Is everything all right?" she called again as she moved across the gallery to the office in the back. Again there was no answer. Maybe he was having a nightmare.

She entered the back room, her heart in her mouth. Ferdie was still on the couch, on his back, his eyes wide open, his breath coming short and fast.

"Are you all right?"

A pair of terrified eyes shot over to Julia. Ferdie's lips trembled, as though he were struggling to say something. He blinked several times, tapped his chest and let out a deep breath. He looked over at Julia again, this time with a softness in his expression.

"I'm really sorry," he said. "I awoke completely petrified. I had no idea where I was, or *who* I was. It's been happening more and more often lately."

"But you're all right now?"

"Now that you are here, yes," He put out a hand to her.

Julia looked away. How to get rid of him?

"Hold my hand, please, Julia. Just for a moment."

Reluctantly, she took his hand. It was ice.

"Should I turn down the air-conditioning?"

"No, no. Only my hands are cold. The rest of me is burning." He smiled, trying to mask, it seemed to Julia, some passionate urge as playfulness.

She freed her hand. "Well, my dear, you seem well rested. I think it's time for you to get up and . . . "

"Yes, I understand, it's time to go. To vanish from your life, dear Julia. To vanish into nothingness. But before we part forever, perhaps you would be so kind as to offer me something cold to drink? My mouth is completely dry."

"Certainly. I'll get you some ice water." She started to leave to go upstairs to the bar.

"Perhaps something a bit stronger. Please."

She gritted her teeth. Be human, she told herself. Then, realizing she was overcompensating for her sudden guilt, but doing it anyway, she asked: "Would you like to have your drink on the roof, in my garden?"

"That would be wonderful."

She took Ferdie's other arm as he negotiated with his cane across the gallery, then up the stairs. He had to struggle on his own on the narrow stairway to the roof. After she got him seated in the huge wicker chair, she went back down to the bar and, cutting up another lime, made them both gin and tonics. She carried the drinks up on a wicker tray and handed Ferdie his drink and took hers to a cushioned metal lounge chair.

Ferdie gulped down half the drink. "So good," he said. He put the drink down on the rattan side table and leaned his head back against the high rounded back of the chair and closed his eyes. Julia thought he may be starting to doze again. His eyes still closed, he said in a low voice: "Julia, I want to apologize for my boorish behavior over the past two days. I have no right to have acted the way I did. We are really nothing to each other, in terms of the past. *I* certainly mean nothing to *you*."

He opened his eyes, looking at her with a hopeful expectancy that she would protest his last remark. She only smiled. He shut his eyes again.

"The truth is I'm just an elderly, lonely man looking to take advantage of a serendipitous situation. I had to come to Puerto Rico for business. I'm trying to help an acquaintance in Spain get a loan from your government to start up a factory here. Shoes. He manufactures shoes. I work on commission. If the deal goes through I get some money. I live on such commissions. Since I knew I was coming here, I started correspondence with you. To try to take advantage of my situation. Not business-wise. But, as I have expressed in such a foolish way before, romantically. We who have been cursed, and blessed, with the Don Juan complex, what does our age matter? To have been able to bed the object of the unending desire of my best friend of the past, that would have been truly heavenly! And, of course, as Don Juan, I have convinced myself that I truly have fallen in love with you. So I will open my eyes now and probably resume my rather ridiculous role of foolish, aging, lonely, though also utterly sincere, Don Juan. It is up to you to continue to show the common sense I knew you possessed from the first time we met."

Ferdie opened his eyes. He smiled at Julia, somewhat hesitantly. (Was the diffidence real?) He picked up his drink from the table and finished it. "It's lovely here," he said, looking around admiringly. "And you are lovely too, *mi amor.*" His eyes twinkled, then teared. "And now I believe I should be getting along, back to my hotel. I have some phone calls to make to Spain."

Julia, somewhat touched by Ferdie's "confession," helped him up from the chair and took his arm again and led him downstairs. At the front door, she said: "I'll walk you to your hotel."

"It's just a few blocks."

"That's fine." She took his arm again and they started up the street. They turned the corner to Calle Cristo. Clouds had reneged on the promise of rain and most of them had cleared away. The late afternoon sun was surprisingly powerful, as though it had reserved its strength for a couple of hours and was now finishing strong in the homestretch of the day. Julia felt sweat glue her blouse to her back.

She would say goodbye, hopefully forever, when they reached the hotel. Yes, she was somewhat moved by what he had said in the roof garden. Compassion could occasionally tap into that hard heart of hers. Especially when she knew she would not have to carry that pity over to another day. You judge yourself too severely, Julia dear, was her last sardonic thought just before she felt Ferdie's arm begin to shake. She looked over at him. His whole body was trembling.

They were a few feet from the entrance to the hotel, in the little square opposite the San Juan Cathedral. Julia led Ferdie to a bench under a large tree. "What is it?" She took his hand. Again it was like ice.

Ferdie clamped down on Julia's hand and gave her a confused look. "I feel strange, weak as a kitten, as though all force and feeling has left my being. I feel . . . unreal."

"Perhaps you should go to the hospital emergency. Have a doctor there examine you."

"Well, yes, perhaps we should do that."

"Wait here while I call . . . "

"No, no, I prefer to wait inside the hotel, in the air-conditioning," he said. "The heat is making it difficult for me to breathe."

Julia helped him up again and they crossed the narrow street to the hotel entrance. As they were about to go through the heavy wooden portals, Ferdie's legs wiggled like shook rope and Julia could not hold him up. He collapsed and lay crumpled against one of the doors, then fell over on one side to the ground. Julia turned him on his back. His eyes had rolled up into his head. He was breathing in shallow, rapid bursts. His skin looked purple.

Julia ran up to the front desk and asked the clerk to call for an ambulance. Ferdie was lying across the entrance. A group of tourists stood staring down at him, looking for ways to circumvent his body to enter the hotel. As Julia came back, the tourists were stepping over his legs, sheepishly excusing themselves.

Julia got down on her haunches. Ferdie's eyes popped open. There was terror in them. Then they closed. Julia took his hand, which was both cold and sweaty. His skin was now clammy and gray, like a damp rag. The hotel's assistant manager and the security officer came by. They looked down at Ferdie, said nothing. A local character known as "the General" strolled up. He was dressed in khakis and had several rows of toy medals on his chest. He wore a visored airman's cap at a rakish angle on his head. He reached to his belt and loosened a toy walkie-talkie and began speaking into it: "Calling the Governor's mansion, calling the Governor's mansion. We have a body here. Send help, send help." The "General" gave a smart salute and started down the street. Then he changed his mind and decided to join what was now a crowd of about a dozen onlookers. Julia pleaded with them to give Ferdie air. They stepped back, then soon crowded in again.

Ferdie continued labored breathing. Fifteen minutes passed and still no ambulance! Julia appealed to the hotel people to call the emergency number again.

Another fifteen minutes went by before the ambulance came whooping down the narrow cobblestoned street outside the hotel. The paramedics worked their way through the crowd, checked Ferdie's signs, then hoisted him onto a wheeled stretcher. Julia could not tell if Ferdie was conscious or not.

"Are you going with him to the hospital, *Señora?*" asked one of the paramedics. "If so, please get in." He held open the back doors to the ambulance.

Julia hesitated. She thought she saw Ferdie's head raise from the stretcher to look at her.

"Well . . . umh . . . yes, of course." She got into the back of the ambulance with the paramedic.

She thought she saw a small smile quiver across Ferdie's lips.

She stayed until close to midnight, while Ferdie was examined and checked into Presbyterian Hospital. He had had a stroke and was in a semi-conscious state. She returned daily for the next two weeks, as Ferdie fought for his life, experiencing another stroke and two heart attacks. She spent two hours in the morning, reading the newspaper to him when he was able to understand, feeding him and holding his hand. She usually ate lunch in the same little cafeteria in the hospital patio where she and Dusty had often had snacks and coffee. She returned to the hospital in the evenings, usually bringing Ferdie special food he had requested, when he felt up to it. She kissed him softly on his wizened cheek before she left.

She didn't ask herself why she was doing this. It didn't make her feel particularly good or noble or kinder or happier. It was, in fact, almost every day, a bother. But she continued to visit.

On a lucid day, Ferdie made what he said was his *real* deathbed confession. "Dusty told me that the Puerto Rican patients he supposedly killed on purpose actually died because of medical mistakes. Yes, radiation experiments were involved, experiments that were carried out on behalf of science, on behalf of the government. But, dear Julia, Dusty had nothing against the people here. In fact, he loved one of them very much." Ferdie's wan smile tugged at Julia.

"You see, Dusty *wanted* the so-called incriminating letter to be discovered so that it would cover up the unfortunate errors. He planned to say later that the letter was a joke, that the patients had died of their diseases, which they soon would have anyway, given the seriousness of their condition.

"You see, dear Julia, what Dusty did, was not out of hate for a group of people, but out of love of his country. After it was over, Dusty said it had all been for the best. He acknowledged that leaving the island had helped his career.

"But I never believed he wanted to leave you. What caused him to invent all this nonsense was his ego. He could not admit publicly that he had made mistakes as a doctor. I'm sure that the regret of his life was having to leave you."

"So that's what you think?"

"That, dear Julia, is what I *know.*"

"And those times you came to see me in Spain . . . ?"

"Were, of course, on his behalf. Though I have to admit, something inside me was not completely unhappy that you continued to spurn him. It showed your strength of character. I did make an extra visit or two without his knowledge. As I said, I was beginning to feel a certain attraction to you myself. Unfortunately, I never got the opportunity to express my feelings those many years ago, which I now regret so completely." Ferdie's eyelids began to flutter. "You see, Julia dearest, I now know that I've wasted so many of my years on things outside myself, which would have taken their course without me. The best we can do . . . The best we can do . . . " His body was beginning shake.

Julia took his hand. "Rest," she said.

Some nights later, Ferdie had a massive heart attack and died in his sleep. When she was told the next morning, Julia cried for several minutes. She arranged and paid for Ferdie's funeral. She didn't know who to contact. Nothing in his hotel room gave any indication of friends or relatives or even business acquaintances. She called in notices to the newspapers in San Juan, Miami and Madrid.

She was the only one to attend the burial.

TWENTY-SIX

The Miami telephone number on Ferdie's calling card was no longer in service. The operator could not find a listing for *Seguros Hispanoamericanos* or for a Fernando A. Méndez y del Río. She gave Ralph the number for an F.A. Méndez y del Río. When he called, a recorded announcement told him that the number had been disconnected.

He spent a day in his hotel room calling the myriad of hotels and motels listed in the Miami-Dade directory, asking if a Pablo Camino, a Paul Rhoads, a Carlos or Charlie Parker, or a John Birks or Juan Gillespie had checked in recently. He described his friend as tall, middle-aged, broad-shouldered, good-looking with a mole on his left cheek, a thin mustache and a large head.

Nada.

He called the Miami-Dade police, explaining he was a reporter from San Juan following the story involving the famous Puerto Rican artist Pablo Camino. The police press officer, Sergeant Wilda González, said the investigation was ongoing and there was nothing new to report.

He repeated the calls to the police daily and got the same answer.

He called *The Miami Herald*, and was told that the reporter covering the story was in Puerto Rico trying to get further information on the case. How long would the reporter be there? As long as it took.

Ralph used a computer at the hotel to look up the stories about the murder that Pablo supposedly was involved in. The stabbing death, he saw, took place in South Beach and, somehow, involved Orthodox Jews and Cuban exiles. The murder victim was Felipe Méndez y del Río. Ferdie's name was Fernando. Were they related? Most probably. Which meant . . . what? Invisible fingers were again tightening the knots Ralph was experiencing lately in his stomach.

He spent several evenings, late nights and early mornings doing the rounds of bars and clubs in and around Little Havana, South Beach and other parts of Miami, showing a ten-year-old photo of Pablo that had run in the San Juan newspapers. Picture him a little older and grayer, he told the bartenders.

Nada.

He checked the rental car agencies. Pablo had rented a car under his own name at Avis two weeks ago and had not yet returned it. It was several days overdue. Ralph flashed his outdated private investigator's credentials, explaining he was searching for Pablo on behalf of his family. He got his first break when the Avis clerk agreed to give him the car's make, a black Buick Le Sabre, and license plate number.

He called both the police and the Miami-Dade Motor Vehicle Bureau asking if such a car had been listed in a recent accident or traffic violation, or had been reported stolen or had been confiscated.

Nada.

He went around to art galleries in the Miami area, asking the owners if they personally knew Pablo Camino, or knew of anyone who may be Pablo's contact for selling or showing his paintings in Miami. They all knew of Pablo's work, a few had met him during exhibitions in Miami, Palm Beach, New York or San Juan.

Fenton Morris, the owner of a gallery on Lincoln Mall, said he had featured several early Pablo Camino drawings in a show of Latin American artists the previous month, but the works had been shipped from San Juan and the artist did not appear at the exhibition. None of the others had been contacted by Pablo recently or knew of his whereabouts.

Ralph checked the cruise lines and the airlines. Despite showing his private investigator credentials, he could not get passenger lists from either.

In his own rental car, he cruised the streets of Miami looking for the Le Sabre, and for Pablo.

He went from boutique to boutique and from restaurant to restaurant along Ocean Drive and in the South Beach side streets. All the owners and employees he spoke to said they saw nothing unusual on the day of the stabbing. He showed the photo. No one recognized Pablo.

Although he hung around the prayer house in South Beach at different times for three days, none of the religious Jews who went in and out of the building would talk to him about the crime, or about the victim. They denied ever seeing Pablo. When confronted with statements they made that were in the newspapers, they shrugged and insisted that the reporter had "made it up."

Nada, nada y nada.

He checked restaurants, drug stores, clothing stores, grocery stores, showing Pablo's photo to waiters, waitresses, clerks and cashiers. Then, after almost a week, he got his first lead. A young guy with wispy face hair and splotches of brown lotion on his pimples said from behind the cash register in a sundries store on Collins Avenue that he recognized the man in the photo.

"He was in here just this morning," the young guy said. "He bought lots of canned food and beer and I delivered it to him a couple of hours ago."

"Where did you deliver it?"

"At the Roney Plaza, just down the street."

"Do you have the room number?"

"It was one of the condo apartments. "It was on the fifth floor. First door on the left out of the elevator. Apartment 502."

Ralph thanked the kid and headed for the Roney Plaza, a huge complex divided into a hotel for tourists and apartments for the locals. On his way up to the fifth floor, he wondered how Pablo was able to swing an apartment. He exited the elevator and went to the first apartment on the left. It was 501, not 502, as the kid had said. He would try it anyway. He rang the bell. He rang again. He rang a third time. Finally, the door slowly opened. Behind it, a tiny, hunched-over woman with what looked like a shrunken head peeked outside. She looked over 100.

"Papa," the woman said. "Where were you? They're beating me and they're robbing me, Papa. Where's Mama? Go get Mama. Please!"

A young black woman suddenly appeared from inside the apartment. She wagged a finger at the old woman. "Mary, you a naughty girl. Why you open de door when I tell you not to?"

The West Indian woman apologized to Ralph. "I was in de bat'room. Is dere somethin' I can help you wit?"

"I must have the wrong apartment," Ralph said.

"Oh, dat's O.K." The woman gave Ralph a dazzling white smile, wagged her finger again at her charge and shut the door.

Ralph went to the first door to the right of the elevator. Number 502. He figured that the kid probably didn't know his right from his left. He rang the bell, his heart pounding again.

A tall, thin, middle-aged man with a gray mustache and a sickly white face opened the door. He was in an undershirt and held a beer can in one hand. It definitely wasn't Pablo. Not even close, except for the thin gray mustache.

"Excuse me, sir," Ralph said. "Did you get a grocery delivery this morning from the store down the block?"

"Yeah?" said the man, immediately suspicious. "What of it?"

"Well, um . . . I'm the manager. We overcharged you . . . um . . . five dollars." Ralph dug into his wallet and pulled out five singles and put them in the man's free hand.

"Hey, thanks." The guy smiled down at his windfall. "That's real white of you. Thanks."

Ralph nodded. He took the elevator to the lobby and left the building.

Pablo started drinking the sour-tasting black coffee out of the container as he headed back to the car after getting his breakfast to go at MacDonald's. There was nothing in the news in the last few days about the search for him. Still, he wouldn't chance going back to his hotel room, or checking in at any other hotel in town. So he lived out of the car, driving up and down the coast by day and switching nightly to locations in the poorer neighborhoods in Miami and nearby towns. He had spent the last week thinking about everything and nothing, looking at sunsets, fighting for sleep that seldom came in the car during the nights, eating fast food take-outs. Until just last night, bags of discarded food had sat in the car; a steady squadron of flies had circled the leftover French fries; ketchup was smeared over the dashboard, clothes bought and worn along the way piled on the seats.

But just this morning he decided to shape up his surroundings. He cleaned up his "home," buying a small vacuum cleaner that plugged into the cigarette lighter on the dashboard. Then, as though shaping up his physical surroundings had also cleared his mind, he realized, both in his head and deep in his gut, what he had to do to put his existence in order: He had to have one more talk with the Maestro.

Didn't the dread-filled message of death in life or everlasting misery in death come about because of the negation of other ways? What had happened to those other ways?

He would find out for sure by going to the source. He would drive straight up to Atlanta, in case they were waiting for him at the airport here. Eventually, they could trace his destination, but he'd worry about that later, devise a way to throw them off once he got there. New identity, no identity.

He would start out right after he finished his Egg McMuffin and coffee.

Waking at eight a.m. on the eighth day after he arrived in Miami, Ralph realized it was time to go home. His return ticket had him on a flight to San Juan leaving at two in the afternoon and he saw no reason to postpone the departure date.

He checked out of the Holiday Inn on Collins Avenue and had breakfast in a coffee shop across the street. He checked his watch. Nine o'clock. He had to return his rental car and be at the airport at about one. He had less than four hours to make one last search for Pablo.

What else could he do, Ralph figured, but spend these last hours cruising around, on the lookout for a black Buick LeSabre, license plate BTW37F? He drove up Collins Avenue, down Arthur Godfrey Road and across the Julia Tuttle Causeway into Miami. He turned off before reaching the Airport

Expressway and searched up and down avenues and through neighborhood streets, realizing he was on the wildest of wild-goose chases.

Although Ralph spotted several black Buicks, none of them had the right license plate. On one street, he saw a tall guy with a lot of wavy gray hair on a large head opening the door of a parked black car and his heart flipped. The guy turned, as though sensing he was being checked out by the slowly passing car. The man had a soft, smooth, un-Pablo face. The car was a Mercedes.

Ralph made his way back on the expressway to the airport. It was over. No way would he find Pablo. Ralph was now sure that his friend, literally and figuratively, was in another place.

He felt depressed as hell. Secrets, searches, whether physical or metaphysical, really were meaningless. Nothingness ruled the world.

Pablo walked down the long street to the corner around which his rental car was parked. He turned the corner, then stopped in his tracks. In the middle of the street, double-parked by the Buick LeSabre, was a police patrol car. A policeman with a large gut was peering inside the car, while a bosomy black woman officer was looking at the license plate and writing in a small notebook. She put the notebook in her bulging back pocket and went to the patrol car and picked up a walkie-talkie from the front passenger seat and started talking into it.

Pablo quickly doubled back around the corner. *Shit!* He hurried down the street, tossing the bag holding his breakfast into the gutter. His car was not parked illegally. The rental agency must have reported it overdue. They were closing in on him.

He kept walking up and down streets for about fifteen minutes, then started back in the direction of the Buick. He saw the patrol car coming his way. He turned another corner and was back in front of the MacDonald's. He ducked inside and stood on the line there like he was going to order a Big Mac. He looked outside the window. The cop car was pulling into a parking lot at the side of the restaurant!

What if they come into the restaurant with a photo of him? Pablo bolted out the door again as the patrol car pulled back out of the parking lot and headed for the drive-thru at the back of the restaurant. He went up the street again and around the corner to his car.

The car was being hooked up to a tow truck. He could no longer drive up to Atlanta.

He turned back again, walking away as fast as he could. After about ten minutes, a taxi passed and he hailed it.

"Where you go, mister?" asked the cabbie with a thick Spanish accent.

"First to the airport," Pablo answered.

"And then back?" said the cabbie, hoping for a round-trip fare.

"No, this is going to be one-way," Pablo said.

Ralph returned his car to the rental lot and got on a shuttle bus to the airport terminal. His carry-on was searched for fruits and vegetables, then he went to the check-in counter. He looked around at the people traveling down to Puerto Rico. Touristy *americanos* (wasn't there enough heat and sun for them in Miami?), Latino business types, families making the sentimental visit back to their homeland. No Pablo.

When he got back to the island, he would go to the police and tell them what he knew about the guy who was killed in Pablo's home, about his mental problems and why he probably broke into the house. At least, that should show that Pablo acted in self-defense, if he were the one who had killed Rosado.

His friend, he hoped, was on his way to, or had arrived at, some place where he would somehow, some way, find peace.

Pablo paid the cabbie, and saw that he was running out of cash. He found an ATM in the airport and took out as much money as he could, a couple of hundred dollars. There didn't seem to be any cops roaming the terminal and checking the faces of the passersby. He went to a counter and was told he had to go through Atlanta, where he would get connecting flights to London and Amsterdam. His heart in his mouth, Pablo presented his American Express Gold Card and showed his passport. The clerk wrote up the ticket without looking up on any list of wanted people. The young woman smiled as she handed Pablo the ticket. She had a space between her two top front teeth.

He had about an hour and a half before his flight took off for Atlanta and he headed for the airport lounge. He would sit in a corner and nurse a couple of beers until boarding time. Heart, pulse, all the vital signs were racing. He had to get there, find out how to go on.

Ralph shouldered his bag and started for the departure gate. He checked his watch. Twenty before two. The plane would be boarding now. He had to make a quick stop in a tourist shop to buy something for his daughter. He got a black tee shirt emblazoned with a sequined palm tree and "Miami Beach" written on the front and the message, "Life's a beach," inscribed on the back. He bought his wife a bottle of Chanel

No. 5. Then he bought his kid another tee shirt. He walked swiftly toward the gate for the plane taking him back home.

Pablo was just about to step inside the bar-lounge when he saw Ralph showing his ticket to a guard at one of the departure gates. His first impulse was to call out to his friend, to hurry over to him, to embrace him, to tell him how much he appreciated his friendship. How deep and important that friendship was to him. But he did not shout, nor did he move.

He stood there, mute, glued to the spot. Ralph went through the metal detector, moved further and further down the long corridor, turned and disappeared.

Pablo took a small table in a corner off from the bar. A waitress came by and he ordered a beer. His eyes filled. He was sure that his friend had come up here looking for him. Reaching into his back pocket, he took out the blue bandana he used as a handkerchief and blew his nose into it. He downed his beer. He wiped the embarrassment, guilt, despair and love out of his eyes.

Grandfather Max was leaning over the rail of a freighter, puffing on a clay pipe. Ralph, a young boy, stood next to him, wondering where they were going. Max looked down at his grandson. His eyes were as green as the endless ocean, as though the sea flowed from them.

"Are we going to look for my father, for your son?" Ralph, the boy, asked.

Max frowned. "He's out boozing. We're going to look for something else."

"O.K.," Ralph said. But he was disappointed. Grandfather Max, he knew, would be hunted down in the jungle and killed. A heavy sadness gathered in Ralph's breast. Max became his father. He would mourn him forever. His breath was coming in short spurts; the tears were in his chest, rising.

A short, quick breath woke Ralph. Before the plane landed, he outlined in his head the beginning of his next book, a novel about Max and his adventures at sea and in foreign ports and the madness that ended his life. A cabin boy would narrate.

Life would go on in all its absurdity and tragedy, Ralph understood, a sort of meaningful meaninglessness, and he would be writing full-time, taking care of his family and keeping Pablo up front in his mind—which he realized was the best he could do.

TWENTY-SEVEN

On landing at Schiphol Airport, Pablo flashed on the face: the bulbous nose; the creased forehead; those wearied, see-all eyes. He went to the money exchange booth at the airport plaza and changed his dollars for guilders, then stepped outside, in his short sleeve shirt, in the dead of winter. Despite the heated idea in his head, his whole body shook and his teeth chattered from the cold while sharp pains shot through his chest. He got a cab to take him to Waterlooplein. At the flea market he bought a Dutch Army woolen sweater and field jacket, a pair of boots, and a hunting knife, which he tucked into his belt beneath the jacket.

He took another taxi to the *Rijksmuseum.* The museum was closed.

Incredible!

Then he saw the signs on the doors of the two entrances on either side of an archway, which said in several languages: Closed Mondays. Apparently, it was Monday.

He spent the next few hours walking the streets and along the canals, and wound up where he realized he was subconsciously headed: Rembrandtplein. It was more than twenty years since he had lived in the city, but the café where he and Ana had spent lots of time together was still there. He went inside and was hit by an almost overwhelming nostalgia. The furnishings seemed more modernized, rugs no longer covered the tables, but the place was as cozy as ever. He took a seat and ordered a *genever*. If only Ana was with him. Why? Because, he loved her. So why had he treated her like shit? He would change. He would promise Ana that it would be different. He would beg her to come live with him again, to forgive, if not forget.

But first, the face-off. Destinies were at stake. He hoped the confrontation would not lead to dire consequences.

After two more *genevers* he left the café and went looking for a room. He found a small hotel off the square. He paid for the night in cash and realized he would be broke by tomorrow. He also saw the top of a folded up note in one of his wallet's compartments. He pulled it out and opened it: half-sister Iris's cell phone number.

He knew she would help, few questions asked, if he told her to hold the questions until later. He would ask her to send money orders to the American Express office here.

He'd call her later.

He went to his room and showered. He hadn't slept all night on the plane and tried to nap. A dark anxiety took hold. They were back, the demons, the furies, working beneath his skin to turn everything inside out. He was having trouble breathing. He heard the shallow wheezing in his throat. He got up and left his room, not waiting for the tiny elevator, hurrying down the two flights of stairs. The streets were crowded, people were coming home from work, it wasn't much later than five p.m., but already it was dark as night. He walked, returned to his room, tried to sleep, got up, went downstairs, walked. He repeated the pattern through the night.

Near dawn his anxiety soared. He rushed out of his room again into the street and walked around looking at bike racks. The bikes were chained to the racks. Unlike years ago, Amsterdamers now seemed to keep all their bikes under lock and key.

Then, along Prinsengracht, across from a row of bikes locked in racks by the canal, he saw a single bike leaning against the wall next to a short flight of steps leading to the front door of a house. The bike was unchained. He hopped on it just as the front door opened and a young guy in a long black leather coat and spiked hair started down the steps. "Hey, hey!" the guy yelled. Pablo raised an arm and turned up the palm of his hand and shrugged in some sort of apology as he pedaled off.

The city was shrouded in fog. Trees, houses, cars, occasional other bikers suddenly emerged out of the mist, as though detached from any moorings, as though floating free from reality. He expected something monstrous, like a Redon cyclops, to pop out at any minute. In the distance, the towers of the Rijksmuseum were vaguely in view, like tops of cloud-shrouded castles. He moved along Herengracht, down Nieuwe Spiegelstraat, crossed the Singel and pedaled toward the museum. A huge banner above the main archway of the red brick building announced a exhibition of Drawings of the Golden Age. The sky was now the same gray color as the fog, as though the world was gripped in a quiet, windless dust storm that continued to settle on everything.

How many hours to go before the place opened? What time was it now? He had left his watch on a dresser in the hotel room. Amsterdamers already were pedaling in front and behind the building on their way to work, but the museum was not yet open.

Pablo rode the bike back across the Singel, raced trolley buses down main streets, cut up and down alongside canals and kept on pedaling in circles until he began to sweat and feel out-of-breath. He might have left his watch, but he managed to remember to tuck the hunting knife under his belt before he had left his hotel room. He felt the leather case pressing on his left thigh.

The sky was now a dirty gray, as though the lifting fog carried back the filth that had seeped into it during its overnight descent to earth. He pedaled back over the bridge to the museum. The two front entrances were still closed. He pedaled around to the back of the building. There was another entrance beyond the gardens. Museum employees were going through the doors.

Pablo found a nearby rack to park the bike. He walked swiftly to the entrance. He noticed the employees flashing IDs in front of a guard sitting at a table at the entrance. He stood behind a woman with curly blond hair. The woman wore a green parka. She flashed her ID. The guard nodded.

Pablo pulled out his wallet, quickly flashed his American Express card and zipped through the corridor. The guard called out to him, then stood and shouted, but he was already weaving in and out of the employees moving to their offices and workstations. People turned to look at him. He quickly found an exit door. Behind it was a staircase. He climbed the steps two at a time until he arrived on the first floor, then strode quickly and stone-faced to the room, crossing the hardwood floor, concentrating on the painting ahead.

He approached the portrait, his eyes glued to the artist's wrinkled brow. He wouldn't stare into the eyes yet. Within each wrinkle of the brow was a crevice of suffering; mountains of wisdom surrounded plains of suffering. He moved closer and rocked back and forth. There, in front of him was the artist as St. Paul. St. Paul as an old man. As the knowing, suffering, sonovabitch who saw, had seen, everything. Who knew everything and forgave everything because he had been man and sinner, sinner and visionary, visionary and saint.

St. Paul held a book with Hebrew lettering. The handle of a dagger protruded from the saint's coat. When Pablo drew his knife, would the dagger also be drawn? Did the artist presage the coming moment? Another clashing blade-against-blade to the death? Could steel cut away the suffering in the soul? When and how did the sinner become the saint?

Where was *his* Damascus?

Soon.

When he struck himself blind, just as Paul had been struck blind.

Pablo unbuttoned his jacket enough to reach in and touch the knife's ivory handle. He grasped it.

First, the saint's eyes. Then, the sinner's eyes.

The creases on the face beneath the turban were deepened by the inner light on the left side of the face and across the wrinkled, glistening brow. Clumps of gray and streaks of silver and gold in the hair beneath the yellowwhite turban and above the ears drew away some of the starkness of the expression. Wisps of sideburns, mustache, goatee. The light sprang from the great brown shadows. The wrinkle-shaded wide-open eyes that saw not only you, but also the world inside you, that mocked and understood you and accused and forgave you.

The eyes, so incredibly heavy with the world, must have caused suffering to all who really looked into their bottomless pity. The artist, seeing what they reflected in others, must also have suffered. He, Pablo, could at least end that suffering.

Pablo lost his breath; then fought to pull in air again. He slid the knife from his belt, but kept it under his jacket. Silently, two quick jabs in the eyes, then cut them out completely and they would no longer transmit their unbearable message. Then plunge the blade through his own eyes.

Eyeless in Amsterdam. I-less in eternity.

Tightening his grip on the handle, he peered once more at that compassionate, quizzical face that was surprised it was being studied so closely.

"That's it?" Pablo asked.

"What else is there?"

"Doesn't pain and suffering mean that man once knew happiness and joy?"

Did the portrait frown?

"No, no. You've got it all wrong. The other side of nothingness is still nothing. *Nada.* In my language, *niemendal, niets, nihil, niks."*

So then, why?"

"Why what?"

"Keep going?"

"I have no idea. Do what you have to do, and leave me alone, for the love of God!"

Pablo's eyes narrowed. They exchanged angry glares. So much for compassion and insight into humanity. Pablo began to draw the knife out from under his belt.

He pulled his eyes away; his gaze moved to the surrounding brown and black darkness. He noticed again the reddish tints in the warm gray shadows that deepened to brown and black. Pablo peered long and hard into the shadows. He had already been blinded by the radiance of the artist's light. But he now realized that he had failed to see the true nature of the shadows. The deepest, most stirring truth was in the shadows. It hit him with the shock of a fist exploding behind his eyes. Pablo was swept up in incredible warmth. He knew it would temper considerably, but at that moment he realized that by looking further and further into the shadows, he would, for the first time, move to the edges of . . . what? Understanding? Mystery?

Whatthefuckever.

Two security guards came into the room. They were soon followed by several more. They surrounded Pablo as he continued to study the painting. Pablo took a deep breath, forced his eyes off the painting and nodded to the men and women in the gray uniforms. He offered no resistance as they led him out of the room.

EPILOGUE

The usual crowd packed the Galería Quiñones. Money laundering art collector Ricardo Rexach appeared, not with wife María del Carmen Bernal del Rexach, but with Sulay Sánchez, the 21-year-old local supermodel turned TV anchorwoman. Rexach's wife was at home recuperating after a second mentoplasty, received in California to correct the botched job performed on her last year in Florida, when her little monkey chin had been augmented to spatula size. The silicone implant was removed and her jawbone was reshaped after an incision in her mouth and now she could barely speak and cancelled all invitations until the swelling of the mandible went down. Rexach expressed great sympathy for Doña María when telling of her plight. While leading Sulay Sánchez around the galley and introducing her to various important members of the cultural community, he slipped his hand from her waist to the edges of her delectably swelling behind.

The middle-aged Ocasio twins, Billy, the sculptor, and Pipo, the muralist, were there, talking in tough street slang and wearing their black leather motorcycle jackets, having parked their bikes on the sidewalk near the entrance to the gallery so all the guests could admire the power and the glory of their machines. Conceptual artist Johnny Arroyo, recently released from serving two years in prison after his latest conceptual work, threatening to blow up a San Juan-to-New York jet in mid-flight, was greeted cautiously by those in the crowd who knew him from his pre-prison days. Other artists were present, as were students and critics and collectors, some down from New York and up from Caracas, who understood that Pablo Camino was an important artist. Julia was being interviewed before the TV cameras, explaining how she had recovered the portrait of Albizu from a police warehouse that stored, among other things, discarded evidence, and how she had it restored, and how the new works, mostly drawings, but also four paintings, all portraits, two of himself, one of an Indonesian waiter and the other of a female acquaintance, showed that the artist had entered a new period that explored both his own humanity and something beyond himself. "Knowing the artist, I hesitate to use the word," said Julia, "but I will anyway. There seems to be in these new works something 'religious'."

Julia said to the TV cameras: "I would like to thank Ralph Camacho, a good friend of the artist, for contacting him in Amsterdam and convincing him to ship the new works now on exhibit. Mr. Camacho was also a great help in getting the police to release the Albizu portrait to me. He told the authorities here in Puerto Rico the story you have already reported. Namely that through his investigation at the behest of the artist's family, he learned that the man killed in the artist's home actually invaded the house to destroy the Albizu painting, for some unknown reason, and that the artist acted in self-defense. As you know, legal experts now say it appears the killing was a justifiable homicide. The important thing right now is that the portrait in question has been retrieved and restored and is being exhibited once more so that people can see it as the profound and inspiring work it is, not only as the portrait of a Puerto Rican patriot, but also as a masterwork of a great Puerto Rican painter."

Julia, who was standing in front of the painting, now stepped to the side as the TV cameras zoomed in on the portrait.

Well, she managed to give her spiel without saying what everyone knew anyway: She was the mother of Pablo Camino. The tears only welled toward the end of the statement and she hid them as she stepped out of the camera's view by wiping her nose with the Kleenex she had in her hand. There have been too many tears lately. So what? Feelings are returning, even at this late stage. Pablo seemed to have come back to life once more through his art. For her, more pity, more tears may be the way to find her own humanity. By reaching out of herself, she had finally realized, she would not lose anything truly important.

She turned to look once more at the painting and once again to admire the restoration work. She was glad she had sent it to that restorer in Boston, even though she would be paying him for the next year. It was certainly worth it. A wonderful job, once again conveying the artist's (her son's) concentrated vision of the old man, less than fiery as he had always been portrayed, but melancholic, pained, waiting uneasily for death.

She realized the personal connections with the portrait. It was indeed a fine work by her son, and the subject was the man who blew the whistle on the doctor, the father of the artist. This also was the man who was the icon for the people who wanted Puerto Rico separated from the United States, which, in truth, was not on the top of everyone's list for ways to improve things on the island, but whose ideals, she realized, were woven into the lives of most Puerto Ricans. So he was portrayed as a patriarch weakened by old age. So that's what life is about. We all lose it. To be human is to lose, thought Julia, nowhere near tears.

The novel was coming slowly. But ten chapters, at least, were on the screen. Nine months work. Ten chapters down, about thirty more to go for a first draft. Maybe the good professor who viewed his first book as a modern-day linkage to the Eternal Voyage that explores the universal themes of blah, blah, blah would also see the adventures of bigamist-murderer Max in sea-going mythical terms. Maybe not. Just write the damn thing!

Now that he no longer taught at the University, he could spend interrupted hours in front of the computer. Well, more or less interrupted. Since Tere decided to take up her practice again—this time as a Legal Aid lawyer—Ralph opened the laundromat every morning at eight and remained until one p.m., when Don Cisco, the 70-year-old retired biology teacher, took over until closing. He went back to his apartment in the front of the building, ate lunch, wrote from one-thirty to three-thirty, picked up Diana from school, either brought her home or dropped her off at a friend's house, returned to his typewriter at about four-thirty and remained for another two hours, until he either picked up Diana or made dinner (if Tere had to stay late at the office). His late afternoon writing sessions had been interrupted recently because Diana, who was now wrapped up in photography since Ralph bought her a camera, pleaded with her father after he picked her up from school to take her to various places around the city so that she could photograph them.

The photo in the mail. Pablo, on a street in Amsterdam, a canal in the background, a short, attractive woman holding his arm. Pablo was in an Army field jacket, looking ill-at-ease in front of the camera. The woman, in a tweed jacket and long scarf hanging outside the jacket, had a small smile on her lips. The photo accompanied the letter, from Iris Rhoades, Pablo's half-sister, whom Ralph had never known existed.

She said she had just returned from seeing her brother and was "writing on behalf of Pablo, who was not sure if you wanted him to contact you. He was concerned that you were angry at him and, although he did not put it in so many words, he felt very guilty about not contacting you soon after he left Puerto Rico. I believe this feeling weighs on him heavily, since he has told me of your friendship, which he values very highly. I sensed a great sadness in his heart when he talked about 'deserting' you. He hesitatingly asked me if I would get in touch with you, which I'm now doing. Enclosed is his address and phone number. Please contact him. A letter or call from you would be greatly appreciated by him, and by me, his loving sister: Iris Rhoads."

Ralph wrote Iris, thanking her for the photo and the letter. The same night, he wrote his friend and they exchanged several letters and phone calls as Ralph kept Pablo up to date on everything that was going on, which included sending him a copy from *The Miami Herald* of the story about the guy arrested for the murder of Ferdie's brother. A homeless Gulf War vet who had been picked up for buying drugs from an undercover agent, confessed to the killing. The vet said he was paid four hundred dollars by the man's estranged wife to knock off the guy. Ralph also told Pablo about Ferdie's visit to the island and his defense of Dr. Dusty Rhoads. Pablo only comment about that in a letter was, "We're all guilty, but some of us are more guilty than others." He added: "I've finally grown my new head, so don't worry about me."

Pablo and Iris sat at a table outside a café across from the train station. It was a rare sunny day and Amsterdamers were soaking up the sun at the outdoor café. Pablo had gone to the hotel where Iris was staying, just a few blocks from his apartment-studio in a converted warehouse facing the Amstel. They took a taxi to *Centraal Station*, then decided to have one last *genever* before she caught the train to Paris.

Maureen, Iris' latest companion, obviously jealous over the amount of time Iris was spending with her brother on their spring vacation, left in a huff the day before. She, at least, Maureen told Iris, would arrive on time for their hotel reservations in Paris. Iris said she would soon follow. Maureen said she couldn't understand why half of their supposedly special vacation was being spent with Pablo. Iris kissed Maureen on her freckled nose and promised she would join up with her the next day.

Now Iris was reminding Pablo again: "If you need anything, just call. How are you fixed for money?"

"I'm O.K. I appreciate the loans. Ralph said since I'm no longer a 'wanted man,' the transfer of my account should come through soon."

"That's good."

Pablo took Iris's hand. "You're a terrific sister. I really appreciate all you've done for me, and the visit."

"I love you, as a brother, brother," Iris said.

"I love you too." Pablo took her hand, kissed it, then let it go.

"When did your ex-wife say she would come to Amsterdam?"

"She said she would try to visit this summer. Nothing positive."

Iris nodded, as though she understood both Pablo's desire to see Ana again and her reluctance for another commitment to Pablo.

"I don't know if I should ask you this, but what the hell. My curiosity is greater than my tact. Do you still have conversations with that portrait of you-know-who?"

Pablo looked into the slim glass holding the gin. He tapped an index finger against the glass, as though testing its material substance. Then he looked up at Iris. "No, not really," he said.

Pablo could see the question marks remaining in Iris's green eyes.

"I mean I still go to see the painting. Most of the guards know me there now. I told you what happened when I first got here?"

Iris nodded. "The arrest. The fine."

"Which you helped me pay. Well, like I said, I go back there, but we don't get into the heavy stuff anymore."

Well?"

"Well what?" .

Iris noticed the defensiveness creeping into Pablo's eyes. She decided to drop the subject.

Pablo finished his gin. "Do we have time for one more?"

Iris looked at her watch. "I don't think . . . "

Pablo ordered another gin anyway. He asked the waiter for the check. "I'll knock this one off real quick."

He shot down the drink, then paid and picked up Iris's luggage as he led her to the train station. He accompanied her to the ticket gate, then put her two suitcases down. They held each other tightly and kissed on the cheek.

"Remember," Iris said again, "if you need . . . "

"Everything's fine," Pablo said.

"Keep in touch."

Pablo nodded, they hugged again, and Iris picked up her luggage and moved through the gate to her train. Pablo turned and left the station. He walked to the island where the trams were waiting and got on a Number Five. After a few minutes, they took off, down Nieuwezijds Voorburgwal over the Singel, into Koningsplein, over Herrengracht, onto Leidsestraat, over Keizersgracht, then Prinsengracht, into Leidseplein. From there it was a short walk to the *Rijksmuseum.* Then to The Room.

Their eyes lock. Neither blinks first.

"O.K.," Pablo says. "Here's what I want to know. Your deepest darks, Bone Black or Charcoal Black? I've tried both, neither gets me where I want to go."

"So?"

"I keep trying."

"You've got it!"

Pablo turns his eyes into slits; his nostrils flare. Then he sighs deeply. "O.K. Thanks."

Pablo tips an imaginary hat to the maestro and heads back to his studio.

Biographical Note

Robert Friedman was born and bred in the Bronx, N.Y. and lived in Puerto Rico for more than 20 years, working as a reporter, editor and columnist for *The San Juan Star*, as well as special correspondent for the *New York Daily News.* His first novel, *Caribbean Dreams* dealt with crime, corruption and colonialism on a fictitious Caribbean island very much like Puerto Rico. He is now Washington correspondent for the *Star* and lives in Silver Spring, Maryland with his wife, Ginny. They have two grown daughters.

Printed in the United States
99561LV00002B/229-231/A